SWORD OF ORION

SHARON LEE AND STEVE MILLER

A PHOBOS IMPACT BOOK

AN IMPRINT OF PHOBOS BOOKS

NEW YORK

PI

PHOBOS
IMPACT

A Phobos Impact Book
Published by Phobos Books
200 Park Avenue South
New York, NY 10003
www.phobosweb.com

Distributed in the United States by National Book Network, Lanham,
Maryland.

Cover by Zuccadesign

The characters and events in this book are fictitious. Any similarity to
actual persons, living or dead, is coincidental and not intended by the
authors.

Library of Congress Cataloging-in-Publication Data

Lee, Sharon, 1952–
   Sword of Orion / Sharon Lee and Steve Miller.
     p. cm. — (Beneath strange skies ; bk. 1)
   ISBN 0-9720026-8-5 (pbk. : alk. paper)
   1. Teenage girls—Fiction. 2. Life on other planets—Fiction.
I. Miller, Steve, 1950 July 31– . II. Title. III. Series: Lee, Sharon,
1952– . Beneath strange skies ; bk. 1.
PS3562.E3629S96 2005
813'.52—dc22

                                      2005010811

∞™ The paper used in this publication meets the minimum
requirements of American National Standard for Information Sciences—
Permanence of Paper for Printed Library Materials, ANSI/NISO Z39.48-
1992

SWORD OF ORION

To Victor Appleton, his son, his heirs, and his readers.

SWORD OF ORION

PROLOGUE

In a highly elliptical orbit around a world without a name in a star system known only by a number, the war-battered spaceship *Valero* complained of its mission in a myriad of ways. Ventilator fans rattled in their mounts as they tried to keep up with the heat. Pressure alarms echoed in compartments full and empty, as they had for close to a day. The ship's skin crackled with random energy, remnants of the rays and blasts the slowly failing force shields had been unable to fully contain.

In similar but not quite matching orbits about the world were the ship's companion vessels. The last dozen of what had been a mighty fleet, they were in the same straits: low on power, low on crew, low on hope.

The enemy fleet was, perforce, also in the system. Each side had thought to use overwhelming force, each side had assumed an advantage in firepower, each had sought advantage in surprise. The result was an epic encounter with destiny.

Within the fading protections of multiterawatt shielding, within the battered hull plates of the *Valero* itself, most of the crew sat mute, strapped into battle stations, awaiting what could be—what should be—a final, and decisive, assault against them. Now they waited, waited for the one last chance, the final advantage, to come to the fore—or fail.

Should the enemy fleet successfully close with the *Valero*, all would surely be lost, for not only did it head the rebel fleet, but it contained the last and most brilliant of the scientists and leaders behind the rebellion.

"Parvair?"

Banin's question came as she sealed the last of the contacts with a touch as gentle as a caress.

"It is done," she said. "The fields are set."

At each end of the couch were lock switches with guards; now on each switch the lights glowed green.

The child was fussing slightly. There was reason enough to fuss, after all. Parvair sighed lightly. One should not, perhaps, use a child thus. Still, it had seemed best to have the security. . . .

"Then we must finish quickly!" Banin whispered. "I have the safe codes ready."

He scanned the instruments proving her assertion— the procedure was successful, the devices powered and connected, lacking now only the touch of the switch that would turn ideas, willpower, and energy into freedom from the Oligarchy. The woman gently detached the cuffs from about the wrists of her child—and it wasn't until the second came off that she saw one wrist was bloodied where the electrode gel had been too thick and pulled the skin with it; the other was marked with a red-purple welt—burnt—as if the very nature of the destructive circuit the child had been part of had left its mark.

She sighed; wiped the spot of blood from the tiny left hand.

"Where is Erazias?" she asked Banin. "He was to be—"

"He is at the controls of the courier. If you'll check these figures, I'll carry the child to him."

She looked at him bleakly, bent to her child, kissed both tiny wrists—

"Yours is the voice he will listen to," Banin said urgently. "It must be you who gives the command. . . ."

The assent came—it was simply the act of handing her child to her husband. Her hand strayed for a moment to his worn cheek, and with a sigh she turned her back on both of them, as much revolutionary and scientist as mother and wife.

Banin quickly placed the child into the carry seat, automatically checked the cover for pressure tightness, and slipped the final calculations beneath the cushion as he sealed it. A brief wild thought—what good an extra hour's air if the ship was holed before he could reach the courier?—but then he was on his way, right palm slapping pressure plates to access the drop shaft from laboratory to main deck.

His own pressure mask was slung over his shoulder, but he abstained from using it as he passed from deck to deck. He recognized many of the faces, human and alien alike, and he shared with them this moment he'd wrought, all with as much to lose as he, though in truth, he was the only one of them to have his heir in hand.

If the crew wondered about his mission they did not ask, both pressing duty and personal dread keeping them to themselves, and of all they would trust none was more hallowed than Banin, save perhaps Parvair herself.

To the captain's deck then, though the captain had been an early casualty, and through to the courier docked where the captain's launch should be.

3

Erazias stood inside the hatch, relief plain on even his blue alien face as Banin appeared, his dark apprentice's robe pointing up to the yellow of fear around his eyes.

"The package is here," said Banin as lightly as he could, "and we honor your willingness to carry it!"

The Turlon gave a sort of half-bow.

"I have sworn to Parvair to advance her work. This is a day unlike any other. . . ."

Banin returned the half-bow.

"The safe codes are here—the shields will drop as you approach them. The dropped shields will surprise the enemy, and they will swarm to the attack."

Banin smiled briefly, let it become the quiet grin he was known for.

"Hurry. We will surprise them this time, and their greed shall be their undoing!"

With that the child was passed into the ship, and a moment later the key with the shield codes.

Banin himself pushed the switch to seal the outer hull of the courier as Erazias reached to seal the inner.

The return trip was faster, with Banin running when he could. Sections of the ship were without lights now; in others the ventilation was ominously quiet.

Then he was back to the well-lit laboratory, where the ventilation was quietly working, with its precious equipment and more precious wife.

"The figures check?" he asked without preamble, settling in beside her on the couch that was—incongruously—the final control center of a battle that was shaking a galaxy.

She nodded and leaned to him, kissing him quickly on the cheek.

Then, a touch of a comm button.

"Erazias, we are ready," she said, as calm as if she released him for a holiday. "Launch, my student, and travel well."

There was no reply; simply the distant *fararump* of the courier's hurried departure.

Parvair touched Banin on the forehead, took his kiss, and then each moved to a separate end of the couch.

Both switches must be unlocked within a moment of the other, both must be activated together. . . .

"Shields down!" came the warning from the bridge, followed by a sharp "Courier away!"

Some crew members cheered, only knowing that something had happened. . . .

Then from the bridge the expected news: "The enemy fleet is in motion!"

Valero rocked under the touch of enemy force beams. It was a glance between lovers and comrades that acknowledged the moment; then the switches were unlocked, the buttons pushed at the same instant—and *Valero*, its companions, and the onrushing enemy fleet fell out of the universe together, leaving behind a stellar system full of strange high-energy particles, a few stray bits of metal and plastic, and no other evidence of the titanic battle that had just concluded.

CHAPTER ONE

Jerel slipped the shaped printout over her slideboard, which squatted on its grav field over the countertop, floating barely above the slender fingers of her left hand. Music leaked through the walls in swirling torrents, which meant her uncle Orned was in his office working.

Peering at the printout, Jerel pushed down in the center of the slideboard with her right hand—hard.

The result was a pinched finger and quiet, somewhat unladylike remark.

"See," she said to Kay without heat once she'd shaken her hand a few times, "this really isn't up to full spec."

Kay shook his head, reaching for an argument he hadn't fully thought out. They were in Jerel's workroom, and should've already left for Simka's Alley if they wanted to be in time to hear Norin and Feter's set.

"You can't believe everything you download off the graynet. What evidence do you have that—"

As usual, Jerel thought nothing of cutting her friend off in midsentence.

"The evidence I have is that I squished my fingers! This board's getting scratched and I'm getting slowed down. Costs me money, and it's dangerous, too!"

Kay was still formulating a reply as she opened the small tool case, removed the neomagnetic rotator, and applied it quickly to the three spots the overlay sheet indicated at the forward end of the printout.

A chirp sounded, and the slideboard clacked to the countertop like a piece of inert plastic.

"Jerel, you're gonna get yourself in trouble!"

"Huh!" was her reply, or maybe it was her reaction to the sharp click of the power module when she applied the rotator to three more spots and the module ejected itself energetically from the board.

Kay dragged one hand distractedly through his curly blond hair. "Jerel," he began again, having at last found the thread of his argument. . . .

"Anyhow, Kay, is the word out at school about Mileeda?" Jerel looked up from her work, peering directly into his eyes. He knew the ploy, and tried to soldier on with his point, despite the offered change of topic.

"You told me when you signed up with Capsule Courier that they have a no-modify clause in the contract for anyone who uses a leased board. You're still leasing yours, right? Else it'd be purple or flashing gold or anything but safety orange . . ."

"*Piff,*" she said, which wasn't so much an answer as blowing her too-long bangs out of her eyes as she peered at the innards of the slideboard, now indecently on its back and open to view.

"Right," she said. "I told you that. But you know, some of the crew has got to be using mods or else they'd be running into the same problems Mileeda and I are. Did. Coming too close to the bottom pavers, scraping on random junk in alleyways, catching on rags and paper, for Thirster's sake."

She took a tool he didn't recognize from her kit and probed the interior of the board as she talked.

"But anyhow, see, I'm not going to mess with the speed bits, and that's what they can check real easy with the standard pre-trip dock, because that'll give them a much different ETA. I'm going for a slightly stronger compression and a little more height. That'll take me over the worst of the gravel on the route, maybe even all of it, and get me there within allowable time. Should work, I bet."

Kay sighed. Once she'd opened the thing his case was lost, anyway. He tried to recall the flow of the conversation, came up with a name mentioned twice.

"What about Mileeda, anyway? What word is there?"

She lifted an eyebrow, *piff*ed again, looked down and plunged back into some adjustment he couldn't follow, talking into the slideboard.

"Mileeda didn't finish her last trip yesterday. Got one of the naugy pouch runs up toward Highsteel. 'Cept she didn't get there. Something weird happened."

She said something beneath her breath which might have been "thirst" or might have been "burst" or even . . .

"There!"

Kay lifted his eyes to the ceiling.

"What weird happened?" he insisted patiently.

Jerel laughed, oddly, alternately rubbing at the small marks on her wrists the way she did when she was thinking, or tense.

"I dunno. No one does. She just never finished the run is what's weird. And she never went home!"

Kay perked up, seeing a shot at some juicy gossip to feed his mother. The more he could keep her busy with what was actually going on around them, the less likely it was that she'd fall back into one of her rants about the purity of the Oligarchy, or his duty to learn the forms of the fifth hand flourish to a sitting Speaker . . .

"She didn't hijack the run?" he asked Jerel.

"Nah. Nothing so reasonable as that. She's just gone, *poof!* The street cops found her board—it was still humming, so they took it in to inspect—and they found her pouch. Clari said the pouch was just sitting on the board along one of the back alleys right near CapCour, like she'd stepped off to stretch or get a drink and just never came back."

There was a slight snicking sound, which was the power module going back into the board. With a flourish Jerel turned the board over, touched the points with her rotator; and the board hung above the counter again, this time significantly higher.

"There! All set."

There was triumph and relief in that, and Kay felt a bit better. At least Jerel'd known that she might not have been able to get the thing back together. But she was off again on another topic.

"Tomorrow I got a mandatory meeting at CapCour and Clari said something about a safety review because of Mileeda going missing. I guess I won't be able to stop by and see you at the zoo unless they don't give me any trips." She squinched her eyes, considering. "They might not," she said darkly. "With Mileeda off I'm back to lowest on the lists. And if she shows up, you bet they'll fire her. You can't just walk away from your board and leave a courier pouch sitting in the middle of the street!" She looked doleful. "So there, I'm stuck!"

Kay sighed. He'd heard all the news about Jerel going up one on the lists when the new girl came on with the company, and about the confusions since people said they looked so much alike. Jerel didn't see it, and he didn't himself. Beyond the fact that they both had brown hair, Mileeda didn't look anything like Jerel. Jerel was—Jerel. You couldn't mistake her for anybody else.

"At least you have some idea what you'll be doing. I can never tell if I'm going to be able to get off to the zoo on schedule or if I'm going to have to listen to my mother talk about the gowns some dead woman wore to a ball fifty years ago, and why it caused a governor to get thrown off a planet on the other side of the sector."

Jerel nodded. She'd been trapped more than once by a sudden bout of Kay's mother's reminisces about the times before the revolution had sapped the Oligarchy's power.

Both she and Kay had been infants when the battles and riots swept the Oligarchy from a century's reign; they'd both lost a father in that strife—and Jerel her mother, too. Jerel, it was known, had actually been on the scene of the last enigmatic battle. Kay's mother never tired of explaining how much she and Kay had in common—including that moment when an overmatched fleet of revolutionaries had somehow disappeared, dragging all traces of itself and its enemy with it.

The Oligarchy had not long survived the fruitless, galaxy-wide search for its supposedly invincible armada, for the revolution's supporters—long victims of the Oligarchs—had been well prepared for the resulting confusion.

Jerel knew that sometimes Kay thought his mother was a victim, too, for whatever dreams she'd had in those days were now gone, lost in an ever more tangled web of memories that failed to match the world she lived in, and most likely didn't match the world she *had* lived in, either.

"I'm hoping to get to work early tomorrow, if you do get a chance to come by," Kay said; "my mom's been sleeping late again."

"I'm sorry, Kay," Jerel said with quick sympathy.

She startled him by touching his hand briefly, and then flung the slideboard at the floor, knowing it wouldn't hit.

A quick jump and she landed on it firmly, the slide-boots locking her feet into proper position.

This, of course, meant another change of topic; with any luck, Kay thought, they'd be able to leave now. If they hurried, they'd still be in time to hear—

There was a shuffling noise in the hall, and an "accidental" rap on the wall or door frame, and then Jerel's uncle Orned appeared.

Kay blushed but Jerel didn't. Her uncle was far too good an insurance man to walk about making such a noise unless he intended it. For some reason he'd decided she and Kay needed a certain amount of privacy, including a subtle warning that he was on the way, ever since he'd found them sitting side by side looking over a copy of the latest *Barst's Catalogue of Alien Creatures*, trying to decide which of the newest crop looked most dangerous.

Uncle Orned nodded to Kay, smiling his slight, neutral smile; seeming not at all dismayed to find Jerel hovering soundlessly in the middle of the room.

"Hello, Kay. Didn't hear you come in."

This might have been true, given the volume of the music, but Jerel doubted very much that he'd been unaware of her presence in the apartment—or of Kay's. Her stomach tightened a bit. Something was brewing.

As if to confirm that, her uncle turned to her, the smile disappearing.

"See your friend to the door, Jerel—you'll have a chance to talk to him tomorrow. As soon as he leaves, bring yourself down to my library. *Yesterday.*"

Now what? she thought, and exchanged a glance with Kay, thinking of Simka's Alley and the promise to Feter. Biting her lip, she looked again to Uncle Orned, trying to gauge if she could talk her way free for an hour—not that it was likely, with *yesterday* in play—but Orned had already gone back out the door.

"Yesterday?" Kay asked, heading for the front door, trying to analyze the slightly odd inflection in the word as Orned had used it.

Jerel sighed, worried, but not so worried that she could resist the urge to lean forward and use the slideboard to take her to the door.

"Yesterday?" she said. "That's one of Uncle Orned's code words for 'right now.' Kind of like saying, 'You're in trouble, triple max.'"

Kay blinked. "But, we didn't do—"

Jerel gave him a wan smile, opening the door and wobbling in a small circle with the board.

"If this was a 'we' kind of problem, Uncle Orned would have included you, I'm sure. Whatever it is, it's mine, double bet. Tell Feter I'll come later if I can."

"Right." Kay left with a wave of hand; behind him he could hear the door sigh closed as Jerel put her shoulder to it, and then heard the unmistakable sounds of the automatic locks—and then double manual locks—as she closed up.

The door to Uncle Orned's office was closed, which was a bad sign indeed. Jerel could hear music on the other side, not as loud as it had been. This was not looking good. Worse, she couldn't figure out what it was she might have done. That she'd done *something* she had no doubt. Uncle Orned was strict, but he didn't make up things to get mad about.

Perforce, she stared into the retina reader set beside the door, and punched her personal code—five two-digit numbers and three letters—into the disguised ornamental key plate.

The door slid silently out of the way.

The music was energetic and orchestral; she took that as an additional sign as to the depth of the trouble and met her uncle's glance instantly.

He nodded very slightly, his eyes cool; and she took her seat carefully.

Uncle Orned's desk faced the door. In fact, in all the rooms of their flat his favorite chair faced the door. In all the rooms there was an inconspicuous holster with a gun in it, right where Uncle could reach it as he sat.

At the moment he was reading from his newsfeed, or his persfeed. That screen was out of her sight, for, as he'd explained to her when she was quite young, his job required him to deal with information he couldn't share. With anybody.

The library itself was old-fashioned, with a couple of ancient bound books for decoration and dozens of shelves of infosource on various media. Her uncle's work also required that he own his own copies of a lot of infosource so that his interest in any particular bit of information *right now* wouldn't be noticed.

It was this fact that had helped lead her to her interest in ship repair, for he allowed her to access any of the information on the three walls not behind his desk. It was there she'd stumbled across a space drive repair training module meant for apprentices when she was barely able to read. Fascinated, she'd demanded tools and a ship to work on—which Uncle Orned had refused to provide.

He had, however, provided her with tools and access to more or less appropriate projects for her skill level.

Uncle Orned was fair—he didn't just order in the age-specified material, but tested her and made sure she was being challenged by her studies, formal or informal.

The music, Jerel realized, was approaching its crescendo. As it did, her uncle visibly relaxed. He stopped reading and keyboarding, let his gaze rest on a distant somewhere he could see and she couldn't, and did one of his breathing exercises.

Jerel bit her lip and tried not to squirm in her chair.

Uncle Orned was still a young enough man that he'd more than once been mistaken for her older brother, a case made for casual viewers by their more-or-less matching looks—smooth tan skin and wiry build, brown eyes, brown hair—and even his hairstyle. It wasn't that his hair was cut like a boy's, it was just that it wasn't as formal or as formidable as the hairstyles worn by many of the older men, men who'd been active adults well before the revolution. If anything, Uncle Orned's hair could be said to be neutral, much like his clothes, and his voice, and his willingness to discuss his own history, though he, too, had been an adult during the revolution.

The revolution was something she sincerely couldn't remember, which made her uncle's unwillingness to discuss his part in it, if any, doubly frustrating. She knew from history lessons how bad it had been elsewhere, but remarkably little about how bad it had been here. When the lessons had first come up, back when she was a kid, she'd searched Uncle Orned's archives for more data, but learned, surprisingly, that what she'd been used to thinking of as the most complete library on the planet didn't hold much information about the revolution at all.

When she asked Uncle Orned about that missing info, he'd promised to tell her later, but when "later" came, he'd only pointed her to the same archives and suggested she look more closely.

She hadn't—and maybe that had been a test of some kind, for when she hadn't followed up for some days, she found that her allowance had been raised a bit, while Uncle Orned directed her reading even more heavily toward the space drives and mechanics she loved so much.

If he'd hoped she'd go into the insurance business herself, he never said.

The music volume fell momentarily—and now she recognized it, though she couldn't name it. Uncle Orned played it a lot, sometimes over and over when he was working. He called it his "thinking music." Now came the rousing finale, with a crash of cymbals and drums and other instruments she couldn't identify, and a brief twitter of what might have been electric butterfly wings. . . .

Then suddenly there was no sound in the room but her own breathing.

The pause lasted a few more seconds, and then Uncle Orned's cool brown gaze was on her.

"Jerel," he said conversationally, as if he'd just noticed she was in the room. "I think we must talk. Perhaps, I daresay, you must talk."

There was silence, and his gaze was unwavering.

Finally, she asked, in a small voice, "What should I talk about, Uncle?"

He ran his hands through his hair above his ears, turning that movement into a languid stretch, hands at shoulder height.

"I suspect first," he said, still in that conversational voice, which was somehow much worse than being yelled at, "we must have you talk about what you expect of me, and how long you expect it."

She was startled, and the amazement made its way into her voice, which shook a bit.

"*Expect* from you, Uncle? How do you mean?"

15

He sat straighter in his chair, and swept his right hand out, indicating the room, and in effect the entire apartment. His mouth straightened, and he might have sighed very quietly.

"It seems you expect me to be here. You expect food in the larder, you expect . . . comfort. I'd guess comfort is about right?"

She thought for a moment, still puzzled, but nodded carefully.

"Yes, Uncle, I guess that's close. I've been comfortable here for all the time I can remember. We've had food, we've had power. I've never heard you say 'I can't' if I asked for something." Here she wrinkled her nose and thought a moment before continuing.

"That's not to say I expect you to buy me everything I want—you've said 'I won't' often enough to make the point that I've got to pay for my own frivols."

"Ah, good," he said, with a glimmer of a smile. "We begin to approach the topic, then."

He stood, turning on his heel as he pointed at the various infosource behind his desk.

"Here, here and here . . . and here, these are the things that have kept you comfortable over the last fifteen years or so. These are my studies and a large part of my work."

He pulled two of the cases from the shelves and flung them onto his desk. Jerel jumped at the paired thumps.

"You know what I do for my living, so you know that sometimes people blame me for what other people pay me to do, just as someone might blame you if a package arrives broken, or a message comes too late."

She nodded, mesmerized by the intensity of his gaze. "Yes, I do know what you do, and that not everyone appreciates it."

He laughed sharply, tapping each of the two cases in turn before sitting down again at the desk.

"These projects here were done years ago. This one"—
he caressed one of the flexible holders he'd tapped—
"this one took a year to set up and another year to final-
ize. This one," he said, tapping the other, "very nearly
put me in the hospital, or worse."

He sighed, and slowly leaned back in his chair.

"Jerel, we live in uncertain times. There are people and
agencies out there in this world, and across several
worlds, who see that my business is thwarting them.
And it *is* my business to thwart them, if I take an insurance job."

He stood again, paced a quick short pace, turned to
face her.

"I wonder, Jerel, if I should send you away to trade
school. I wonder if you've been paying attention?"

"Trade school? Send me off Arantha?" That came out
as a squeak. She was going to trade school part-time
right here, plus there was her job and—

"Paying attention?" he repeated brusquely, leaning
forward, hands flat atop the folders. "I don't think you
have been paying enough attention. I find, for example,
that someone you work with, someone your age, has
gone missing in extremely strange circumstances. I
learn this not from you—the source I would expect to
hear it from—but from someone who owes me a favor
and who knows where you work. Someone who saw
the description of the missing girl and said it sounded
like you!"

Jerel shook her head *no*, looking her uncle in the face,
the knot in her stomach tying itself a little tighter.

"I guess," she said unsteadily, "we do look something
alike."

Orned nodded. "I guess you do. And that is why I ask
what you expect. How do you expect me to keep you
comfortable and in food if you won't pay attention? How

can you expect me to make sure you're safe if you don't tell me little things like this?"

She opened her mouth to explain, but he waved her off.

"What's Rule One?"

Jerel lifted her gaze to the ceiling and gritted her teeth.

"Jerel?" Uncle's no-nonsense voice, that was. She grimaced, knowing it was going to be a long afternoon, and started reciting.

"Rule One is *always be alert.*"

Orned raised his hand silently—now with two fingers showing.

She went on grimly.

"Rule Two is *take as few chances as possible.*"

Three fingers showed now.

"Rule Three is *be concerned about anomaly.*"

She had the rhythm now, continued as he raised the fourth finger.

"Rule Four is *don't attract unnecessary attention.*"

The fingers moved, showed five, but it was Uncle Orned who finished, coldly.

"And Rule Five is *stay in touch*—which for our purposes today means 'keep Orned informed.'" He paused, lips pressed into a grim line. "At the very least, you have failed to recall Rule Five—or else you have failed to observe Rules One, Two, Three, *and* Five. Am I right?"

Jerel's stomach actually hurt now. She wanted to yell, but, what would she say? She'd meant to mention Mileeda to her uncle as soon as she'd had a chance—

Orned slapped the table, and he smiled grimly.

"You're in for the evening, as you have probably guessed already. If you think of anything else I should know about, do let me know. If you don't think of anything else, study."

She nodded, and he flipped his hand toward the door in dismissal.

"We'll talk more about this tomorrow. Come right home after work. Got that? Right home!"

She got up to leave—

"One more thing, Jerel."

She turned, saw his face still serious.

"Promise me you won't do anything stupid tomorrow?"

Jerel grimaced, replaced it quickly with a slight smile.

"I promise, Uncle. And thanks for worrying about me."

He harrumphed, the set of his shoulders showing that he was still not quite relaxed, and waved her toward the door again.

She went, pleased to escape without a full self-defense test.

Chapter Two

Smug" was not too strong a word for Jerel's mood as she lounged almost anonymously in the company lecture hall. Around her were dozens of other couriers, many of them years her senior. Some had long ago moved into the freight divisions; others were trainees, though none were as young as she was. She was surprised to see so many office staffers, and so many others she couldn't identify, mostly closer to the front. They were obviously not couriers, because they were dressed for office, and not street, and besides, they didn't have a slideboard propped next to them on a seat, or leaning against a knee.

In front of her was a paper copy of the safety manual, and she had no doubt what was going to happen—someone eventually would read the thing to them, and they'd have to sign each page and hand it in. She'd taken a couple of minutes to read through her manual just in case they also threw a test at them before or after.

She'd been part of the first group in, and had been able to claim a choice seat in the middle back, where the office staffers and drivers at the front might obscure her, and where her coloring might aid invisibility. The rest of the early arrivals didn't have much to say to her, since she was low board until Mileeda came back or somebody else got hired to fill her slot. That was all right; she didn't really want to draw attention to herself, as per Uncle Orned's Rule Four.

And anyway, as much as she liked being singled out for jobs, she disliked being noticed by the staffers who didn't actually deal with couriers, who couldn't appreciate the kind of balance and reactions and speed that the travelers needed to do the job.

This morning she was particularly pleased with balance and reactions. Her uncle was sharp when it came to timing things, and he'd have noticed if she left too soon or too late, so she'd carefully left exactly as she would on an ordinary day. That meant she missed Kay, ducking his mom by going off early to the zoological preserve. That was just as well, though, because she had plenty of time to work out the feel of the revamped slideboard.

And did it feel different! She definitely had a bit more height on straight-line travel, and much firmer cornering. All that meant that she had to readjust the grips on her boots for the optimum ride. She had to stop three times before she got it right, but after that everything was smooth.

What she hadn't quite expected was that, with the proper technique, she could up the speed out of a corner considerably, and go deeper into corners before needing to slow. On some routes she'd easily be able to chop time, or maybe take on side jobs. . . .

The thought of side jobs triggered a line of speculation about Mileeda. Her body learning the new parameters of her board, Jerel wondered if Mileeda had gotten greedy on a "tipper"—a job run on the side for a tip, or sometimes even a favor. Tipping was risky, according to Uncle Orned, because the kind of folks who wanted to send an unregistered package quicktime might not be, as he put it, the very best people.

Tipping was a topic the company didn't like to talk about. As long as they had a policy of supplying new slideboards and requiring on-call couriers to have them available at all times in case of special jobs coming up, the risk of a boarder making a little spare money off side jobs was always there.

Jerel had stayed away from outside jobs, partly because of Uncle Orned's caution—though he often enough asked her to slide somewhere to pick things up for him—and partly because she wanted her study time free. She was going to be ready, the next time there was a challenge exam for ship-engine school!

"We'll be starting in a moment," a slightly nasal voice announced from directly in front of her, startling her out of her thoughts. The company didn't stint on training equipment, so the seats all had locational stereo, as well as a nifty fold-out keypad. Everyone in the place would have heard the voice as if its owner had been standing directly in front of them. She sighed; if she'd been following Rule One she'd have seen the bustle up front subside as the training director settled into the podium. . . .

"Ready?" came the voice again, and Jerel saw the training director point to someone. The lights came down, and the straggled edge of conversations cut off.

"Thank you," the director said. "We'll begin our safety review in a moment. First, though, Vice President Vasindo has a few words to say about the tragedy of the third line-of-duty death in company history."

The words took a moment to hit, and then Jerel's stomach felt as if it were in free fall. Dead? Not just missing or gone AWOL, but *dead* in the line of duty? Mileeda?

Around her the rest of the room seemed split between those who'd known something had happened and those who hadn't. The announcement also explained why all the office workers were present. The exclamations of surprise had given way to whispers, but then they faded as the lights on the front podium brightened.

Vice President Vasindo was a lanky young man not particularly well dressed in his young-executive outfit, nor particularly attractive. Jerel had seen him maybe twice in the time she'd worked for the company, and both times had thought him nothing more than an upper-level office worker. Of course, she thought now, that might still be the case; there were about half a dozen vice presidents on the company letterhead.

Whatever he did, he hadn't made much of an impression in the past, and his monotone, semi-solemn voice wasn't making much of an impression now, especially after the semi-shuffle he used to get to the front. It didn't look or sound like Vice President Vasindo was pleased to be there.

Jerel frowned at herself, wondering what he felt like, standing in front of a bunch of strangers and trying to act sad about a person he'd probably never met. For that matter, he might be afraid of talking to crowds; Uncle Orned had told her public speaking was often a bigger fear for people than going to war.

Jerel alternately gripped and stroked the slideboard in her lap, her eyes not really focused on the vice president, minding maybe half of his words. Without pausing or changing his tone, he went from telling them what a good worker and nice person Mileeda had been to announcing that they'd find police questionnaires in their go-boxes in the courier room, that failure to respond was a misdemeanor worth a fine—and that there would not be a public funeral, at the request of the family.

Public or not, Jerel knew the death and funeral would be a real problem for her now. After Uncle Orned's talk about sending her away to school . . .

Absentmindedly Jerel rubbed her right wrist, catching the phrase " . . . if you want to authorize a donation to the family from your paycheck, simply . . ."

She slid the board out of the way a moment, tapped the required ID info into the keypad, authorizing a donation amounting to about a half a day's pay. She could afford that, she guessed.

What if Uncle Orned did as he'd threatened? she thought as she settled back into her chair again. Pulled her out of school, pulled her off her job, sent her to some "safe" boarding school, off-planet? She'd hate it! Most of the nearby planets weren't much more than big farms, and if he sent her to one of the habitat schools she'd be stuck watching the same projected, and fake, outside view for weeks on end, with no real outside to go to. Besides, all those other planets were just—places. Arantha was an administrative hub. Most planets only had one little fourth-level spaceport, if they had any. Some really backward places, the only way you could get to them was by gate. Arantha, though, not only had a prime class spaceport, it had four big gates. Plus, she bet there wasn't anything like Simka's Alley on the habitats—and nothing like the formal garden, or—

This, she thought despondently, had the potential of going seriously not well. . . .

Vice President Vasindo had stopped speaking, and shuffled away from the podium. There was a moment of uneasiness while people wondered what was supposed to happen next. Jerel reached for her slideboard, hugging it to her as if it were a pet, or a friend, and let her fingers stroke the bright orange surface. Smooth and cool, smooth and cool, a comfort to touch, a comfort to ride . . .

Finally the safety director came to the podium.

"I'd like each of you to please open your copy of the manual to page six and read the company's pledge of safe working conditions. That's the second block of text, right after the company motto and the mission statement. . . ."

Jerel's wrists itched; she rubbed the right one absently, sighing. It was being just as bad as she'd feared it would be. Not only wasn't there anything new, but reading along while someone read what she was reading out loud to make sure she understood it was going to put her to sleep. There were whole sections of the manual she could have repeated from memory anyway, so this nonsense was worse than a waste of time, and wouldn't do anything for Mileeda either.

Along the way a lot of the office workers were getting dismissed back to their jobs, a small group first, then another, then another.

"Internal Slideboard Regulations is the next section," said the safety director. "Those of you from shipping who are not backup boarders, and anyone left from finance, or routing, please turn your signed manuals in at the front after you use the keypad to indicate your agreement with what we've covered. . . ."

Jerel sniffed, shifting in her chair. It was comfortable, but that didn't mean she wanted to sit in it all day when she could have been out in the streets. And now with these people getting to go to work and her needing to sit even longer she was irritated as well as restless.

Apparently the suits and staff didn't need to know all the stuff that the boarders did! Well, Uncle Orned always said that one of the joys of being on the spot was needing to know more than the people who boss you and get paid better.

The other stuff he said, like the Rules . . . well, they were pretty useful sometimes.

And the Rule about being alert . . . A quick glance around the room showed her that the remaining people in the room were boarders, security people, a couple of bosses—and two policemen, one leaning about midway down the right wall, the second leaning a little closer to the front against the left wall.

Jerel sighed, and listened as all the regulations about care of equipment, using only certified contact boots, not tampering with company-owned boards, and the like rolled by. Then they went on to road rules, and then to the awareness and office notification points and . . .

Eventually the book was done. Jerel touched the keypad to signify her agreement and prepared to take the book down to the table.

"Now," the safety director said, "we're going to ask all boarders not on a current run to please bring your board and manual to technical services."

There was some mumbling and grumbling going on, but Jerel wasn't among the grumblers. Rather, she was quiet a moment, then gathered up her board and book, a weight in the pit of her stomach. Technical services, huh?

She stood, as did the other boarders, and headed down the aisle, where several members of security were directing them to the left, toward the tech lab. She remembered Kay's well-meant, and unheeded, warning—and knew that if she fled now she'd certainly be breaking Rule Four.

The tech section had four board bays, each with multiple inspection and work desks, but today the staff was working one board to a bay, with a supervisor of some kind—the tech on the far left had Vice President Vasindo himself as a helper!—standing by. More ominously, a couple of the security crew were also standing about, and the two policemen, not nearly as inconspicuously as Jerel would have preferred.

She was third in line at the far right bay, which meant she got to see Atran, first in line, catch heck from the tech guy for applying tacky purple stickit dots on the top deck of his old-style, and a note in his folder for not reporting that his board needed a refinish to look "professional and sharp."

Problem was that Atran shifted from foot to foot so much it was hard for Jerel to see exactly what was being examined. She saw the board go into a check-it bin, but after that, nothing.

Next up was Coren, and she was shaking so hard Jerel thought she'd vibrate the whole tech bay. She didn't, but it was probably a close call.

What she did do was hold on to her board a bit too long, so the tech had to practically yank it out of her hands.

Jerel bent her head to hide the smile. One glance made it obvious why the girl was so worried. Coren's boyfriend's name was written all over the board in multiple colors of some glittery paint.

Jerel's view was clearer now than it had been with Atran. She saw the tech shake his head and the administrator, the woman the boarders all called the Galloper because of how she moved between desk and counter, actually grimace.

Other than the scribbled graffiti, though, Coren's board passed with flying colors. The tech suggested a complete beauty dip for it, and there was that note for the folder again.

Jerel'd been watching the other lines as she could, and realized that they were moving at about the same rate as hers, with most of the riders being upbraided for the condition of their equipment, which was unfair because most of them were proud of their boards.

The Galloper practically smiled at Jerel, who numbly advanced as the jittery Coren moved on, her board scheduled for a re-skin at her own expense.

The tech took Jerel's board almost gently, carefully showing its lack of stickit dots or outlandish markings to the staffer, who nodded and smiled, obviously pleased.

A flip and the board hovered over the diagnostic pad—

At which point a small red light flashed on the tech's 'nostic panel. In a moment a dial twitched and twittered, and the tech deftly used his override to turn the board full ON.

It sat perfectly still. The Galloper still beamed. The tech glanced at his gauges, and reached for a hand scanner, tentatively pushing down on the board with his free hand as he did.

Without using the scanner the tech looked at Jerel. "Ah, well, might need a bit of adjustment on this," he said without heat, "looks like it's a bit tall, as we say."

He held his hand under the board, thumb on the bottom, pinky not quite touching the tabletop.

"Right," he said, "a bit tall." He thumbed the scanner into life, pointing it at a spot Jerel recognized.

He sighed then, and turned to the Galloper.

"Someone's been inside this board, it looks like. They didn't know enough to reset the seal orients. One's close on, but the other's a good twenty degrees out of true. Hard to see the alignment if you're not running with a bit of ultraviolet in your light when you open it up."

Jerel, feigning serenity, looked on with interest. It was all she could do. That, and cuss the instructions she'd followed, which had never mentioned seal orients. . . .

"These orients," the tech said, lecturing the Galloper while keeping a half an eye on Jerel, or so it seemed to her, "these are telltales a good tech shop will use. Helps make it clear why things are scummed up, if they are. Now this board's riding high, which it oughtn't do. Be real useful for someone as slight as this rider. Could give her an extra ride or two a week, say. Course if it's been really messed with . . ."

That fast he'd shut the board down and put it on its back in the cradle. A quick, practiced motion, and the board was open.

The tech turned to face Jerel, no longer pretending to be talking to the Galloper.

"See, if you was someone with a real tool shop, and some experience, this could have been done so I wouldn't have found it on a quick check. Might be, oh, 20 percent of the boards going through here have been to a pro shop . . ."

Jerel started to say something, but her mouth didn't seem to want to work.

The tech turned back to the Galloper.

"It's up to you. This board's been opened and adjusted. It's not set to spec and before I'd certify it I'd want to tear it down and do a complete safety and mod check. You want I should issue another board until this one's straight . . ."

But the Galloper was staring at Jerel, as were some of the people from other lines.

"Is this true?" she asked. "Did you know about this?"

Jerel raised her left hand to her eyebrow in a kind of salute.

"Yes. I did know. Would have been pretty stupid of me not to know if my board had been opened, wouldn't it?"

She hadn't meant to sound like a smart mouth, but as soon as the words were out Jerel knew she'd overstepped. The woman's eyes got wide and color drained from her face.

She spun, looking down toward the vice-president, and made a kind of huffing noise, like she'd tried to whistle and it hadn't worked.

"Impound the board," she said to the tech. "Our rider will be having a talk with security and sign over three days' pay as a fine. There will also be a note in her folder. That, or she's fired!"

Jerel sensed someone closing in behind her. She reached for her board but the tech snatched it from the diagnostic cradle before she could grab it.

"You can't fire me!" she shouted at the Galloper's astonished face. "I quit!"

All of a sudden, without really having decided to do it, Jerel was running.

"Hey!" somebody called. "You!" But she didn't stop.

"I quit. Leave me alone, I quit!"

It was the work of but a moment to leave the gaping security guy behind, and another to rush by the police officer who'd been leaning, bored, against the wall.

Turning the corner, she dashed down the hall, angry and upset. The elevator was open and she reached in to punch the Down key before rushing on, toward the stairs.

Her steps sounded loud in her ears; it was a wonder everyone in the building hadn't come running to see who was making such a racket. Her boots weren't clodhoppers, but they did have the contact and control blades for the board built in and the edges clicked as she ran. She skidded slightly as she approached the manual door, the side soles of the boots bringing her to a satisfying halt so she could twist the old-fashioned knob.

Then it was down the stairs, out the emergency door with its blatant blaring horn, and down the side alley.

If she'd had her board, it wouldn't have taken her half as long to get to the end of the alley as it did.

If she'd had her board, she probably wouldn't have been grabbed by two men as she turned the corner.

CHAPTER THREE

Once she'd said she'd quit, there hadn't been anything else to do but leave. She hadn't thought to run, exactly; if she'd thought at all it was that she would walk out calm and tall, head high and showing everybody there how little the job meant to her, but it was as if the thought *Run!* got stuck in her brain like a bad song, driving her down the stairs and out the first door she came to.

It was wrong to go out the emergency exit, but Jerel doubted she was breaking any important laws. No matter—she wasn't going to stand around and listen to them prose on about a bunch of silly rules meant for beginners.

She'd been down this particular alley only once or twice, since to get there without using the emergency exit you had to skirt several aging lectrofences and a trash compactor whose existence was probably the reason for the alley, with those same impediments facing you in order to sneak into the side lot up the alley.

As it was, the whiff of old crushed lunchroom garbage and worse was enough to remind her of the other reason the place was never bothered: It stank. She was breathing in the wretched air as she ran, the paved surface feeling funny against her boots. Boy, did she miss her board!

Just ahead of her was a bright red rental truck that she'd need to duck around to get out of the alley; she could hear the whir of an engine as she approached and then heard someone yell, "Zingo! Grab her!"

She turned to see who was yelling, the contacts in the soles of her boots slid in the grit, and she stumbled, just a little.

An arm with a black thing in its hand appeared around the side of the truck. She had a moment to realize the black thing was a stunner, and tried to yell, "Let me go! Stop! Let me go!"—but the universe went strange.

For one thing, everything felt slow, and her legs stopped working. So did her arms. She could see the world, but the sounds didn't seem to reach her in synch with the action. The yell never got out of her mouth.

You're falling, do something!

That was her mind, but it was disconnected from her body. She could tell she was falling but she couldn't really feel it, not even after her bemused mind realized it. Worse, she couldn't rally her body to do anything about it.

In a moment the slow-motion feel stopped, but it was because *she'd* stopped moving, not because it was over. She could smell the sidewalk her cheek rested on, but she barely felt it.

There was something in her view now that hadn't been there a moment before. A foot, in a dark brown military-style boot.

"Think it's the right one this time?"

"Just throw her in the back before somebody comes after her, and let's get out of here. We'll check details later!"

The voices were urgent; motion started again. Jerel couldn't focus all that well, but she really didn't need to focus to know she was in bad trouble. She ought, she thought laboriously, to be scared, but mostly she was just—tired. Heavy. Too heavy to move.

It was about then that her face began to sting—not when they threw her in the cargo bed of the hauler, but before.

A far-off thought came into slow focus: stunner.

Right. Stunners were designed to stop, not to kill. Certain functions—vision, smell, and hearing among them—weren't nearly as affected as the sense of touch. The main effect of the stunner's ray was to delay certain nerve impulses.

"Tie her tight! We got to expect it'll hit her before we get there. . . ."

She struggled, or meant to, but nothing happened. Her face hurt, she couldn't think straight, and all she could see was the floor of the hauler, bouncing as she was driven away.

Wherever "there" was, Jerel wished they'd arrive soon. What would happen then she didn't know, but enough of the stun had worn off that, by concentrating, she'd managed to work up a certain level of anger. She was mad enough to let them know they'd made a *big* mistake. Just wait until Uncle Orned caught up with them! Hah. You don't mess around with an insurance man.

That thought seemed to chug around her brain for a time, waiting for another. It finally arrived: Wait until Uncle Orned caught up with her! She'd be lucky if *all* he did was send her off-world to school!

She could tell the stun hadn't completely worn off because the idea of Uncle Orned being as mad as he probably had a right to be for this stunt was . . . not nearly as appalling as she knew it should be. In fact, it really was like her thoughts were moving slow, without energy. She knew it didn't feel good, but she couldn't do anything about it. Trying to think harder just made things go slower.

She felt the hauler turn a corner, and wondered if she might be able to reach her phone when she got untied. That would have a position sender in it, if she could reach it to trigger it. Uncle Orned might be able to trace her, then, if he wasn't busy with a job.

The hauler was slowing. She guessed they were almost there. Or hoped, anyway.

Her face was starting to feel funny, and so were her feet. That didn't make much sense . . . somewhere there was more information available, if she could just get her brain to work . . .

The hauler stopped, beeped loudly from a point almost directly beneath her ear. It moved again, lurched. They must be backing up!

She tried to listen for sounds or talking, but couldn't really hear anything past the beeping in her ear. The floor was starting to slant, like they were backing up a hill or something, and she started to slide downhill, away from the door. Her legs were beginning to twitch and push against the tie cords—and her arms, too. Not only that, but she was suddenly *really* angry, or maybe it was scared.

No, it was anger *and* fear she was feeling, and besides that she was getting even more scared because the motion in her legs was going from twitches to outright pushes, like she was trying to run, and her arms began to twitch then, and her fists—she could feel her fists trying to flail about!

In very short order her face was stinging and her eyes were tearing. Her arms, tied as they were, weren't doing much, but her legs weren't tied as well and she was pushing herself all around the back of the hauler, scraping her face even more, while the whole time trying to *stop* herself.

Now she could feel her throat moving, knew, as her brain was suddenly back up to speed, that she'd be making some noise because—

"Let me go! Stop! Let me go!"

A couple more words came out after that, words she'd said—or tried to say—after the yell hadn't worked. Not words she usually used, either

But, wait, she thought—that might be good. Maybe someone would hear her and come to help her now!

The hauler lurched one more time and rocked to a standstill about the same time her legs stopped trying to run. Her fists stopped, too, and she felt exhausted and sweaty, the sound of her heartbeat loud in her ears. Not only that, but now her face really hurt.

A sharp snap as somebody worked a maglock, and the rear door of the hauler opened up. Two men stood outside, each with a stunner in hand. Both were dressed in grayish brown work clothes that looked sort of like old soldier uniforms.

"Well there, that wasn't so much fun, was it?" asked the older of the two, who was wearing a saucer-shaped hat, the gray almost exactly matching the color of his hair and sideburns. He didn't have a mustache or beard, but all that meant was he wasn't one of the Orthox refugees. The stunner was in his right hand, and a cord-cutter in his left.

The second man had brown hair, and it was hard to tell where his gray clothes stopped and his gray skin started. *A slow-soldier,* Jerel thought; she'd seen them on the newscasts. A cache of Alimen had been found stashed away in a secret cold-hibernation bin a few years back. They'd apparently retreated into hibernation as a last resort; the equipment hadn't functioned exactly as it should have, so some of them had brain damage from being low on oxygen, as well as permanent skin conditions.

That one—the slow-soldier—seemed inclined to point his stunner directly at her, while the older one smiled slightly.

"Good," he said. "I see you got enough sense not to yell now you had your little fit. Much smarter than the other one."

He turned to his companion, impatiently motioning him to put the stunner away.

"What we'll do, is we'll have you carry her. I'll walk behind, and if she makes as much as a peep, or tries to hit you or kick, I'll stun her again. This time on high, and at close range."

For some reason Jerel wasn't sure of, that made the slow-solider laugh. The laugh made her skin crawl, but not as much as the feeling of being picked up and slung over his back like a garment bag.

The man in the hat walked directly behind, smiling, his stunner almost touching her nose while her chin bumped up and down on the slow-soldier's back

Jerel lay on her back on the dusty floor, eyes open, aches and tingles in arms and legs, and a bad taste in her mouth. There wasn't anything to see, since the closet was dark and her eyes hadn't adjusted yet. She could stand, she supposed, but at the moment there didn't seem to be anything to be gained by it, and staying still might help settle her stomach and head.

On the other side of the door were her two abductors and someone else. Not just any someone, but a red-crested Turlon she was sure she wasn't supposed to have seen. It was an accident that she had seen him—she could tell by the size of his head crest that the lizard person was a male—reflected in the old-fashioned passive-plastic mirror still hanging on the wall of the abandoned apartment.

Wits, she could hear Uncle Orned saying, in his most exasperated voice—*where are your wits, girl? How could you have been caught like this?*

A surge of anger and upset flowed through her, and she almost jumped up—but thought better of it when her right foot twitched on its own, again.

This wasn't something that being mad or scared was going to get her out of, she thought. What was going to get her out of this was—

In the dark, she frowned, not exactly sure *what* was going to get her out of this.

At least, she thought, she ought to be able to see where she was. She closed her eyes, lightly, not squinching them but merely letting her eyelids cover the pupil lightly. Kay had told her that people—at least human people—could see much better in the dark if they closed their eyes for a while and then looked around with averted vision. He'd even said "averted vision," as she recalled.

I wish Kay was here, she thought, and then sighed, because of course she didn't wish Kay was there, no matter how much he might know about biology. You didn't wish for your best friend to be stuck in a closet guarded by scary men with stunners. Not even if you really wanted their help, and maybe even a hug.

Eyes dutifully rested, she looked partially away from the door, using the corners of her eyes—that was averted, or indirect, vision—trying to see useful amounts of light, or even get a peek beyond the door. Maybe if she knew where they were she could find a way to push the door open and rush out!

Her forearm stung, as if to remind her that the stunners weren't the scariest part of her situation. When they got to the apartment, the slow-soldier had heaved her down off his shoulder and held her with one hard arm around her waist while Gray Hat got all her things out of her pockets and stripped off her belt pack. Mindful of the stunners, she hadn't dared to try to stop him. After he'd taken all her stuff, he pushed her sleeve up and pressed a sample pad against her skin. Then the slow-soldier had walked her across the room, still holding her hard against him, and shoved her into the closet, closing the door with a bang and a laugh.

That sample pad, she thought—that wasn't a good sign. A normal med-reader pad, crisscrossed by tiny detectors, would have left little behind to irritate her skin. But a sample pad meant they'd got some of her skin, some of her blood, maybe a reading on her temperature and pulse, and some DNA.

The DNA part was worrisome. If they were making sure she was Jerel Telmon they might be the kind of crackpots her uncle had been warning her about since she was just a little kid—people who thought that by hurting someone from the family they'd somehow gain revenge against her dead parents.

If she put her cheek on the cool, dusty floor of the closet and looked sidewise out of her right eye she could see almost nothing. The floor on the outside was the same as the floor on the inside.

She thought that if she watched long enough she might be able to see shadows or reflections of feet if her kidnappers walked around, but she didn't know what good that would do. She wouldn't be able to tell them, because even Turlons had two feet and two arms, looking a bit like humans who'd somehow gotten lizardized.

No, wait! Likely the Turlon wasn't wearing the same kind of boots. And from her quick glimpse in the mirror, she'd seen that he was dressed a lot fancier than the guys who'd grabbed her, in bright, glittery colors. It might be important if she could figure out who was who from their shoes.

Jerel slithered along the floor, and put her cheek and ear against the door. She pushed hard enough that if the door had just been closed it would have popped open. She hadn't expected that to happen because the latching sound had been pretty distinct when they'd slammed the door behind her, but she figured she ought to be sure.

The door wasn't soundproof, though she could hear nothing more than a couple of distant mumbles and what might have been pacing footsteps.

She sat up, leaned against the door edge.

Hah! At the proper angle she could see a bit . . . and look!—the plaskit frame was so warped that she could even see through a gap there if she squinted.

The cheap construction and the abandonment of the place probably meant this was part of the briefly used way-housing from the war. For all she knew the Alimen and other refugees still lived here, stuck in between by a war that had never really finished, had never really been won or lost.

Oh, true, the Families here on planet had been deposed, but that had been almost an afterthought, and as much because they'd run up bills they couldn't pay than because they'd lost the war—and anyway, it was all over and done with. Ancient history.

She tried peering out the other side of the door, scooting around on her bum rather than standing. She still didn't quite trust her legs and arms.

It was then, face pressed close to the crack—through which she could vaguely see a wall—that she heard the slow-soldier talking.

"Looks like them colors are close, don't it, Mosey? Wouldn't you call them close? I mean, if I was to look across the room and see them two colors side by side I'd . . ."

There was a mumble, then a liquid voice saying something quietly, then the soldier's voice again.

"Well, that's what I thought. That means we got the right one this time, don't it? You gonna want to take her with you?"

More mumbles, more of the sibilant voice.

"Oh, no problem with me, Captain. I can wait for your confirming sample to get here. Go ahead, take your nap. We'll sit watch as long as we have to. All I have is time. Plenty of time, with nothing but waiting in it. If we're leaving in the morning it's the same to me as leaving now. Wonder if she likes spaceships?"

Spaceships?

Jerel's anger spiked along with the fear; she was afraid for a moment that she'd be sick. *Spaceships* probably meant that she was being held by exactly the kind of people her uncle had warned against. She swallowed hard, her thoughts skittering around her head like they were looking for a place to hide. She clenched her fists and did one of the breathing exercises Uncle Orned had taught her. Slowly, she got less scared, and her thoughts smoothed out.

One thing she figured was for sure. She wasn't going to just let them stun her again and drag her to the spaceport like a bag of rags. Her parents hadn't given up, and neither would she.

She'd fight.

Or maybe, she thought, thinking about the slow-soldier and the stunners, escaping would be better.

What she needed now was a plan!

CHAPTER FOUR

Jerel stood quietly in the closet, counting. She'd already hit twelve dozen once, counting slowly, and at each dozen she'd carefully moved. First she moved her right hand, making sure all the fingers were responding, then her left hand. She rolled side to side, exercised her right foot and then her left.

When she was sure her legs were working, she stood, being as quiet as possible, not wanting to give away the fact that she was mobile. She'd seen enough bad media plots to know that someone couldn't just shake off a stunner blast, so she didn't want to rush. On the other hand, she had the feeling that Gray Hat thought she'd be sicker than she was, so if she *could* get moving, that was an advantage. Above everything else, though, she absolutely never again in her lifetime wanted to be stunned.

Now she was standing tall in the darkness. For the count of twelve, she just stood there, giving her stomach time to make up its mind about being sick. It decided against, and though her head still hurt, and her face, she figured she was mobile. Carefully, quietly, she stretched, then flexed her knees while keeping firmly centered on her feet, and leaned this way and that, as if she were on her slideboard. She wasn't on her board, of course, and when she leaned too hard there was a slight grinding sound from beneath her feet—that would be the contact blades in her boots.

The counting had been a good idea, she decided. Both elbows were working. Both knees were working. Wrists and ankles were fine. Her hands and fingers moved to order, and so did her feet and toes.

Besides counting, she'd been trying to "tote up her assets." When she'd been a little kid, Uncle Orned had a game he'd like to play. They'd pretend they were stuck someplace—in the elevator, say, or in the shower room at home—and then they'd take all the stuff out of their pockets to see what they could use to escape. "Toting up the assets" meant sorting through everything they had on them for the things that were most likely to be useful.

This was a little different from that, she acknowledged, on account of Gray Hat having taken all her pocket stuff and her carrybag, too. But, she still had some things with her.

She had, for instance, a belt, her clothes, her boots. It might be she could use the belt to swing at somebody— she'd bet getting snapped in the face with the tip of a belt would sting—or she could put it around somebody's neck; but that wasn't her first best option. Slow-soldier and Gray Hat were stronger than her, and the stunners had range over a belt. She didn't want to fight with them directly unless there wasn't any other choice. The question was—did she have another choice?

She rubbed her right wrist, listening for more sounds from the outside, shifted her weight slightly and heard that grating noise again. . . .

Wait! She still had her boots, which even now were etching lines in the cheap flooring almost every time she moved.

Quickly, she sat back down on the dusty floor, fingertips caressing the seals on her boots. With a quiet little hiss the seals parted and she carefully took them off, right and left on the proper sides. Biting her lip, she pressed the tiny adjustment button on the left boot. A small LCD glowed in the dimness. She pressed the button three times . . . saw the "?" symbol, which meant "Are you sure?"

Since she wasn't very likely to stumble over a slideboard keyed to her boots in the next little while, she pressed the button once more, for "Yes."

The twin blades of the slideboard contacts slipped part of the way out of the boot sole.

Usually she used gloves for this, but her boarding gloves were in her carrybag, along with her tool set. Teeth drilling into her lower lip, she worked very carefully, not wanting to bloody her fingers on the polished veramin. The blades finally came out, and she held them balanced across her palm, knowing that the slightest squeeze would cut her.

Now what? she thought. She hadn't gotten much further than realizing she had a potentially useful tool on her, but now that the blades were out, she needed a way to handle them safely. Leaning the blades against their boot so they wouldn't fall flat—if they did, she'd never be able to pick them up again!—she reluctantly took off her socks, and wrapped them around the two naked blades.

Realizing that she'd been holding her breath while handling the blades, Jerel sighed, and did the breathing exercise again, forcing herself to relax before she picked up the right boot and touched the button.

Now she had a fine collection of extremely sharp, extremely thin blades. She was surprised to see they were shiny enough to pick up some of the light that leaked in beneath the door, flashing it into her face.

She put her boots back on, grimacing at the slightly clammy feel of the temperature and pressure reactive "sure-cush" lining. She'd paid a lot for these boots, just because of that lining, made especially for slideboarders and the heavy workout they gave their feet.

Though she was being careful, she accidentally clunked the door with one boot and held her breath. Nobody came to investigate, though, and after counting very slowly to thirty-six, she finished putting her boot on—her eyes on the blades braced along the wall.

They really were mirror-shiny, she thought. Maybe she could angle them to see what was going on outside!

"Go ahead and yell, kid," Gray Hat called unconcernedly through the door. "Ain't nobody can hear you! Might just as well save your breath while you got some!"

While it wasn't the news Jerel had been hoping for, it was what she'd expected—her captors weren't afraid of being bothered.

What she'd discovered with her limited spying was that Slow-soldier and Gray Hat were alone in the room at the moment, and that the left wall of her closet was against a wall to another room, if not another apartment. This was, she told herself firmly, hopeful. What she needed to do next was to find out what was in that other room.

Her blades bundled together in a double layer of socks, she tried to pierce the shared wall by putting the blades against the wall and leaning her weight against them.

This actually worked, but it was slow going, partly because she needed to be quiet and partly because her weight was a little on the light side. Usually, she didn't care about being skinny, but now she was sorry she wasn't solid and big like her sometime friend Sherina.

She was through! Jerel almost shouted with relief, her hands and shoulders so cramped, she was tempted to tears.

Putting her eye to the hole, she glimpsed another room. There was a piece of furniture blocking one edge of her vision, but what made her heart leap was the sight of a window, dead ahead.

The spyhole she'd made was barely the size of a pen; obviously she was going to need something larger. The wall itself was kind of a plaskit sandwich, with an easy-to-penetrate foam core about as thick as her thumb between two sheets of firmer material.

Surprisingly, once through, she found widening the hole was easy, now that she could bring the much sharper sides of the blades into play. The work went quickly, but the sawing made the plaskit panel reverberate with a low drumming noise.

She heard voices outside her closet, and put her ear to the door.

"Hear that, Mosey?" the slow-soldier asked. "Sounds like a copter or something."

There was an answer she couldn't exactly hear, maybe something about "the kid crying, just ignore it."

The slow-soldier had heard her working at the wall. Jerel bit her lip. She couldn't stop now! But if she kept on, the slow-soldier would hear and might even convince Gray Hat—Mosey—to check the closet, and—wait. Gray Hat expected her to be scared—to cry and maybe yell. She'd been so intent on not giving them the satisfaction, and on her plan for escape, that she'd missed sorting another asset into her "useful" pile.

She began to yell, and kept it up, begging to be let out, promising her uncle would give them a reward, telling them they could keep her pocket stuff, all the time working furiously at the wall. A fine flaky powder built up on her hand and all over her socks as she continued sawing and yelling, and she'd cut a section wider than her shoulders, and another down the side. Soon it would be big enough for her to climb through!

Someone banged on the door, scaring her enough that the next scream was almost real. She half-turned, almost yanking the blades out of the wall.

"Shut it down before you wake the boss," Gray Hat yelled. "Any more and we use the stunner again!"

She yanked down hard on her saw, and the cut panel leaned away from her, into the next room.

"Please don't," she whimpered. "I'll be quiet. I'll be quiet. . . ."

There was ugly laughter from beyond the door, and a half-muffled "Yeah, you'll be quiet, all right."

Light streamed through the hole in the wall. Jerel pushed against the panel, which quite willingly creased, folding down and away. She took a breath, and stepped through, gripping a slideboard blade bound with a gritty sock in one hand.

The sight that greeted Jerel when she stepped through the wall nearly stopped her heart. It looked like they had a torture setup in place—there were binding ropes and what looked like some kind of lie graph hooked up to a chair—and on the bed among it all, a red-crested Turlon slept, wrapped in several blankets despite the warmth of the room, and curled around what was probably a portable heat rock.

Keeping a good grip on her improvised knife, Jerel slipped to the window and saw she was barely her own height above the ground. If she could open the window and get out without waking the Turlon, or making the soldiers in the next room suspicious . . .

She fumbled with the old-fashioned manual lock, each sound ringing like an alarm bell in her ears, but finally got it open. Pushing the window aside was another matter; it barely budged the first time she shoved it.

She tried again, holding her breath, and this time got a squeak for her trouble. She held her breath, ears straining.

No noise from the other room; the Turlon on the bed slept on undisturbed.

Oh, no!

There on the table next to the bed was some of her own pocket stuff, including her house key!

While she struggled with herself, she pushed again at the window, applying steady pressure, and felt it yield. It crawled upward ever so slowly, in a series of jerks. By the time the opening was wide enough for her to fit through, she'd decided that Uncle Orned wouldn't want her to leave her house key with such people, and she took a deep breath.

If Kay was with her, he'd know how soundly Turlons sleep, or where she should stick the sharp blade if he woke up and rushed her. . . .

There was a sound in the other room—the distant mumble of voices, and maybe a door opening!

Risking all, she dashed close to the bed, where the shut-eyed sleeper lay with limp crest, face toward the heat rock, and grabbed up her key and her minimulti. If she'd had that useful all-purpose tool with her in the closet she could have been out of the place a long time back! Heart pounding, she leapt toward the window; there was movement on the bed as she did so, a languid stretch, as if the sleeper was coming awake slowly. . . .

She dropped the wrapped blade on the floor and threw herself out of the window, the shock of landing nearly jarring her key and other stuff from her hands.

She didn't dare look to see if anybody was watching, but fled down the hill, toward the center of the city—and home.

CHAPTER FIVE

Jerel was in good shape—she had to be to qualify as a courier. Still she was more than a bit out of breath as she exited the elevator and headed for the door to home.

For one thing, she'd used the elevator to the third floor, then ran to the fifth floor and across to the other wing to take the elevator to the seventh floor, and from there she ran back past the convenience store in the other wing and walked two more flights of stairs before picking up the express from the ninth to the twenty-ninth floor. In the whole time she was in her building she hardly saw anyone who might recognize her beside the convenience-store girl— and she'd been too busy flirting to notice Jerel rush by.

It had been risky, but right, she decided, to grab her keys off the table near the sleeping Turlon. None of the stair doors would have opened for her if she hadn't had a key; and the express 'vator would have sealed her in and called security if she'd tried to use it without giving it her key to scan.

Besides her being out of breath, there was a stitch in her side. She'd quick-marched herself out of Oldside, going through an overgrown patch of vegetation that some community improvement group had planned to turn into a park but never finished, and then alternated walking and running until she was on her side of town, using some of the shortcuts she'd discovered as a courier. She'd managed to scrape herself up some more in her rush through the silly park, and her feet felt funny in the boots without her socks.

She sorely missed her slideboard, but probably drew less attention as a walker through the more crowded parts of the downtown city anyway.

Now that she was at her own place, she tried to breathe deep and steady as she pulled out her key. The palm reader checked out her prints, the door took her key and codes . . .

There. The seal slid aside and she entered, after checking the hall one more time to make sure no one else was in sight. If she'd been followed, it was by somebody really good.

As soon as the door closed she threw all the locks on it she could and entered the shutdown code, which would even keep emergency crew like firemen, or maybe more importantly, police, out—and then leaned against the wall, eyes closed.

She was immediately rewarded for not having screamed for Uncle Orned when she got in—she could hear him talking quite loudly in his office. It was unusual for him to bring work home, so the visitor must be one of those rare friends from his past. It was interesting, too, that he'd left the door on only one lock. There was almost always a reason for what Uncle Orned did.

The stitch had eased out of her side. Jerel sighed and opened her eyes, coming out of her comforting lean against the wall.

All things considered, and no matter who was with him, she was going to need to interrupt. "Rule Five," she muttered. "Stay in touch."

She strode toward his office, hearing him so plainly that it must be the door was open. And Uncle Orned never kept his office door open.

"You will not," he was saying sharply, "simply 'take the child' with you! You may have had her from my brother's own hands fifteen years ago but she is not quite the pliable youngling you think her, nor am I the fool you apparently believe me to be."

Uncle Orned, thought Jerel, was really mad. This was daunting enough that she paused outside the door, even though he wasn't mad at her. Yet.

The answering voice was quiet and slightly sibilant. It reminded Jerel of another voice she'd heard recently, but—

"Coming of such genes and with your excellent tutelage I am certain that she has been prepared and held in readiness. I do not doubt that young Jerel is accomplished! And, you—brother to my—"

"Held in readiness!" Uncle Orned interrupted, which wasn't like him at all. "No, she has not been *held in readiness*, Erazias. She's been raised per the instructions you brought from my brother—*in safety, and with kindness and respect*! Which is why—" His voice cut off, which Jerel figured meant he'd taken a look at the status board.

"Enough! I see that she's home and I'd guess she's lurking in the hall. She may as well take part in this now."

Sighing, Jerel straightened her shoulders and walked forward. *Might as well get it over with*, she thought fatalistically. She crossed the threshold on the mark of Uncle Orned's shouted "Jerel!"

He was out of his chair faster than she'd ever seen him move. She stopped, and saw that the other person in the room was an ornately robed blue-crested Turlon seated in the chair she usually used, and her stomach cramped. Another Turlon? What was this, a tour ship?

Uncle Orned was at her side; hand on her arm, he led her to his own chair, which she'd not dare sit in otherwise, reached out and slid two fingers under her chin, tipping her face toward the light.

"What happened?" he asked, and he didn't sound angry anymore, but as cool and calm as usual.

Jerel sat back in his chair, relief making her eyes water. She was home, and Uncle Orned would take care of everything now.

Jerel had always thought the phrase "green around the gills" had something to do with fish, or with being sick, but as she looked now, a glass of her favorite soft drink in hand, the Turlon—Erazias was his name, introduced curtly by Uncle Orned as a former student of her mother's—was distinctly greener than he had been, his hands and the skin around his eyes blue-green, instead of the dark blue color they had been when she'd entered. His robes were—amazing. Among the shimmering colors and folds upon folds of cloth it was hard to get an idea of his real size; hard to know what the various buckles, belts, and strings led to, or meant.

Uncle Orned had been a real dear for not yelling at her in front of company for her stupidity in quitting—or, well, she admitted, might as well strike the "quitting" and let "stupidity" stand for it all—but his questions seemed to have a point she wasn't quite getting.

Erazias leaned forward. He'd been asking questions, too, and his were about the visibility of weapons, and threats, his tongue sometimes appearing very circum-spectly between his lips for a moment. When he began to speak it was as if he needed to loosen his tongue, or wet it, to make speech possible, so often he began with a *ffftt* kind of noise.

She'd happened to be watching him when the threat of spaceships was mentioned, and she'd seen the area around his eyes tinge greener, almost to yellow. His visible hand had clutched one of the silver harnesses among the folds of his robes as if he sought assurance of some object buried within.

"You did well not to call the police in on this," Uncle Orned was saying to her now. "I'll have to do some research to make sure the news hasn't gotten out; we may have to arrange a surprise for the people who . . ."

"We have already moved beyond that, Hunter," Erazias said, punctuating his statement with a fluid movement of his right hand. Jerel saw that his thumb looked really bright green now; she'd been sure that it was blue moments before.

"We have arrived at the cusp I told you of," the lizard man said, "and our enemies are very nearly before us. This red-crest she speaks of—this bodes not well, I fear. We shall need to leave—and very soon. Revenge must wait until we return, victorious."

Orned leaned his face into his hands for a moment as he sat at the extra chair he'd brought into the room while ministering to Jerel's various bruises and scrapes. His touch had been both gentle and professional; clearly he'd had experience tending to the wounded.

He dropped his hands, but didn't look at Erazias, apparently finding the rug worthy of study. "If we must move on this, we can," he said quietly, and not as if he liked the idea at all, "but the timing is not good. I have things in progress, and to come to us without warning—

in fact to come to us *as if we should have known* of this—I am without words."

He sighed, straightened, and gave Jerel a measuring glance.

"I think you should get something to eat," he said briskly. "In fact, we all should eat something. Would you please get us some food, and bring it to us here? Erazias and I have some more talking to do."

Jerel took the hint, feeling sore muscles in her legs as she rose to leave. She first strode toward the kitchen, then changed her mind and went to her room, where she gratefully took off her altered boots, stretched her legs, and put socks on, glad to have something beside the sticky lining against her feet.

Then she put on her old pair of slideboots, not because she was expecting to go sliding but because she didn't want to get out of the habit, and besides, she didn't feel right in regular street shoes anymore.

Her mail-drop light was flashing on the desk—might be anyone, might be Kay!

She checked with a touch on the switch, and the screen came up blank, except for a couple words.

Kay it was—a simple note that said, "I'm here. Let me in! Important."

She laughed, because the message was such a normal thing—and then frowned. "I'm here"—that was all right; just their usual way of telling each other they were on the way to visit. But the stress on letting him in, that the visit was important—that wasn't usual at all.

She grabbed her hand phone from its dock and tucked it in a pocket. Uncle Orned frowned on her using his phone, and Gray Hat had taken her pocket unit. If Kay needed to check in . . .

She ran to the door, used the video to make sure that only Kay was in the hall, then raced through the opening sequence, checking the video again when the door was ready.

Kay stormed in, surprising her with a quick, hard hug.

"You're fine?" he asked, as if he knew she wasn't. He realized of a sudden that he was close to her—and wrinkled his nose as he sidled away.

"Hey, you smell like a physician's office!"

She stepped back a bit, too, nodding, sorry he had moved.

"Yeah, I guess I do. I had . . . I had an accident and fell on my face. Uncle Orned said I had to use some antibacterial junk and all—you know how parents are!" She jerked her head toward the kitchen. "C'mon, I need to get some food together."

Kay nodded, and looked around as if making sure Uncle Orned wasn't close by at the moment, and walked behind her to the kitchen, talking low.

"Listen, I think there's trouble. Police are looking for someone like you off on the other end of Oldside, that's what my mother told me. And she's been on the comm unit talking to people for the last hour. She said she saw a Turlon she'd recognize anywhere wandering around the building. You aren't hiding a Turlon, are you?"

He made a goofy face, like it was a joke; it faded when she hesitated.

"Jerel?"

"Well, we're not *hiding* him," she protested. "But he's here."

Kay looked aghast.

"You've got one of the most famous people on five worlds just calmly visiting you?" he demanded, then looked sheepish and added, half-apologetically, "My mom says."

Jerel opened the coldstat, pulled out a couple of random quick-meals, and threw them into the 'wave with a practiced toss before snapping the door shut. The machine beeped happily to itself as it read the heating instructions, and then hummed into action.

"I don't how famous he is," Jerel allowed. "He's someone I met when I was a baby and I haven't seen him since. He knew my parents. But—the police are looking for *me*? Is your mom sure?"

"Ah, you known how she is—always checking the comm links, listening to the police and the emergency bands, in case the counterrevolution gets started. And talking to all kinds of people, trying to hook up with the ones that are 'still loyal'"—Jerel could hear the quotation marks in Kay's voice when he said that—"and who'll make us rich when the Oligarchy comes back. Anyhow, somewhere she heard that there'd been a fuss at Capsule Courier . . ." Here he looked into her face; disbelieving, she felt her face heat. Blushing! What a dork.

"And," Kay finished, "that the police were called in."

The 'wave bleeped its "mission accomplished" noise and Jerel gladly turned to deal with it.

"Yeah, there was a fuss," she said over her shoulder. "We had an inspection and the tech found where I'd altered my board, and they were going to fire me, so I quit and left. But—the police? Why would the—unless they thought I had something to do with . . ."

She didn't finish the sentence, but Kay did. ". . .with Mileeda's murder?"

That made her shiver, despite holding the hot meals. She grabbed a couple of disposable plates, then looked him in the eye.

"That doesn't sound good, does it?" she asked

He shook his head. She was very pleased he wasn't doing an I-told-you-so about the inspection and her alterations.

Jerel opened the food packs, arranged them on a tray—and then remembered Erazias. She'd just grabbed what came to hand without even thinking—

A quick hunt found some nitrogen-packed phalanas—a kind of tubelike veggie pancake stuffed with yummy bean cheese, according to the package; the Food Compatibility Code dots were blue, red, and green, meaning almost anyone could eat them—and a pack of irradiated soy snaps that showed both red and blue dots. She stared at the code a minute, then decided it didn't matter who *couldn't* eat them as long as she and Uncle Orned and Erazias could.

She got the rest of the food onto the tray along with three bottles of water, and smiled at Kay.

"I gotta go. Might be you should go on home. I'll drop you some mail or we can talk later, depending on stuff. Right? And thanks for being worried about me and checking up."

Then she thought of something else.

"Kay—maybe you might not want to mention to your mom that we've got that Turlon here. I mean, it isn't like you've seen him, is it?"

He grinned, a little lopsided, and nodded.

"Right. My mother'd be on about it for years. I'm gone. You know where to find me!"

The conversation stopped when Jerel entered. She put the tray down in the center of Uncle Orned's desk, where they could all reach it.

"Kay was here," she said to her uncle. "His mom says the police were looking for me after I left CapCour."

Uncle Orned froze, his hand on a bottle of water.

Erazias also froze, his eyes suddenly outlined in yellow. Jerel knew some people who would love to be able to change their eyeshadow like that.

Her uncle recovered first; wordlessly turning his back on Jerel and Erazias, his hands busy at the computer. In a matter of moments he turned again to face them.

"That woman has connections to be envied. I can't imagine that it's an accident she lives in our building."

Face grim, he motioned Jerel to sit.

"Eat. We're all going to eat. I've set some inquiries in motion. I hope you'll remember your Rules in the future, Niece; it certainly looks as if they might have come in useful today!"

"Rules?"

Jerel looked away from the questioning Turlon—family Rules weren't any of his business. Orned waved a hand at him, saying impatiently, "Eat, will you? You're the one who wants us ready to get on the road!"

They ate in silence, Erazias not commenting on Jerel's choice of food, but not eating very much of it, either. Well, Jerel thought, for all she knew he had a season's supply of food stashed about his person. Those robes could have hidden a slideboard and had room for another.

For that matter, Uncle Orned didn't seem to be noticing much except whatever he could see of his various computer and comm devices. Jerel didn't have anything to say, sure that whatever was going on was her fault and glad that Uncle Orned hadn't elaborated about the Rules to the visitor.

Five Rules, she thought, forcing herself to eat. Five Rules ought to be easy enough to remember and to follow and she'd really messed up most of them in the same day this time! She wondered if that might be some kind of record—not that she figured it would be a good idea to ask Uncle Orned, even after Erazias was gone and he was over being mad.

Thinking over the Rules one more time, and all the mistakes she'd made on the day, Jerel suddenly realized that she was staring at Erazias. It wasn't that he was ugly, which he wasn't, or that he was being rude, which he wasn't. Only, she wasn't used to watching someone wrap their tongue over a phalanas and then around it, and using that to pull bits of it into their mouth. She knew kids who ate a lot messier, using both hands and a full set of utensils, and if your tongue could do all that, why not?

Uncle Orned muttered when a small beep sounded behind him; he turned to his computer, then cursed mildly. It was perhaps the first time Jerel had heard him curse since the day some years before when she'd managed to break a supposedly break-resistant dish he'd been particularly fond of.

"That would be police news," said Erazias to the room in general. "And I am not at all surprised. This will be an effort by the Families to force our hand yet again. I gather they still have their supporters in place here; and what better place for a supporter than with the local security forces?"

Uncle Orned said something under his breath, at the same time pushing against his desk drawer awkwardly, as if trying to pull it up rather than out.

To Jerel's great surprise and to Erazias's bland acceptance, the top of the desk lifted and slid open.

"Finish your meal quickly," Uncle said to Jerel, "and here. Don't touch the safety unless you really have to!"

His motion was a casual toss. Jerel instinctively caught the object in her left hand, and suddenly felt even less like eating. She held a tiny four-shot gun, very much like the one she'd admired and practiced with at the local firing lanes, wrapped in a nycloth holder. It was small enough to tuck easily in under her belt—or inside her clothes—if she needed to. She'd thought it belonged to the armsmaster at the gun shop . . . but it or its twin was in her hand.

"First, we'll need to . . ." Orned was saying, just as Jerel's phone went off. She'd forgotten to change the ring to vibrate!

She snatched the phone from her pocket, saw the number 77 glowing on the screen.

"It's Kay," she explained to her Uncle's raised eyebrow, and he nodded, giving her permission to take the call.

"Go," she said to the phone, and Kay's excited voice burst in.

"I'm here," he said quickly, "and with big news. My mother—anyhow, I *am* here."

Uncle Orned looked at Erazias, who was still calmly eating. The Turlon made a small motion like the fluttering of a bird with one hand, and Uncle nodded to Jerel.

"Let him in as long as there is no one else in the hall. If anyone else is there—*anyone* else—don't open the door."

Jerel rushed to the front, still carrying the gun wrapped in its holster. The video showed a clear hall except for Kay, who was carrying what looked like his hiking pack. In fact he looked like he was tricked out for a hike, or for giving a lecture at the zoo.

She opened the door, grabbed his arm, and pulled him in.

His eyes went wide as he saw the gun in her hands.

"It *is* happening," he whispered. "My mother was right!"

Erazias watched Kay carefully, glancing back and forth between him and his pack. Kay didn't notice; he was running on, all his attention on Jerel and her uncle, with hardly a glance for the other visitor in Orned's suddenly cramped office.

" . . . but I didn't tell her you had company or anything. She's been excited the last few days like she gets sometimes if she got a note from one of her old friends. And then she's been scanning all the news, all the time, staying up late and getting up late. Anyhow, when I got back just now she told me I was going to have to make a decision, because she was sure you wouldn't let Jerel go to jail . . ."

"Did she say what exactly Jerel might be going to jail for?" That was Uncle Orned, uncharacteristically breaking in while someone was talking.

Kay glanced at her; she smiled to show she knew he was only repeating what his mom had told him. He sighed and put his attention back on Orned's face. "She said she figured that the police were going to say that Jerel was involved somehow in Mileeda dying. She said the new government's so incompetent that they'd rather blame the wrong person in a hurry than spend time to do things right. And she said you wouldn't put up with that."

Uncle Orned fluttered his hand much the way Erazias had earlier, and looked firmly at both Kay and Jerel.

"What decision did she expect you to make? Did she say?"

Kay nodded seriously.

"She told me that it was my duty, as true-blood Vanion, to do whatever I could to help a friend in trouble. To do anything else would be dishonorable, and she was sure I wouldn't want to, to disgrace my father's name and family. That I would make the right decision, but that I had to understand that it *was* a decision. Then she said she was proud of me, and that she'd stand behind me."

He kind of shrugged, and looked directly at Jerel. "This is the worst I've ever seen her," he muttered, apologetically. He looked back to Uncle Orned.

"I'm not really sure what she meant, sir. Sometimes it's like she makes up stories and then forgets they're nothing but made-up. Anyhow, she gave me money and some of her jewelry, and told me to get ready to travel, in case Jerel needed help. And, she said it wouldn't be good for the police to come to our house and find out how often Jerel and I talk or see each other, because if you left, they'd question me and her and want to search our place."

"*Fffttt*," said Erazias, or something very much like it. "Tell me, youngling, is there something about your relationship with *terama* Jerel that would worry the law-protectors? Have you been stealing lane markers off the streets? Robbing old soldiers of their medals and certificates? Are you performing illicit acts together?"

Kay's face reddened and he dared a glance at Jerel. She was beyond amazement at this point, however, and didn't catch the implication at first. By the time she did . . .

"But see," he said seriously, "I did know that Jerel had messed with her slideboard. I guess it wasn't illegal for her to do that, but I know it was against company rules, 'cause Jerel'd even told me so."

"Hold!"

That was Uncle Orned. Jerel blinked. Sitting behind him on the desk were two more weapons—he must have pulled them out of hiding when she went for Kay. This was starting to look even badder and scarier than being held by Gray Hat and the slow-soldier.

"Kay, I'm afraid you're caught up in something beyond your control, and I'm sorry for it," Uncle Orned was saying in his cool, calm voice. "Your mother's predilection for conspiracies has brought you here for a second time tonight and I'm afraid she may be correct in saying that you must make a choice. You must know that she does have an odd point to what she's saying. If you knew that Jerel was adjusting her board without permission that means you could be guilty of violating a very minor civil law—'conspiracy to violate a lawful contract.' Any competent lawyer should be able to defend that with scarcely any inconvenience to yourself. But, if the police are trying to tie Jerel to Mileeda's death, that's a far more serious thing. In a murder investigation, anyone associated with the suspect will be questioned. Not only questioned, but perhaps held and investigated. Maybe even hypnoed."

He paused to sip his water, then revved his hand up into a flutter again like he was thinking before he went on—

"You'd have to admit to being associated with my niece, wouldn't you? And what if they claim that Jerel's tinkering was part of a criminal conspiracy. Poof!—they can hold you for years while they investigate, especially if Jerel isn't here to dissuade them."

"But Jerel didn't . . ."

Uncle Orned laughed, almost meanly.

"No, you are correct. Jerel didn't. And for reasons far beyond this poor planet, we can't let her whereabouts be as definite as a jail cell." He smiled crookedly at Kay. "So you see, your mother has told you nothing but the truth there, too."

Jerel sat in near shock. Somehow the events of the last few days fell into one tangled pile of accident and came out looking like she was part of a plot against Mileeda—and that Kay was, too. She'd take a lie detector test if she needed to, but she frowned. The problems with the police and even Gray Hat and the slow-soldier were only one side of what was going on. There was something else—something that had brought Erazias here, demanding that Uncle Orned give her to him, and nobody, she suddenly realized, had exactly told her what that was about *at all*.

"What do you mean, sir?" Kay asked tentatively. "Are you going to hide Jerel from the police?"

"Why, yes," Uncle Orned said. "In a way."

He looked at Kay, then at Jerel, then at Erazias, and then at all of them at once.

"We are leaving the planet as soon as we can get to a spaceship or a gate. All of us. It's not safe for Jerel to stay, which means it isn't safe for me, nor for Erazias. And your mother has told you true again, Kay—you must make a decision: Come with us, or run the very real risk that the police will try to use you to find Jerel."

He sighed.

"Your mother, for all her silliness, has put you into a conspiracy, even if it didn't exist until you walked through the door just now. She'll owe you for that, I'm sure."

"You're serious!" Kay exclaimed. "I mean—I thought I'd just have to hide out over here until Mom found something else to—sleep in the media room or something. . . ."

Against her will, Jerel chittered a laugh, the idea of Kay throwing a sleepsack on the floor in front of the display somehow hitting her funny bone.

Uncle Orned nodded. "You're right, Jerel. It would have been great fun if that's all that was going on. But as it stands, I think we're going to be out of this place tonight. Probably permanently. And you're in, Kay, up to your eyebrows."

Kay turned to Jerel and grinned.

"Remember when we used to play space chase? This'll be just like it! Nobody will be able to keep up with us!"

At that, Erazias rose, and bowed a sinuous and complex bow to Kay, his robes swishing gently and adding greatly to the grandeur of the motion.

"All will be well if that is the case, youngling. When a journey begins in optimism it is more likely to end in success!"

Jerel watched, surprised, as Kay returned the bow—no, he did something subtly different—and then said something, or spoke something, or maybe just sneezed.

"Your accent is execrable," Erazias said, "but you have the gist of it. And the bow is commendable in all ways. And so we start. Comrades!"

They all bowed again, to each other, and with various degrees of grace. When the bows were over, Uncle Orned took charge.

"I see that Kay is already provisioned," he said crisply. "And I have bags packed for us. We'll be out of here in a moment. Right now, everyone will have to stay close to me; once we get going we'll all know our destinations ahead of time in case we get split up."

"Now, Jerel, open that closet over there. It'll need your print to do it!" This partly in emphasis as Kay, closer, tried the door unavailingly. "I'll get my bag from . . ."

Jerel opened the closet quickly. Inside was a worn backpack with one of her light jackets draped across it. She put the jacket on, and slung the bag over one shoulder. Okay, she thought. They were going off-world for a little while, until the police found whoever actually had killed Mileeda. Maybe she'd find out what Erazias's problem was and maybe she wouldn't, but, really, things would settle down pretty soon and she and Kay and Uncle Orned could come home and get back to normal.

A buzzer—another—and another went off on Uncle Orned's desk.

He turned, surveyed the situation, and cursed, briefly.

"The front lifts are all on emergency control. We'll have to use the locals and the stairs to get out."

He looked at Kay very seriously. "Listen closely to me, Kay. If you go out the door with us, you may be risking your life. If you don't want the risk, I can knock you out, and you'll be an innocent victim, with a lump on his head to prove it."

Jerel saw Kay's face go white.

"I'm coming with Jerel," he said firmly. "Part of this is my fault anyway—if I'd tried harder to talk her out of messing around inside her board maybe none of this would have happened."

Uncle Orned touched his forehead in a quick salute.

"Brave man." He turned and pointed toward the rear of the apartment. "We're going out this way," he said, which didn't make any sense at all, Jerel thought. The only thing back that way was the laundry and utility room and a recycle bin—and the triple-barred door leading to those old stairs.

There was a pounding on the front door then, and almost immediately, on the side door.

"Open up! Police!"

Uncle Orned pushed a button on his desk, and the office door, open all this time, slid closed, locks engaging audibly. He pushed another button and music flooded the room—Uncle Orned's "thinking music."

"Hurry," he said calmly.

Jerel grabbed Kay's hand and pulled him down the hall. Before them, the door locked with three strong metal bars waited.

CHAPTER SIX

They were almost at the seventh floor when they heard a muted boom, and then another.

"Faster," came Uncle Orned's breathless voice from behind them, "they'll be through very quickly!"

They ran, Jerel in the lead, Kay right behind her. In a weird way, it *was* like the space-chase game they'd played as kids; her in the lead, Kay so close behind he was in danger of walking on her heels. She knew it was Kay because she recognized the fall of his feet, and because Erazias moved with a surprisingly noisy *slap*, *slap*, *slap*, as if his boots were unfastened. If Uncle Orned made any sound as he ran downstairs, it was too slight for Jerel to hear.

Her boots hit the sixth landing, and she ducked in toward the right wall, Kay beside her, Erazias opposite, allowing Uncle Orned to pass, gun in one hand, key card in the other. He set the card in the slot, but didn't push it in. He looked to Jerel and Kay.

"The top deck of Anthol's car park is on the other side of this door," he said, his voice just as cool and calm as always. "We'll want to keep close to the left wall—the security cameras don't cover any of the left wall on this level—and stop in front of the green Nethor van with the roof racks and the spoiler above the rear glass. There should only be one, and it will be parked with its back to the wall. When you hear the doors unlock, get into the cargo bay. Pull the cargo slide over you immediately. Once you're in, stay quiet until the music starts."

There were more sounds from overhead, and maybe a noise from below as well; Uncle Orned slapped the key card home.

"Comfortable?" Kay whispered.

"Quiet!" Jerel hissed. After everything she'd done wrong today, she was taking her uncle's advice seriously. Kay, on the other hand, seemed to think the whole thing was some kind of game, or a holiday that would be over maybe tomorrow or the next day.

She still couldn't quite figure out what the whole problem was between Erazias and Uncle Orned, but she'd heard enough to understand that there wasn't anything but a serious and life-changing event going on. Certainly she'd never been shot with a stunner and held by criminals before, or ever heard her uncle quite so vicious in describing the police. And that boom they'd heard when they were running down the stairs? She thought—and hoped she was wrong—that it might have been the seals blowing off their front door. . . .

Kay and she were lying side by side in the absolute dark beneath the cargo cover, arms touching, her left hand in his right. She didn't recall quite when that had happened, or even who had grabbed a hand first. Maybe it was when he helped her into the van after jumping in headfirst, pack still on his back. She'd not been able to fling her bag quite so easily.

Still, she could have let go when she'd pulled the door closed, if that was how it happened.

The van shook as someone else got in, and then again as a door—or maybe two doors—slammed shut quickly. They both squeezed the other's hand a little harder.

In a moment there was a click and a whir as the power cell switched in and the electric motor beneath them gave a small whine. At the same time she could hear the compressed-methane engine that charged the power cell come to life.

Jerel sighed. Hadn't she already played this game earlier in the day? Pretending to be cargo was getting really old, really fast. How was she supposed to stay alert, she thought irritably, if she couldn't even see where she was going?

Her mood wasn't improved by the truck's sudden rapid acceleration, which had her and Kay sliding toward the back of the compartment, and then from side to side as the van ran down and around the car-park ramps.

"I've got handholds on this side," Kay whispered. "What about you? I think there's even a belt or a tie-down."

Jerel groped in the darkness, found a gripper molded into the wall of the cargo bay, and grabbed it just in time to keep herself from sliding all over the place when the truck executed another rapid turn.

There was a sudden gray glow in the corner of the cargo bay. Jerel squinted. Maybe all the moving around had vibrated a 'nostics screen on, or some—

"Hey," she whispered. "Kay, look. There's a live feed over here."

"Over here, too," he answered, forgetting to whisper. "See that? We just passed the first level. Now, we won't be getting thrown around so much."

Jerel turned on her side, both hands on the grip bar now, and watched as the van approached the exit gate. Jerel didn't see anybody hiding in the shadows, or any police uniforms. In fact, the area looked empty, except for the attendant's scooter, parked with its nose against the gate's control box. The van moved forward; the bar lifted smoothly, and it passed under and out to the edge of the street. There it hesitated a moment, then merged right.

Immersed in the video, Jerel wasn't ready for the sudden *blappty-blap* of the music system kicking in, which helped mask the sudden *chupp-chupp* of the methane engine as the onboard computer decided it was time to charge the power cell.

"What in farkaction is that?" Kay wasn't talking quietly now, he was almost yelling to be heard over the rumble and thump of the noise that was shaking the whole van rhythmically.

"That's Slypo," she said, keeping her eyes on the feed screen. "Like Uncle Orned said, it's music." The van stopped for a traffic-control device. To the right of the screen was an alley, its interior lit with crazy loops of colored lights, each flashing in its unique pattern and speed. Simka had put the lights on early, she thought; it wasn't even true dark yet. Still, there were already few kids around, most of them round the Dance Wars game. She squinted, but couldn't really tell which silhouette was who—or even if there was anybody she knew in the crowd.

"Music?" Kay yelled. "That's not music!"

Outside the flags flickered from red to blue and the van accelerated mildly, moving past the ZipiCash kiosk on the corner and the skin art studio where Sherina worked . . .

"It's music," she told Kay, irritably. "The technos and repair geeks listen to it."

70

A scooter shot out of the side street and across the nose of the van. Jerel threw her free hand out to grab Kay as they braked suddenly. The van's horn blared, and the guy on the scooter flipped a gleeb in their direction before darting off to cut somebody else off.

"Farkin streetlolly," Kay muttered.

"Playing blink with traffic is just stupid," Jerel agreed. The van was moving again, at a relatively sedate pace, and the volume of the Slypo went down a notch. She realized she was still hanging on to Kay's arm and let him go, stretching her arm out and resting her head on it.

Kay sighed. "Are you *sure* that's music?"

"Look," she said, "I didn't invent it, so don't blame me. But there's a lot going on in Slypo; you kind of catch more every time you hear a spome."

"Come on. Spome?"

The van turned into the Cross-Grid Mall. A bunch of little kids were in line in front of the aquarium, a few older kids posted along the length to keep order.

"School trip," she said to Kay, and then, "Spome, yeah. You can't just call it a song, and it's not a poem, and it's not like there's a track, and there's not really an end, though there's changes that feel like ends. I mean, where is the 'end' of a wavicle? But anyhow, it's more like sampling a particular spectrum or belt of sound. Somebody called it a spome, way back when they were trying to write about it, and the name stuck."

Jerel didn't think now was the time to convert a non-tech to listening to Slypo, and probably telling him that the original Slypo had come from a couple of AI computers that had been analyzing music from cultures around the universe—looking for similarities and differences for someone's thesis—and they'd gone AWOL, refusing to work, instead going into cybercrime to move themselves about and make music of their own.

71

They were past the feelie museum, the van moving into the lane that bore round the City Gardens on the opposite side of the zoo where Kay volunteered. It looked, Jerel thought, like they were maybe going to the port—or to her grandmother's residence, which amounted to the same thing.

Jerel had only seen her grandmother three times, and none of those visits had been really comfortable. It seemed the Granvayle, as she was called in the newsies, was still peeved with Uncle Orned not going into the family business, and even more peeved because he'd insisted on keeping Jerel with him, down in the city, where—according to her—it wasn't safe. What had been worse, though, was the last time they'd gone to visit. The Granvayle had sent Uncle Orned to wait in the library while she tried to talk Jerel into moving into the big house at the port, with the rest of the family. Jerel hadn't been exactly polite in saying no, but it had made her mad that the Granvayle had snuck around behind—

Their vehicle slowed, and then slowed again, brakes humming. The music, on the other hand, got louder, with the bass so low Jerel felt it shaking in her lungs. Off the edge of the screen, she could see the flash of a spot-checker's wagon.

"Now what?" Kay complained.

"Quiet!" she hissed.

The van came to a stop. There was a small click-whir sound, and suddenly the compartment was filled with the smell of raw sewage. It was so intense that Jerel held her hand over her nose, but it didn't help.

The music suddenly dropped in intensity from heart-shaking to only loud, and down again, to quiet. In the screen, a brown-haired man in a green jacket that she knew must be Uncle Orned, despite his sloppy posture and the stim-stick smoking gently between the first two fingers of his left hand, was talking to the spot-checker. She was sorry for there not being any sound on the feed, but suddenly the checker burst into laughter, and walked away, waving her hand in dismissal. Uncle Orned climbed back into the van and they waited while the wagon zipped past them and back down toward home.

The van moved—the power cell giving off quiet clicks. Not very fast . . .

The click quickened; then, almost as suddenly as it had come, the smell of sewage left them; Jerel could feel an actual breeze move through their compartment, and the music blared louder than it had yet.

The van turned so hard that the companions were thrown together in a heap, with hands reaching for handholds and not always finding what they were expecting.

"Sorry," said Kay as the vehicle's vector straightened and they got themselves unsorted.

She laughed low. "Me too. I didn't hurt you?"

He laughed, discernible only because of the proximity of his mouth to Jerel's ear. "I'm set. Had worse in a pickup tackleball game. And I don't think they were an accident!"

They held hands silently for a while, watching the familiar streets pass by, thinking their own thoughts.

"I regaled her with the story of the backup I'd just come from—and asked if she wanted a sample. . . ."

Jerel and Kay laughed, which was clearly what Uncle Orned wanted them to do.

They were all standing in the dark on Grand Hill West. The sky was mostly obscured by light despite it being dark night now; and a slight haze hung over one of the biggest sources of that light, which lay below them, even more lights arcing above it, moving to and fro, rising and falling.

"I hadn't seen what the van said when I got it," Kay admitted. "We didn't have much time to admire it!"

Orned bowed a flippant bow, as much unlike him as the rumpled hair and untidy jacket.

"Chaklit Seven Chaklit at your service, young sir."

On the van's side was a sign: SEVEN C EMERGENCY SEWER AND RECYCLE SERVICE—ALL HOURS, ALL WEATHER, ALL DISTRICTS. Which explained the smell, Jerel allowed, and she didn't wonder why Uncle Orned might have need of such a vehicle. An insurance man on a job needed to be sure he wouldn't be bothered at a crucial moment. And who was going to bother a sewer jockey?

"In any case, the ruse worked. But the problem that comes now is *there*." He nodded down at the spaceport, dazzling the night with its lights. "I don't believe the same ruse will work at the gate. Not tonight."

Erazias was on the edge of the hill itself, peering at the spaceport through some kind of device; his fingers were nearly yellow in the spill of light. His robes, by contrast, absorbed a surprising amount of light, or perhaps they were colored for camouflage, and so he was harder to see than Jerel would have expected.

He folded the device and slipped it out of sight among the voluminous folds of that same robe and came to stand with them at the side of the van.

"*Fffttt*. It will be difficult and dangerous," he said. "It may be that it is too difficult and dangerous."

Uncle Orned glanced over his shoulder as a slow thunder rose around them, and soon a bright spot moved and became three flaring drive jets.

"It had seemed quickest and surest," he said. "The matriarch of the Vayle Trade Consortium would surely have extended her protection over the daughter of her most favored son, as well as her granddaughter's friend."

"But not you!" Jerel turned to stare at him. "Uncle Orned, you know she said you weren't ever welcome again, for having—"

He raised his hand, and she swallowed the rest of it. Right, she thought. Neither Erazias or Kay needed to know family business.

"Had we been able to simply drive in . . ." Uncle Orned continued. "But see, all the gates are guarded, not only by the port guards, but by police. No doubt someone has done their homework or run a crosscheck and assumed that the daughter of Banin Vayle would run to Vayle if she were threatened. They dare not let Vayle have her, for then it would be years of arguments between lawyers to shake her loose. So they must be vigilant, and stop her at the gate."

Kay spoke up diffidently.

"Sir, isn't there a way to smuggle people in? We keep hearing stories . . ."

"Yes," Uncle Orned answered seriously. "There are ways. Most of them involve time, careful planning, and lots of money. They also depend on luck, and a bored police force. You'll note that the police force isn't bored at the moment."

Erazias said "*Fffttt*" and scratched at his neck, tugging on a small section of skin. The skin peeled off; he glanced at it, said something Jerel couldn't catch, and began to throw the patch aside—

"Don't!"

That was Uncle Orned, the imperative enough to make the Turlon stop.

"You are right, of course," he said, after a moment. "Why provide more evidence that we were here?" He tucked the skin patch into some inner pocket or purse in the robe and turned back.

"Perhaps now," he said to Uncle Orned, "we may attempt my path?"

Uncle Orned sighed; and looked out over the port.

"I don't like it," he said finally, to which Erazias replied with an unusually emphatic *"Fffttt!"*

"It is more desirable that the hope of all the galaxy fall into the hands of brigands and traitors? You hold strange likes, Orned Vayle."

"And you hold strange and dangerous technology," Uncle Orned said, his voice mild in that particular way that meant he was really starting to get mad. "And reasons which are only your own."

"Fffttt," Erazias said gently. "Gate technology is neither strange nor dangerous. My own beloved master— your niece's revered mother—expended her genius to insure their safety. You may be easy."

Kay frowned.

"The gates? Do you think the gates won't be guarded? Or are they easier to smuggle people through?"

Erazias held up a hand as if warding off the questions.

"After we decide that our first choice will not do, then we will choose from the other choices. We should not give up too soon, nor wait too long."

"True words," Uncle Orned said quietly. He turned his head for one more long look at the port, then looked at Jerel with a smile, as if she'd just done something he approved of.

"Everybody in the van. Kay and Jerel—backseat."

CHAPTER SEVEN

Jerel tried to sleep as the van traveled west, but the Slypo—now scaled back to a mere murmur of its former volume—kept catching her attention long enough to keep her awake. She yawned yet again and tried to settle more comfortably into the reclined backseat, just awake enough to catch the next twisting of sound and try to follow it, to predict the flow—and of course that was part of the reason the techno community listened to it and had it on all the time: Geeks were often called on to work odd hours; if they didn't, necessary things stopped working. So they had to be awake when they were wanted, and they had to be alert.

Around her, now that she and Kay were in the passenger compartment of the van, were windows and viewscreens. Uncle Orned had thoughtfully turned the backseat's auxiliary control panel to view so they could see how fast they were going, how the power cell was charging or discharging, what the pressure was in each tire, and even a radar image of the traffic stream on the road behind them.

Jerel sighed and shifted in her seat, the part of her thoughts not engaged with the Slypo kind of fuzzy and unfocused. She realized in a lazy sort of way that Kay probably really didn't care that Slypo was a synthetic human music—not that it wasn't real but that it was synthesis of all the various human music that two self-aware computers could find and analyze and interactively re-create. That was okay—why should he care? Kay liked animals and plants and biologic systems; he not only liked them, he was good at biology and genetics and stuff like that. For a while he'd even talked about taking the entrance exam for some famous xenobiology college on Bornitor—and then he'd stopped talking about it. She didn't remember why. . . .

She could feel by the slant of the van that the roadway was slowly curving; that meant they were reaching, or rather avoiding, another urbcenter, the fifth or sixth so far. It made sense, she guessed, to try the gate at Charadale. It might be that the security guards there would be bored enough for Uncle Orned . . .

As the van leaned a bit more into the turn, Kay's presence beside her became more pronounced. He was apparently immune to Slypo and was wide asleep, as he'd been through the last two urbcenters. Now, he was slowly slumping against her, which she found oddly comforting.

Up front, a strange conversation was going on, weirdly threaded through the Slypo. Uncle Orned would mention a name, and Erazias would either—usually—say no or go on at length. Every so often, Erazias would take a turn, and Uncle Orned would have to say no or talk.

Some of the words sounded like people's names, some like planets, some like they were either—or neither. The numbers—some of the numbers might be communication codes, and others were surely planet-designation codes. Her mind stuck on that thought, as if it were a jagged and particularly interesting bit of Slypo. She ought to know those world codes, she thought, even if she wasn't studying to be a pilot but to be a space-drive repair tech. Somehow it didn't feel right that there was so much she didn't know, when she was one of the smartest people in any of her classes.

She opened her eyes and watched some overtaking traffic briefly on the radar, and then the man with the stunner shot her again and her legs ached and refused to move and she wanted to run but she couldn't and—

"Jerel, what?"

The voice was Kay's and it was right next to her.

With a gasp she snapped awake, the thread of the nightmare snapped by a cramp in her left leg.

"I have to move," she gasped. "Let me stretch my leg out—it hurts like you wouldn't believe."

Kay straightened and gave her room to flex her leg and ankle energetically. She could feel the tightness lessen, but it was still there when Erazias took note of them rustling about and turned to look at them over the back of the seat.

"Youngers, I suspect it is not yet time for you to be awake. Rest is important when one is under stress, and the future is less than certain!"

"Being able to move is important, too," Jerel muttered under her breath. "Don't you just think?"

"*Fffttt.* Indeed, being able to move is important," he agreed, showing her that she'd not been quite as quiet as she thought. She really didn't know that much about Turlons; maybe they could hear a lot better than humans.

Uncle Orned's calm voice broke in before she could decide if she owed Erazias an apology.

"Jerel, and you too, Kay, let me apologize! We'll stop shortly so we can all stretch."

Jerel concentrated on working her left leg and didn't answer, hoping Kay's quick "Thank you, sir!" counted for both of them.

She shifted in her seat to stretch the right leg, bumping Kay by accident—or maybe not. He was definitely pressing his leg slightly against hers. She pressed back a second, then patted his arm lightly in thanks before bringing the seat up out of recline, and trying to straighten her hair, which hadn't done well with her sleeping on it.

It was then that she realized that the Slypo was off, and wondered if its absence was what had finally let her fall asleep—or maybe that was what had woken her up?

Kay, in the meantime, had brought his seat up, too, and if he'd fixed his hair Jerel hadn't noticed. He was intent on the instruments, and when he saw she was looking at him, he pointed to the rear-scan radar.

"This is kind of fun. Bet it really helps when the fog rolls in."

She shrugged. She'd had a driving course in school but hadn't bothered with a license since so much of what she needed was within walking or boarding distance; she didn't think she'd ever sat in the backseat of Uncle Orned's other car, since when they went somewhere there was only the pair of them. She had taken the mandatory driving course at school and qualified for a Light Driving Permit, but she'd opted to spend that money on tools. . . .

She must have gasped out loud at the thought of her tools, because Kay's worried glance was suddenly on her face.

"Leg again?"

"No, not my leg," she managed, trying to quiet what was threatening to become an emotional storm complete with tears. She took a deep breath and plowed ahead. "I didn't have a chance to get my tools. None of them. I didn't even think of them until now!"

"None?" His voice had a trace of incredulity in it.

"Well, I mean I've got my minimulti, but I've always got that."

He looked at her speechless, and Jerel realized she was crying. Crying! What a stupid useless thing to do! But her tools—all her tools—and her books, and her advance-placement certs and . . . and everything! Left behind and likely never to be seen again, because the police were stupid and—

She slammed her fist into the seat beside herself, grimacing the tears into submission.

Kay—poor Kay! Now it looked like he was shaking, and if not in tears himself, close to it. She grabbed his hands in hers and tried a brave smile. It failed so badly that he laughed despite himself, and then she did, both with faces slightly red and damp.

"Rest stop coming up," Uncle Orned said over his shoulder. "Don't want to surprise you with a sudden light."

Erazias may have said *"Fffttt,"* but if he did it was covered up with Jerel's own indignant *"What?"*

Kay swallowed whatever he was going to say, and patted Jerel on the arm as she'd done to him a few minutes earlier. She pulled slightly away, scowling, then relented and offered him a weak smile. It wasn't Kay's fault Uncle Orned always had ideas.

"While the two of you have been napping," Uncle Orned went on, "up here in the cockpit we've been discussing the situation. While Erazias assures me that the conditions at Charadale Gate will more than answer his necessities, he agrees that there may well be extra guards on, and thus increased risk." He paused, then added, "In case you missed it, Erazias is convinced that this is more than just a local misunderstanding."

"Fffttt. It is almost certainly no misunderstanding at all. Those who abducted *terama* Jerel knew very well

what was required, else they would not have discarded the one taken in error."

Discarded, Jerel thought, and shivered. He meant *killed*.

"That being the case," Uncle Orned said blandly, "he has agreed that it is not unreasonable to attempt his . . . procedure . . . at the auxiliary cargo gate at Pwesta. So, that's where we're going."

Kay stirred, and subsided as Uncle Orned added, "If Pwesta Gate doesn't yield the correct conditions, then we will, indeed, hazard Charadale."

Jerel knew that among the many good things about Arantha was that it had been colonized with one purpose in mind, and it had been colonized from a single colony base.

That meant that wherever you went you could find the hot-water tap on the left side of the sink and the cold on the right, that the restroom signs for male and female humans and aliens were consistent across the planet, that urbcenters had the same core arrangement.

Way back when they'd taken Extraplanetary Geography together, Jerel and Kay had learned that some worlds had mountains so high a climber needed an oxy mask to be able to breathe on the summit; and some had environments so unfriendly that whole cities lived under domes.

One of the reasons Arantha had been chosen as the admin hub was that it was stable. The plate tectonics were mild. The weather was more or less constant, the solar cycle having a variability of a few tenths of a percent, and the planet's inclination was useful to create a bit of a winter and a summer with neither of them overwhelming. Stability, as they'd already learned in Theory of Government, was important, even if Grand Hill West and Grand Hills East, North, and South would hardly make a real mountain, even if they were piled on top of each other.

Yet there had been more changes than the original planners had foreseen, for they had planned for a world that would administer a subcluster of planets held together through space travel.

And so Arantha depended on the major spaceport when it was being constructed, and, once it was colonized, five subsidiary ports were built, each capable of dealing with some portion of the traffic the major port carried in case of an emergency, for the flow of goods and people needed for regional administration should not be allowed to be interrupted by mere emergency.

Then had come the gates.

While the science of the gates was beyond Jerel's interest, the fact of them meant that spaceports—that ships—were no longer the sole means of entering a world or leaving it; it meant that goods and people needed to be moved in new directions and in new volumes, that new roads had needed to be built—and that not all the urbcenters were identical.

Pwesta, now . . .

The auxiliary gate at Pwesta was a good distance outside its urbcenter. The necessity of moving goods to and from the center had spawned a freight line, and a couple of lorry roads lined with cheap-eat places, bars, and adult service facilities.

"Funny," Kay said, looking out his window. "You'd think there'd be lots of trucks and stuff."

Jerel frowned at the dark shops they glided past; even the red lights at the adult facs were off.

"You don't think the gate's closed, do you?" she asked, meaning a joke, because Charadale Gate never closed; a steady stream of people and goods came through at all hours.

"That's a good question," Uncle Orned said from the front seat. "Pwesta used to be accessible—"

"Welcome to Pwesta Gate Approach," an automated voice said, coming out of the speaker between Jerel and Kay. "Please be advised that the gate operates during daylight hours only. Cargo vehicles arriving outside normal hours of operation are directed to the security shed."

Uncle Orned said something under his breath, and pulled into a bar's deserted parking lot. "Well?" he said to Erazias.

"*Ffttt.* We will attract attention, at the least. A moment . . ." He shifted in his seat amid a rustling of robes. Jerel craned to see what he was doing, but it only looked like he'd taken a device about the size of a courier's satellite positioning reader out and was studying its screen intently.

"No," he said, slipping the little device away. "Not enough."

Uncle Orned sighed. "So, to Plan B." He set the van in motion, out of the parking lot and back the way they had come.

The night wasn't particularly cold or windy, but Jerel shivered as she stepped out of the van.

"Here." Kay leaned out of the half-open door and shoved her jacket at her.

"Thanks," she said, and pulled it on, sealing up the front and slipping her hands into her pockets.

Over her head a number of the giant diodes cast a cloudy blue light, their covers cracked and scarred. Several light poles were empty, and beneath a pole at the far end, where one of the great diodes was clearly damaged, were dozens of stones and assorted pieces of junk.

Vehicles were parked in the dark patches created by the damaged lighting, clustered together without regard to the guide markings on the pavement and apparently without recognizing the prominently displayed NO LOITERING signs as having meaning for them.

"*Fffttt*," said Erazias, and then he said it again more loudly as he got out of the van, while Kay and Uncle Orned stayed. When they got back, Orned and Kay would make their way to the facilities. And then they'd get on the road to Charadale.

This place—a public rest area just a little past the intersection with the lorry road to Pwesta Gate—this place, Jerel thought, was . . . creepy.

She wasn't used to feeling watched this way. Sure, any slideboarder was likely to hear comments while traveling, the topics ranging from the fit of their clothes to the way they moved their boards to others less savory. On more than one occasion she'd been followed by a couple of gleebs who seemed to think she ought to be grateful to them for paying attention to her.

These watchers were different. Expectant almost, and perhaps even hostile.

"*Fffttt*," Erazias said as an ugly word or two floated from one of the half-hidden vehicles. He rustled within his robes for a moment, then straightened.

"Short-term contract labor," he muttered, maybe to her. "Not allowed at the gate during the off shift."

"But—why are they here?" she asked. "It's hours until Pwesta Gate opens."

"Perhaps they have no other place to go at night. Perhaps they come to socialize before the day's efforts. . . ."

Jerel almost had to skip to keep up with the quiet-walking Turlon. He padded quickly toward the buildings, his bare feet making only a very slight ticking noise against the surface of the walk.

"Hey, where are your boots?"

"In the van, where I hope they will forget themselves as mine and discover a home they prefer. I have not been embarrassed so much by clatter and clumsiness since well before your mother accepted me as her apprentice.

That I might stumble and betray us all because of those boots—*mortified* is the word I think of."

A loud whistle rang from one of the vehicles, and somebody yelled, "Hey, we can use some of that over here if you're giving it away to a skin-shed!"

Jerel gasped and hurried on, not breaking into a run but wishing she could. But then there was Rule Four to think of. There was no doubt in her mind that running would attract attention . . . as if the fact that she was walking with a Turlon in the middle of the night hadn't!

"*Fffttt*. Ignore them, *terama* Jerel. They are of no consequence!"

Erazias, in fact, had slowed; he now stopped altogether and set his robes in order with deliberate care, showing how little the rude comments meant to him, Jerel guessed.

And she guessed she should do the same, then. Ignore them, and keep her reactions private. She'd had some practice keeping reactions private, with her mother among the most famous of those missing in the war. In fact, it was when she'd been badgered at school during the observances for the anniversary of the battle that had eliminated both the Oligarchy and rebel fleets that Uncle Orned had prosed the Rules to her in the first place.

Thinking of the Rules was—comforting—and gave her an idea of what she ought to be doing. She glanced around, making sure that no one had gotten out of their vehicle, and that Erazias and she were alone on the walkway. That covered Rule One. As far as she could figure, they were already taking a lot of chances, but she guessed Uncle Orned covered Rule Two by taking as few as possible.

Rule Three—this whole rest area was an anomaly! Lights broken, rude loiterers, no police or security guards to be seen—she was concerned, all right!

That left only Rule Five—but, she thought, Uncle Orned could see them and the situation from the van almost as well as she could. Rule Five covered—at least for the moment.

Erazias had finished with his robes and was moving again. She stretched her legs, and he said *"Fffttt"* as she gained his side. A moment later, they passed a scarred and battered sign warning that bare feet were not permitted for hygiene reasons, and he repeated himself, rather more forcefully. The doors opened automatically at their approach, and Jerel felt relief that they worked.

"When the lights are broken on purpose," Erazias said just before they parted, "when behavior is rude, when civil signs are ignored, that is a warning that a slide has begun. It is well that we leave here soon!"

Jerel had imagined, brushing her hair, and trying to put a semblance of nonchalance into her freshly washed face before leaving the restroom, that she and Erazias had made a fairly neat entrance, given their situation, and that perhaps Erazias had a point about the planet going downhill. Murders, abductions, police trying to arrest innocent people—none of that was stable, or usual.

Their exit was not nearly as neat as their entrance, for as soon as she got out the door and looked through the window she could see a bunch of people in workeralls circling the van, maybe yelling at it; some even reached out and pounded on it with gloved fists.

Erazias emerged and stood beside her, contemplating the scene, then touched her shoulder and waved her out the door; she could see green and yellow stains on his fingers.

As soon as they were outside, Jerel could hear Slypo pouring out of the van, like it was shouting back at the people who were yelling and hitting it.

"*Fffttt.* Distraction. Orned endeavors to center them upon the van. It is well. Make haste, *terama.* I am your shield and your blade."

Jerel ran, thinking, *Stupid, stupid, stupid! You left your gun in the van!*

A woman stepped inside the circle around the van, hefting a long piece of pipe. The crowd hooted and howled as she swung at the windscreen—and howled again as the van lurched forward. The woman jumped back, dropping her weapon. The van lurched again, Slypo roaring across the car park, and a man reached out and yanked the woman back into the circle.

A boom sounded—and another. Jerel realized that somebody was shooting at the van, and not with something as benign as a stunner, either. She slowed—and then stopped as Erazias grabbed her arm.

"*Fffttt.* Tarry a moment, bold heart. Let us observe the hunter as he toys with his prey."

The van backed up in a rapid zigzag, brakes screamed; the methane engine shrieked as the vehicle leaped forward, sideswiped the man holding the weapon, and continued accelerating, scattering its circle of tormentors. Erazias pushed her. "Now! Fly, *terama!*"

If only, Jerel thought, racing toward the van, Erazias a billowing presence at her back. Some of the cars lurking in the shadows were moving, she saw. If one of them rammed the van—

A group of runners burst from behind the facilities building, shouting. Jerel saw sparks come off the walkway, heard sizzling noises—

There—the van! It braked suddenly, throwing gravel and broken glass as it skidded. The back door came open and she threw herself forward, falling across Kay's knees, as the van came out of its slide with a banshee scream of Slypo and charged the mob following, leaving Erazias out on the lot.

Jerel heard the door slam and then Kay was helping her get upright, yanking the grab bar up from the floor—

"Hold on!" Uncle Orned yelled over the Slypo, but he needn't have; the rush and the music's volume and the adrenaline were already telling her to be ready for almost anything, even the strangely familiar smell. The world twirled as the van careered around the lot, and there was Erazias, standing tall and peaceful in his robes while a man in greasy orange workeralls closed, swinging a metal pole at his head.

Jerel shouted, her voice lost in the chaos of the music.

Out on the lot, Erazias accepted the challenge. There was a swirl of robes, and the pole was suddenly in one hand, while in the other was a knife. He slashed at his attacker; the man screamed and backed away, dropping something else. . . .

It took half a second for Jerel to understand what had happened: Erazias had cut the man's arm off!

Uncle Orned spun the van hard, presenting an open door to Erazias, who piled in, metal pole still in hand.

"*Fffttt!* House guard!" he shouted, his eyes completely encircled in yellow, and his hands so pale they were almost white. "Remove us!"

Orned accelerated toward the exit—and the ragged line of workeralled figures before it. From the right roared a sudden vehicle, obviously intent on ramming them. The van veered, hard; in the backseat, Jerel was flung against the door and Kay against her.

"Ow!"

"Sorry, I just. Sorry!"

The van came round again and Jerel looked out the window; the other vehicle was close, close enough that she could see faces. Familiar faces!

"That's them!" she yelled. "Those are the people who stunned me!"

As if that was the signal he'd been waiting for, Erazias reached beneath his robe and brought out a small pistol with a very large muzzle.

Orned's glance took it in, and he changed course, revving the engine ruthlessly, and bore down on the other vehicle. The window rolled down and Erazias took a bead.

There was a slight chuff—a much smaller noise than Jerel had expected—and Erazias's arm jerked. Then the other car skated off to the side, back end snapping, brakes squealing, green smoke pouring out of the windows.

"Choke gas!" Kay hollered. "What a shot! What a shot! Great!"

If Erazias heard this enthusiastic praise he said nothing, but quickly sealed the window and settled his weapon again beneath the robe. The van accelerated, hard enough to push them all into their seats.

It wasn't until they were on the throughway that Orned shut the music off, the sudden change in sound pressure as bad as the noise. Jerel slumped against the seat back, as if the music had supported her and given meaning to what had just happened.

"Jerel," Kay was saying from his collapse at her side, "I didn't know you could run so fast, and you just did it like you've being doing it all your life."

But Uncle Orned was talking, too, calm and cool, though it took a second for her to understand him, as if the Slypo was still clogging up her brain and wouldn't let the words through—

"Jerel, did he hit you?"

"Hit me?" She blinked, and looked at Kay. His eyes widened.

"True farkaction, Jerel," he said explosively. "They burnt off half your hair!"

CHAPTER EIGHT

Listen up," Uncle Orned said as he stopped the van. He turned in the seat to face them, eyes serious. Jerel recognized his lecture pose, though this time he wasn't, apparently, trying to teach her a lesson.

"We're about to do something heinously illegal. It's so illegal that neither Admin nor GateTech will publicly admit that it can be done, though some law forces are approved to use the technique."

He paused to make sure he had their complete attention. Jerel felt Kay's hand near and slipped her fingers between his.

"*Fffttt*," Erazias interrupted. "The technique in use by the law-protectors differs in theory and practice from that which we will utilize." He brought the satellite finder he'd consulted last night at Pwesta Gate out of his robes and displayed it.

Jerel frowned. Seen up close and personal, it didn't look all that much like a satellite finder. In fact, it didn't—

"We lack the time needed to thoroughly explore either the math or the philosophy of these matters, though both are entertaining and worthwhile. Perhaps, after we have achieved our goal, there will be time for the joys of shared study. Presently, however . . ."

He paused, absentmindedly scratched a colorless patch of skin on his palm until it flaked off. Beneath, the new skin showed so brightly green it was almost yellow. He looked up and again showed them the little device.

"*Fffttt.* This device permits us to interact with the fields which produce the gate phenomenon. It is a much smaller version, in many ways, of the Chalibar Projector which as you know is so necessary to the stability and duration of the larger cargo gates. Yet, we have no need to make so great a hole in else-time, nor may we avail ourselves of the standard infrastructure of power supply."

Jerel was struck by how much Erazias sounded like Uncle Orned when he was in full explanation—except for the *fffttt*s.

"When a gate is used, it creates vortices of power; and each of these might itself act as a gate if it were not in an ungainly location, and if it did not manifest in a quasi-random fashion.

"So our intent is to use this device to locate and utilize one of the not-quite-random potential—"

"Erazias," Uncle Orned said. "Time . . ."

"Ah, yes," the Turlon said. "Apologies."

He paused, and the area around his eyes suddenly became greener.

"*Fffttt.* So," he rushed on, apparently needing to get some of the science out of his system, "what we will do is use this device in an axis-symmetric three-dimensional field, revealing thus the hysteresis loss inherent in large gates set improvidently on spinning objects, and heterodyne the frequency of the power we find there, unveiling a gate which already potentially exists but which does not fully manifest itself. These manifestations are sometimes called 'wild gates,' and we can, with prudence, use them just as we would any other gate."

Kay used his free hand to gesture for attention.

"Sir, I think I'm not understanding this. It sounds like you're cutting a side door into a gate—"

Erazias hesitated and shot a look at Uncle Orned, who gave him no sign that Jerel could see, and looked back to Kay.

"In essence, younger, that is what we shall do. It is, as was said, more nearly a matter of philosophy than mathematics, but yes. In layman's terms, what we shall be doing is making use of spilled energy, which would otherwise be wasted. Practically, it does not matter if we create a gate, as some suggest, or merely open one which already exists, as others argue."

"If making a wild gate is so easy," Jerel asked, "why don't people just use them all the time?"

Uncle Orned gave her his slit-eyed grin, which was as close to making a goofy face as he ever came.

"Because, dear niece, we're stealing energy. If everyone did it, the large gates would go unstable. You can't imagine the problems that would cause."

Kay gestured again, his eyes squinched up the way they did when he was thinking hard.

"But if we're stealing energy from the big gate, doesn't that mean the gate we'll be using—the wild gate—will be unstable?"

The pair in the front seat exchanged glances. Uncle Orned, thought Jerel, looked amused. Erazias looked— like Erazias.

"*Ffftttt*," he said finally, "in fact it does. But 'unstable' is a term open to many shades of definition. We should have a large enough radius of torsion that the gate we use will be stable for a day or more, on average."

Jerel started to say something about average, having long ago found out that while adding forty-nine and fifty-one could give you an average of fifty, so could adding one and ninety-nine, then swallowed her argument. It looked like a bad time to dispute the point.

"Time!" Orned spoke as if he'd heard some private signal, and gestured them out of the van.

"Jerel!" he called as she stepped out, and tossed her something. She caught it without really looking, then held it up for inspection: a slightly grimy green cap with the legend *Seven C* stenciled on the front. She wrinkled her nose and glared at Uncle Orned, who touched his hair over his right ear, where hers had been burned ragged.

Right, she thought. Rule Four.

She put the cap on, sitting it at a jaunty angle that hid the worst of the damage. She hoped.

"Good," said Uncle Orned. "Let's go."

Jerel was starting to get seriously worried. Beside her, Kay was looking tired beneath his pack, and for that matter, so was Uncle Orned, with his business case in hand.

The only one who didn't look tired was Erazias, who was bluer and perhaps happier than she'd ever seen him, using the pole he'd taken from the man at the car park as a staff, and holding in his other hand the gate-finding device.

Part of her worry came as a direct result of Rule One. She couldn't help but notice as they wandered through Charadale's Oldside that people were staring at them, and that they had passed a number of parked or abandoned vehicles that looked too much like the ones hiding in the dark at the Pwesta car park.

Ordinary city sounds reached them as from a distance; there was little traffic here; despite the occasional distant roar of an aircraft they could have been in a residential quiet zone.

They passed a fried-noodle place, the smell of salt and hot grease reminding Jerel that her last meal had been— years ago, it seemed like, back in Uncle Orned's office, when everything was still more or less normal.

She glanced back over her shoulder and saw a woman peering round the door of the noodle shop at them, a frown on her face. Jerel bit her lip. If somebody decided they were *too* strange, and called the police . . .

Sighing, she hitched her pack up on her shoulders; and wondered again what was in it that made it so heavy. Or maybe, she thought, she was just tired. If she had to run, the pack would slow her down.

Erazias, in the lead, turned down a side street and they followed, she and Kay walking together, Uncle Orned a little behind them.

The right side of this street was a long continuous brick wall, doors and windows barred and sealed, with an air of neglect about it. An old manufacturing plant, Jerel thought, maybe even left over from Phase One itself. Charadale had been one of the first urbcenters con-structed, so that wasn't impossible. But, why hadn't they recycled the bricks, if nobody had wanted to refit the plant to do something else?

There was a noise to her left; she glanced over, trying to look like she had just happened to do it, and saw three kids a little younger than her and Kay peering at them through the empty window of a burned-out store. One of them saw her looking, grinned, and flipped the gleeb. Jerel stared at him until his friends laughed, and all three ducked out of sight.

"Rule Four," she muttered.

"Rule *what*?" Kay asked from beside her. She couldn't tell if he'd seen the three kids.

"Rule Four," Jerel repeated. "That's *don't attract unnecessary attention*. We're breaking that one, I think."

"I guess we might be," he agreed, shifting his pack with a soft grunt. "But whose rule? Slideboarders?"

"Nah, they're Uncle Orned's Rules. Five of them all together." She recited them in order, ticking them off on her fingers as she did.

"Seems like we might be breaking a couple of those," Kay commented. "Rule Two's pretty much in pieces, after that thing in the car park last night. Rule Three, too."

Jerel frowned. "How you figure?"

"Well," Kay said, shifting his pack again and hooking his fingers through the straps, "if we're supposed to be concerned about anomaly, that's not just what other people do or don't do, right? We have to make sure not to make an anomaly that other people will notice."

She blinked. "I didn't think of that," she admitted. "Yeah, I guess Rule Three's pretty bad off, too. How long do you think we're going to have to walk around here? I thought finding this energy spill was going to be *easy*."

"Sir and madam," Uncle Orned said quietly from behind them, "your attention is required ahead."

Jerel looked up sharply, saw a flutter of blue robes as Erazias disappeared into a narrow way between two buildings.

"Now what?" she muttered, and stretched her legs, feeling Kay keeping pace beside her, and Uncle Orned behind.

The alley was narrow and looked like the ground crews hadn't been by for a while—or ever. The footing was tricky, with all the broken bricks, shattered plastic, and old drink cups littering the surface. Overhead ran several sets of power lines, and there were CAUTION and

DANGER signs posted at regular intervals along the walls, still mostly readable beneath brightly painted curse words, name pairings, and art.

Erazias strode on ahead, his whole attention seemingly on his device. For sure he didn't notice the kid who had tossed them the gleeb from the burnt-out store peer out of a thin door in the right-hand wall. He grinned at Jerel, and leaned out, deliberately making eye contact. She slowed, and stopped.

"Gimme cashcoin, lightweights, or I smoke you to the Pearlydons." He showed a phone, call number glowing on its input screen. "Cashcoin, or bad trouble. Choose."

Kay grabbed her arm. "C'mon, Jerel, we don't have to deal with this zwinget—"

The kid's grin got wider. "Ever seen bad trouble, hirise?"

"Have *you*?" Uncle Orned's voice came from behind. His arm shot past Jerel's shoulder and plucked the phone from the kid's hand.

"Hey!"

"Get out," Uncle Orned said, in a voice so cold that Jerel shivered, and then, even colder, "Now!"

The kid gaped, then ducked back into the doorway, slamming the broken plastic door behind him.

Uncle Orned dropped the phone to the alley and brought his boot heel down hard, as he scraped them with a look Jerel had never seen before. If *that* was the face the alley kid had seen, she didn't blame him for running!

"Forward," he said quietly. "I believe Erazias has found what he's looking for."

The three-tone warble of a police cruiser sounded in the distance, answered by another—and a moment later by a third. Jerel flinched.

"It's okay," Kay whispered. "They're probably not looking for us. Prolly after a Pearlydon or six."

She giggled weakly. "You think that kid was a Pearlydon?"

"Freelancer," Uncle Orned answered. "If he'd had standing in the tribe, he would have called on his *dris* to help him deal with us instead of trying to shake us down for money." He put a firm hand in the middle of Jerel's back and propelled her forward. "Close up, please. We need to be in position in case—"

"*Fffttt*," Erazias said, bent over his device in the center of the alley. "There is no 'in case.' I have located our matrix and centered our position. Quickly now! We are ready!"

Leaning his staff against one shoulder, he manipulated the control bars on the face of the device, his hands greenish and his dark blue crest standing full up, like a kite caught in a strong breeze.

The world around them flashed with a sudden coruscating rainbow of light, and there was a smell of ozone. The overhead wires moved and jumped as sparks dashed between them; there was a sudden loud noise, as if someone had ripped apart a long piece of heavy cloth.

And there, instead of the dull brick and hardtop of abandoned factories, empty houses, and near-endless city, was a plain of tall golden grass waving in a breeze they could neither feel nor smell. In the near distance, several large orange machines moved among the grain; in the far distance was a towering row of green-leaved trees, and arching above it all a cloudless sky the color of Erazias's crest.

Jerel was mesmerized. This was no big-screen image, no projection, no hologram. There was a real world right there, hanging at an odd angle and slightly off-center before her.

Then, as if they'd somehow come around this apparition, Jerel saw three people: two humans—one wearing a gray hat—and a red-crested Turlon.

She yelled, wordless, and snatched the four-shot out of her jacket pocket. Erazias turned, sighted the three, and squealed heart-stoppingly, as he lashed out with his staff, knocking Gray Hat down.

"Go!" he shouted, and swung the staff at the slow-soldier, who ducked, amazingly quick, and raised a weapon that didn't look at all like a stunner.

A hard hand shoved her forward, toward the gate; she got her feet under her and ran—and there was Kay beside her, staggering as if he, too had been pushed. Somewhere behind them was the crackle of an energy weapon being discharged—and she was in the gate—

A sudden low humming filled her ears, vibrated in her chest; the golden world shivered before her eyes, and the humming increased, as if the air were full of winged things or the emissions from an off-kilter amplifier. The golden world came back, vividly sharp, and she hurtled forward, gripping her small weapon. The hum filled the worlds and the gate between; sudden darkness fell and Jerel faltered.

"Hesitate not, *terama*!" Erazias shouted from behind her. "We go forward! To the Sword of Orion!"

CHAPTER NINE

Oh *hah!*"

Kay's voice rang out in the darkness, waking the hint of an echo lost. He said it again, louder, but the echo was no more definite.

Jerel, standing still in the dark, reached for her belt pouch, thinking about the sticklight she always kept there, and only then remembered that Gray Hat and the slow-soldier had stolen it. With the memory she was mad all over again—not only stunned, and chased, but made to stand around in the dark like a—

There was a slight hiss, and a pale, diffuse light glowed into being to her left. She turned and saw Uncle Orned, sticklight in his right hand, looking about him interestedly. He was still holding the gun in his left hand, muzzle pointing politely at the stony ground.

"Well," he said mildly, and looked over to Jerel. "This is unexpected."

"But what happened?" Kay demanded. He was standing on Uncle Orned's opposite side, face indignant. "Where's the field and the trees we saw? Where did this old pile of rocks come from? *Where are we?*"

"Peace, peace," Erazias murmured. He was seated on a big boulder, his device on a knee while he calmly peeled a ration stick. "Soon, we shall know where we are, and, by comparison, where we are not. In the interim, I suggest that we rest ourselves, and perhaps partake of such rations as we may have with us. Until we have established our location, we cannot form a rational answer to our predicament."

That sounded sensible to Jerel, especially the part about getting something to eat. She slung her pack off her with a sigh, and caught Kay's eye.

"Sometimes, you gotta let the equipment work," she said. She rummaged in the outside pocket of her backpack, trusting that any travel kit put together by Uncle Orned would—yes. She pulled out two cereal bars and held them up so Kay could see.

"Fenilberry. Want one?"

He sighed, shoulders slumping, and came over to her. "Sure," he said, taking one of the offered bars. "Thanks."

"No problem."

They ate in silence, while Erazias paid alternate attention to food and his gate-calling device, and Uncle Orned stood by, gun still in hand, nibbling on a cereal bar of his own.

"What *did* happen?" Kay asked then. "Why are we here—wherever here is—instead of wherever there was?"

Uncle Orned laughed, low and amused.

"We have just experienced one of the many definitions of 'unstable,'" he said with a grin. "Luckily, we survived it."

"*Fffttt*. It is well that your heart remains high, O Hunter," Erazias said from atop his boulder. "But it is not mete to turn a student's earnest question with levity. Young Kay, in order to understand what has happened, you must first know that there are many possible solutions to the equations which invoke the gates. To maintain a permanent cargo gate requires an unvarying level of power, as well as an unerring precision of mathematics. We must ask the correct question, you see, in order to receive the correct answer. The answers to the question I asked, through this"—he tapped a finger against the device on his knee—"included the world of grain and trees—Ubentyle, as it is named—and also this world upon which we find ourselves. I stress—both answers are valid. There has been no malfunction."

"But," said Kay carefully, "why did we end up here, when the, the answer we were shown was Ubentyle?"

"*Fffttt*. A masterly and precise rephrasing. You have the mind of a scholar, young Kay. So. When we deal in equations and energy states, it is important to the equation—the question, if you will—that the energy state remain constant. Alas, as we were transitioning, someone was fool enough to discharge an energy weapon within our field of influence, which served to alter the question. And thus we were given a second—and, I allow, less satisfactory—answer."

The device on Erazias's knee gave a small hiss, and he bent forward. "And now we have the answer to your earlier query, as well. We are in the Nagara System, upon the fourth planet. Hah. You will of course know from your studies of history that the Nagara System suffered greatly in the late hostilities. The fourth world took particular hurt, as the enemy utilized the gates to bring in forces of occupation. When the people rose up in protest, their first act was to destroy the gates—a boon to the revolution, but at great cost to themselves. The population and much of the arable land were destroyed. This world is now abandoned, somewhat like the buildings we passed by in our quest for the most potent spill site on your homeworld."

He raised the device, peering at the screen in the dimness.

"And, since this is not the world you wished to be on," Uncle Orned suggested, "we'll be leaving soon."

"Indeed, we shall leave as soon as practicable. We must, however, wait for a short time while the the last of the four energy-generating satellites returns to the position most felicitous for the formation of a gate. When that satellite is in position, we will be able to form a gate very quickly, though it will be of relatively short duration, so we must not wander apart from each other."

"Can," Jerel said slowly, almost afraid to ask the question that was worrying her most. "Can they find us? Reproduce the math that opened this gate and come after us?"

"No," Erazias said, most of his attention on his device. "They cannot trace us in that manner, *terama*. It would require them to ask precisely the question which we had asked, and given that randomness influenced our asking, the chance that they might follow is vanishingly low."

"Okay," said Jerel, feeling a little easier for that assurance. "Thanks."

"It is my very great pleasure, *terama*. You must hesitate to ask me nothing."

The sky overhead was dark, nearly empty. There was no glare of distant lights, no glow of aurora, and startlingly few stars. They were moving, single-file, following Erazias like, as Kay whispered to Jerel, baby water-cooters following their hen. She had choked back a laugh at that: water-cooters were kind of flat-footed and bulky on land, even the young ones, and the idea of a cooter-hen dressed in rustling formal robes like Erazias wore was pretty funny.

They were walking because when the fourth satellite came back into position, the gate finder indicated that the area of most stable power was some distance away from their resting place. So, they were walking again, the footing so bad that Jerel thought of the broken alley at Charadale's Oldside with longing.

"Here," Erazias said, holding a hand up. Kay, directly behind him, stopped, and so did Jerel. Uncle Orned kept moving until he was next to Erazias.

"Allow me to assist you," he said, forcefully polite.

"I assure you, no assistance is required," Erazias returned, maybe not so polite. "The device is constructed so that one operator—"

"No," said Uncle Orned. "I insist. For it would be a terrible thing if we were to walk out onto Ubentyle, instead of—" Erazias raised a hand, shot a look over his shoulder at Jerel and Kay, and moved his fingers as if shooing them away.

"Walk at some distance, my bolds, and amuse yourselves. I will call when the time is come."

As hints went, thought Jerel, it wasn't real subtle. She was about to ignore it, on the grounds that she didn't take orders from Erazias, but just then Uncle Orned looked at her over the lizard man's shoulder and lifted an eyebrow. Jerel sighed and turned away, grabbing on to Kay's sleeve as she did and pulling him along with her.

"I guess," Kay said, with a sigh, "if you studied rocks, this could be real interesting."

"I guess," Jerel said. "But these aren't ordinary rocks, are they? What Erazias said, about there being a revolt that the military put down. This would be burn-off and slag, wouldn't it?"

Kay thought about that for a couple steps. "You're right," he said. "They must've used a lava cannon—the military. That's pretty harsh."

"Well—it was a war," Jerel pointed out. She pushed the cap back off her forehead and squinted around. Rock, rock, and more rock, until the horizon bent away—not quite.

"What's that?" she asked, pointing.

"What's—I see it!" He wrinkled his nose. "More bones?" he suggested.

"Doesn't look like . . ." Jerel started toward the odd tangle. It looked almost like downed branches, with dry leaves still attached, except there weren't any trees. Or, she thought, it might be—

"Bones," Kay said. Jerel stopped, but he pushed past, bending to get a closer look.

"Human," he said over his shoulder. "Funny . . ."

"What's funny about bones?" Jerel wanted to know.

"Well, there aren't any predators or scavengers here, right? What would they live on? And yet there's a pile of bones, all picked clean and—hey!" He bent even closer, rummaging around in the bones and the tattered bits of cloth. . . .

"Kay!" Jerel protested. "Don't—"

But he was already straightening, holding something slim and beautiful in his hand. Jerel took a step forward. "What *is* that?"

He turned it over, head bent in study. "There's writing on the blade," he mumbled. "In this light I can't really make out—"

"Jerel! Kay!" Uncle Orned yelled.

"C'mon!" Jerel half-turned.

"Wait! Help me put this in my pack!"

105

She stared at him in horror. "You're not taking it with you? It belongs—" She stopped. Who did it belong to, anyway?

"He's not using it," Kay said, nodding at the pile of bones in a weird echo of her thought.

"Jerel!" Uncle Orned called again. Cussing under her breath, she jumped forward, took the knife from Kay, slipped it—carefully—into the long pocket on the outside of his pack, and squished the self-seal over it.

"There. Now let's go before the gate leaves without us!"

Erazias was muttering over his device as they approached, and Uncle Orned raised a hand, stopping them some distance away.

Sighing, Jerel sat down on one of the numerous boulders; Kay flopping onto the stones next to her.

"Why would you call a planet like this the Sword of Orion?" he asked her.

She blinked at him. "What?"

"Erazias said, when we were in the gate—"

"Oh." She did remember that, now. It had seemed a weird thing to say, but no weirder than most things Erazias said.

"Sword of Orion isn't a planet," she told Kay. "It's an asterism—a group of stars that make a picture if you look at it the right way."

Kay frowned. "A constellation, you mean?"

"No, *part* of a constellation," she said, remembering her astrogation-for-techs seminar. "The constellation is Orion, after an old soldier, I guess he was. When you look at the constellation, if you sorta squint, you can see he's wearing a sword on his belt. So, this planet here is somewhere in the sword part of the constellation."

"*Fffttt.* A most wise and concise explanation, *terama* Jerel. Indeed, we stand on a world within the Sword. As it happens, wild gates of the type we travel by are far more common among the stars of the Sword than elsewhere. It is a matter of star swarms and energy levels and gravitational disparity, and many other things."

That didn't sound right, Jerel thought, frowning. But maybe she had it wrong. She'd been required to take certain pilot-prep courses, but that didn't make her an expert on—

"Ah!" Erazias said, and looked up from his device.

"Be prepared friends, be ready. Power rises. We shift very soon!"

Jerel sighed and got up off her boulder, very aware of the gun tucked into the inner pocket of her jacket.

Kay climbed to his feet, and shrugged his pack into a better position, then started, his head swiveling quickly in search of the source of a sound that seemed to emanate from the stones themselves.

Uncle Orned had been stretching, hand casually on his bag; he spun, apparently also searching for the sound. "Erazias?"

"*Fffttt*. No, this is nothing of mine. The energy levels—"

"Jerel," Uncle Orned said calmly, and she saw that he had decided on one particular pile of rocks as dangerous, and had leveled his gun at them. "Stay behind me. You too, Kay."

Ozone crackled, and Jerel felt static dance over her skin. At first she thought it was coming out of the rocks; then she realized that there was a glow *behind* and somehow *through* the rocks. She reached out and grabbed Kay's arm, pulling him with her as she went back a step, two—and there was a booming pop of air, a scintillation of color and shadow. Overhead the sky was webbed with flickering light while on, or through, the rocks, a picture was forming. Not a picture, she reminded herself; she was seeing into another world.

But which world? It didn't look like Arantha, and even less like the world they'd missed; the colors were all of steel and chrome, the light too bright, and suddenly there were three figures carrying weapons blocking her view of that other world. The figures, though, hesitated, milling around as if they couldn't quite see, as if their too-bright light didn't penetrate the dim and rocky world they were trying to enter.

"You are under arrest!" The lead figure waved a gun vaguely in their direction, and moved as if she were going to stand forward onto the rocks.

Uncle Orned fired—not at any of the silhouetted figures but into the ground ahead of them, sending up a shower of gravel and sparks.

"Halt," he shouted. "You have no jurisdiction here!"

The woman in the lead had drawn back, though she was still pointing her gun in their direction. "We are in pursuit of the fugitive Jerel Telmon—"

Jerel felt herself go cold. They'd come for her! If they were from the police then the badges on their uniforms had recorders, cameras, sensors, microphones—and they'd have evidence that Kay was with them, too.

"Pursue somewhere where you have standing," Uncle Orned shouted, and he sounded, Jerel thought, entirely angry. "From here flee! Return home before we dissolve your gate!"

Briefly, Jerel wondered if they *could* dissolve the policemen's gate, but apparently the threat, true or not, was a good one. The police went back another step, and paused.

Jerel didn't know what the policemen might be able to see. Could the four of them look that ferocious? It was then she realized that her gun was in her hand . . . so the police were outnumbered.

"Jerel Telmon," the lead officer called. "Give yourself into my custody. Good behavior now may mitigate any judgment placed against you."

"No!" Jerel yelled. "Go away! I haven't done anything wrong!"

"If you are innocent," the woman called, and cut off sharply as Uncle Orned fired again into the ground at the edge of their gate.

"You have your answer!"

Silence. Then the garish light dimmed, the portal grew smaller, and the police scrambled unceremoniously back the way they had come, their gate shrinking, shrinking— and with a pop it was gone, leaving not even a glow against the rocks.

"Quickly," Erazias said. "Our gate forms! Keep close!" He moved to the left, robes rustling. Jerel and Kay went after him, Uncle Orned at their backs.

Once again came a pop, and the filigree of light formed overhead. The gate snapped into existence; beyond, Jerel could see brickwork and not much else. Erazias threw himself into the aperture.

"Go!" Uncle Orned shouted behind them. "Don't stop—run!"

CHAPTER TEN

Bricks!" Kay called, and then "Ow!" as Jerel caught up against his shoulder.

"Sorry," she gasped, trying to get her feet under her without shoving him harder against the wall. "Didn't expect that first step to be so steep!"

"Quiet," Uncle Orned said sharply, which, Jerel thought, was easy for him; *he* hadn't gone running off a ledge at top speed—no, she corrected herself, he had; he'd been right behind them. He'd probably just had the presence of mind to look ahead at where they were running into. Rule One, she thought with a sigh.

"You okay?" she whispered to Kay; he nodded, ruefully rubbing his cheek.

"Yeah. . . ."

Jerel turned, carefully slipping her gun into its inner pocket. Her nose wrinkled slightly. The place smelled moldy and damp, odors that didn't mix too well with the tang of ozone given off by the gate. She sighed and tried to ignore it while she surveyed their new environment.

Erazias had his back against the wall to their right, and was busy with his device.

"We're inside," she said to nobody in particular, which was good, since nobody answered her. Kay had moved off a couple steps to the left, head tilted back as he surveyed the tall ceiling, and Uncle Orned was facing the gate, gun held ready, as if he expected the rocks from the world on the other side to come rolling through or something. The gate itself looked odd—deformed. Maybe, she thought, the mass of the building constricted it? But, no, that didn't make sense, did it? The gate the police had used had punched itself right through a solid wall of rock. And besides, the room they were in was big—easily as big as the shop at CapCour; the gate had plenty of room to spread out.

"What's all this stuff?" Kay pointed—and shifted his shoulders apologetically when Uncle Orned gave him a hard look.

Jerel moved over to his side, squinting to see what he was pointing at. The lighting came from small blue glowstrips set at intervals in the brickwork wall, so the farther you went into the larger room, the dimmer it got. As she reached Kay's side, she could see that the other walls weren't brick, but some kind of structural metal; the roof was supported by a network of girders. Light leaked through a pair of dusty skywindows directly over Kay's head, so it was actually slightly brighter where he was than in the rest of the room.

Some of the dusty light reached the scaffolding and shelving built into the far wall. There were a few crates on the shelves, and a couple of machines sitting dark and silent beneath. One had an articulated arm folded down along its side.

"That looks sort of like a lift ladder," she whispered, pointing. "Maybe this used to be a warehouse, and they used it to get things on and off the top shelves. The other ones, though—"

"Old tech," Erazias said, not quietly at all, from behind them. "It would appear that we have raised your preferred port, Hunter."

"It looks a little dusty," Uncle Orned commented.

Erazias shrugged inside his robes. Beyond Uncle Orned, the gate they had come through flickered nervously and then popped itself out of existence.

"Before we proceed," Erazias began—and then cut off sharply as a girl's excited voice reached them from outside.

"Hurry, Mauder, hurry!"

"Fee, now," an older voice replied. "If ye placed as much effort into yer chores as duckin' em, Masy Dernsdatter—"

"I saw it! The wires flashed an' the roof thundered, just like Fantgaffer—"

"Fantgaffer's another got no taste for chores," the woman said tartly. "Run me out here for a gandlesnitch at dinnertime! You'll eat cold if—"

A blade of light showed along the far away wall to Jerel's left, accompanied by a shriek of metal and a noisy clatter. Then two shapes were outlined in the doorway.

Jerel froze, berating herself for not having tried to hide behind one of the machines, maybe—but it was too late now. Beside her, Kay was likewise frozen—and Erazias, hands hidden inside his robe.

Uncle Orned, though—Uncle Orned walked slowly forward, empty hands held slightly away from his sides, and stopped when he was midway between Jerel and the figures in the door.

"Darnay?" The woman said sharply. "Is't you?"

"Fanter!" The shorter figure broke forward, running, dodging her mother's outflung hand.

"Masy!" she cried, missing another snatch at the girl's arm. "Bring yerself back here!"

"It's all right," Uncle Orned said quietly. The girl stopped with a wail, and the woman hurried forward until she got both hands on the girl's shoulders and held her firm.

They were near enough that Jerel could see them despite the continued glare from the open doorway. The girl's hair was a tangled mop of red curls; she was wearing a set of beat-up workeralls and no shoes; Jerel thought she was a little older than the kid. The woman had red hair, too, pulled back hard from her pointy face. Like the kid, she wore old workeralls, though she had boots on. Both were dark-skinned and stocky.

The woman stared at Uncle Orned, who raised his hands slowly, showing her that they were empty.

"It's all right," he said again. "We are gate travelers who have become lost in our direction."

"Ach," the woman said, "lost fer certainsure." She hesitated, and Jerel saw her fingers tighten on the girl's shoulders—then blurted. "What news from yer travels of Darnay Dernsmate er Pulvar Conikmin?"

Uncle Orned's shoulders moved; maybe he sighed.

"I'm sorry," he said softly. "I have no news of either."

The woman closed her eyes, mouth thin and pinched. The girl—Masy—swallowed hard and looked down at the floor.

"Here, we're poorly husts," the woman said suddenly. She patted Masy on the shoulders, then came forward, one strong-looking hand out, palm up. "Be welcome to Fraderione, travelers. I hight Dern Vasdatter. Here be mine own datter, Masy."

Uncle Orned extended a hand and put it against Dern's, palm to palm.

"We receive your welcome with gladness," he said, still speaking softly, as if he were afraid of scaring the woman and her daughter. He moved his free hand, and Jerel caught the signal *come here*. She stepped up to his side.

"Here is my daughter, Jena," Uncle Orned continued, and Jerel concentrated on not blinking, or turning to stare at him. "I am Ondrew. We travel in company with my daughter's first-choose, Kain, and with the honored scholar Zendig."

Kay and Erazias each stood forward as Uncle Orned gave their new names, and Dern considered them solemnly—with an especially long stare at Erazias—before giving a heavy tip of the head toward Jerel.

"Veyadank, lady. Our howzen lies a bare step to seaward. After yer travel, ye must be hungry. Set and eat, and say us out what news ye may."

Now what? Jerel thought, and sent a quick look to Uncle Orned, who only lifted an eyebrow and waited politely for her to decide for them.

Rule Four, she thought, feeling a little sick to her stomach. But the question was, were they more likely to attract attention in Dern's company or by themselves?

She swallowed and inclined her head, hoping she looked serious and solemn and not like she was making fun of Dern's manners.

"Thank you," she said. "We'd be glad of a rest and some food."

"As we will be glad of news," Dern answered. She addressed her daughter over her shoulder. "Masy, run down and bid yer auntie warm the dinner, and say it's travelers from the *vildegatter* come to share with us."

"Aye, Mauder," the girl whispered, and that fast she was gone, running quick and light out the door.

Outside, the warehouse was a hulking, sagging building, its façade a dusty monotone that might have once been white. On its roof were sensors and dishes, most of them pointing dejectedly downward.

At Dern's insistence, Jerel walked beside her, Kay, Uncle Orned, and Erazias following.

"Porthouse sits there," Dern said, pointing up a long hill to a building only slightly smaller, it seemed to Jerel, than the warehouse, and in about as good repair. Three pennants flew from poles atop the roof, each snapping in the breeze that threatened to snatch the cap from Jerel's head. She grabbed the brim and pulled it down tighter.

"Breeze come sprightlike off the sea," Dern said comfortably. "She'll turn, come sundown, and quiet." They rounded the corner of the warehouse, and Jerel stopped, staring out and across at a great glittering and rush. A thousand moving reflections dazzled her eyes, making them tear, and a chorus of booms and crashes came to her ears, riding the waves and the high calls of birds.

"Lady Jena is a datter of the sea?" Dern asked politely. Jerel started and shook her head, embarrassed, and yet, her eyes wandered back to the wide wonder of it.

"I've never seen a sea before," she told Dern in perfect honesty.

"Ach," the older woman said, and for the first time her tight lips softened, almost into a smile. "Ye'll catch the best look from our own cap'n's porch. Might be later, ye and yer young man will go down with my Masy to the spit. Tide'll be turned by then." She nodded to the left, and Jerel took the hint, walking with her along a narrow path that meandered between small, crabbed buildings, built in awkward and unstable locations along the side of the hill. There were abandoned vehicles about, being allowed to fall, unrecycled, into rust amid the scraggly plants and rocks behind the village. There were boats, too, though in better repair than the cars. Some were turned bottom up, some were just sitting by the sides of houses, their windswept rigging casting weird shadows. Others sat in cradles, cocooned against the elements by shrink-wrapped plastics, the paths to them showing no signs of recent use.

They crossed what had once been a paved road, now silted and cracking. Jerel was finding it peculiarly difficult to walk. She felt—heavy—and the hill they climbed seemed steeper than it had looked from the warehouse.

"The village of Fraderione," Dern said, with a note to her voice that Jerel didn't understand, "what remains, when government and gate have done with us."

Jerel blinked.

"Oh, aye," Dern went on, "ye may think we're a poor place, but we were a good village, a sound village, before the gate took our contacts and our routes away. No need, then, for our menfolk to take their turn in the barrel and risk the chance of the *vildegatter*." She sighed, and slanted a quick glance at Jerel. "Pardon, lady. Yer no stranger to these risks, yerself, I see."

"I—" Jerel began.

Dern pointed ahead, where the path became a steep flight of stairs carved into the rocky side of the hill. Above them, the pennants on the porthouse roof snapped loudly in the breeze.

"Lady first," she said.

Jerel ground her teeth, and forced her tired, heavy legs to carry her up, one step at a time.

The house was the largest in the village, and had the proudest history. For hundreds of years it had served as the administration center for the Fraderione fishing fleet, which Venren, Dern's sister, assured them had been among the greatest on any world in Crantor, "sister space," as she called it. When the corporation abandoned the village, the house had passed into the hands of the Cap'n's Family, of which Dern was the elder daughter. It was her husband—Masy's father—Darnay who had finally gotten the elder daughters and the lesser captains to agree to use the wild gate to establish "contacts" and bring trade back to Fraderione.

"A cast into a stormy sea, it was," Venren told them, as they sat round a heavy table made of scarred yellow wood and worked at the food that had been provided. "The great cap'ns, they all have the way of bringing gain out from loss, and our Darnay is a great cap'n, certain-sure. Three times he walked the *vildegatter*, each with a different of the less-cap'ns. Three times came they back with goods and contracts, and draws on central banks."

"And the fourth time," said Dern, "Darnay comes not at all."

"Ssst," her sister said, and put a hand it out to cover hers where it rested on the table. "The fish ran further from shore this voyage, Elderess. Home he'll come, and Pulvar, too, the ship sitting low in the water for wealth."

Dern's lips parted, as if she was about to say something. Then she pressed them firmly together and looked down at her plate.

Jerel did the same, and tried, for politeness' sake, to eat something of her meal of seared fish and boiled seaweed. She'd already drunk two mugs of strong, unsweetened tea, which she thought now might not have been such a good idea. But—food that wasn't rated, or sterilized, or—Masy had told them, proudly, that they'd find the seaweed fresh; she'd gathered it at the tide mark herself, that morning. You could get sick, Jerel thought, from eating food that hadn't been properly pre-prepared. She sighed to herself and looked around at her companions.

Erazias had eaten his fish with apparent relish, complimenting Venren on her cooking. Uncle Orned had likewise complimented the cook, and eaten the fish without any qualms that Jerel could see, and was just now finishing up his seaweed. Kay—Kay met her eyes and gave her a grin, raising his fork with its piece of fish neatly speared in a kind of salute.

"The lady does not care for fish?" Dern asked.

Jerel bit her lip. "I'm—" she began, and was saved saying anything else by Erazias, of all people.

"Lady Jena fasts in preparation of her third-level initiation. She may consume but tea and water until the ceremony is complete."

"Ach!" Venren cried, with ready sympathy. "And here we tempt you!" She waved a hand. "Masy, take the poor lady's plate. The fish will go fine in the chowda, and the 'weed, too!"

Masy got up and did as she was told, but not before she gave Jerel a frowning look, which told her that the Dern's daughter, at least, wasn't buying any third-level initiations—and good for her.

"More tea, Lady Jena?" Venren asked; Jerel shook her head, feeling her stomach slosh.

"No, thank you," she said, and Venren smiled.

Dern leaned forward suddenly, pushing her plate back to rest her folded arms on the table.

"To travel the *vildegatter* is desperation in action, so said my Darnay, who knew it better than any," she said, looking only at Uncle Orned. "The sea will feed our folk, just as it always has—but what will feed our village? Every sea-change we lose more, till there's only the old and the desperate to home."

"A tradition it is," Venren said, looking at her worriedly, Jerel thought. "A tradition that they should leave us. A tradition that they should come back."

"More leave and less return," Dern said, still staring at Uncle Orned. "When the master of the *vildegatter* came to us, it was desperation made us pay the toll. Hard money up front and a tithe of the fishing, plus a percentage of whatever contracts come back."

Uncle Orned inclined his head seriously, and Dern sighed sharply.

"What news have you, Ondrew, of Peliot, cap'n of the *vildegatter*?"

Silence. Uncle Orned didn't look at Erazias so hard that Jerel felt her neck muscles ache in sympathy, and Kay looked up from his now-empty plate to glance between the two of them.

"I have not heard of Peliot," Uncle Orned said at last. "The wild gates which we travel are risky, yes, but we paid no toll to use them."

"Ach." Dern closed her eyes. Venren looked at her in concern, then turned with a smile.

"Masy," she said to her quiet niece, "take the lady and her chosen up to the cap'n's porch, why not? No sense youngers being cooped when elders want to talk dry bidness."

Jerel frowned and shot a look to Uncle Orned. It didn't sound like a good idea to be separated, but to her surprise, her uncle smiled and nodded easily at her and Kay.

"That sounds like a wonderful idea," he said.

More stairs, which Masy ran up, her bare feet making soft thumps on the slick wooden steps. Jerel followed more slowly, hating the heaviness that still clung to her, despite having rested. She wished she'd left her backpack with Uncle Orned, instead of slinging it over one shoulder and bringing it with her. What had she been thinking?

"Hairy up, slowbees!" Masy called from somewhere above them.

"Give us a beat," Kay shouted from behind. "This is heavier than we're used to!"

Jerel blinked, feeling dumb for not having realized it—and obscurely better, too. The heavy feeling wasn't just something weird that was happening to her; it was the local gravity. Kay and Uncle Orned were feeling it, too.

A series of soft thumps sounded from above. Jerel looked up to see Masy poised like a bird on the landing three steps away.

"Ye're out from a light world?" She tipped her head to one side, curls falling into her eyes. "How's it like to fly?"

"Not that light," Jerel told her, stumping upward. Masy danced up a couple steps, blithely backward, and Jerel mounted the landing with relief.

"How much further?" she asked, moving aside to make room for Kay.

"Nowt far," Masy said negligently. "Take yer time, lady. The sea, she's always there."

The view, Jerel admitted some time later, was almost worth the effort. Sweaty and breathless, she dropped her pack by her feet, leaned on the peeling wooden railing, and looked down at the rolling, glittering fabric of the sea. The steady breeze was cool against her hot face and she pulled off her cap to welcome it.

"What happent to yer hair?" Masy asked. "Catch it in the cookfire?"

Jerel started, and put her hand up, remembering too late why she'd been wearing the cap.

"You heard your mom say it was dangerous to travel the wild gates, didn't you?" she said. Masy nodded solemnly.

"Well," Jerel continued, "what happened to my hair is that somebody shot at us with a lectrosnap. I was lucky they only burned off some of my hair."

Masy digested this in silence, while Jerel looked out over the sea again. There were small objects coming in toward land—boats, she guessed, and wished she had her binocs with her.

"Ach," Masy said. "The for'ard runners. Here, ye'll like the long-glass for this. . . ." She moved lightly to the wooden chest sitting against the wall, opened it and rummaged inside.

Jerel breathed in the salty smelly air and started to feel hungry. She had still had cereal bars in her backpack, but figured it wouldn't be smart to eat one, since Masy had heard the story about her only being allowed water and tea. She sighed, and hoped that Dern's business didn't keep Uncle Orned too long and they'd be off soon to somewhere more—comfortable. She wanted, she thought, her chest suddenly tight, as if she was going to cry—she wanted to take a shower. She wanted to sleep in her own bed. She wanted to get back to her classes—she wanted everything to be *normal*. Jumping from world to world with the police thinking she was some kind of dangerous criminal—it was all wrong—crazy. They shouldn't have run, she thought, rubbing her right wrist. It had seemed reasonable at the time, but—shouldn't they have stayed, and told the police she hadn't done anything to—

"Here, lady, try this!" A metal tube was thrust at her. She grabbed it instinctively, and blinked at Masy, who mimed putting it up to her eye.

Jerel lifted the heavy tube in both hands and set her eye to the peephole.

The sea leapt up to meet her, swinging wildly, glittering like knives.

"Hold 'er steady," Masy said. "Focus yerself on a vessel, now."

Taking her eye from the glass, she peered down at the sea, located a small object, lifted the tube and by dint of a little moving around found it. Magnification showed her a boat, a man in the faded workeralls that seemed to be standard dress here poised on the front, a rope held carelessly in one hand. As he approached a post, he threw the loop of rope around it, then pulled gently, until his craft was nestled softly against the soggy wood. He grabbed a ring set into the post, holding the boat near while he ran the rope through several times and tied a complicated knot.

Jerel lowered the tube and tried to hand it to Masy, who shook her head. "Mayhap yer chosen will want to see, eh?"

Kay, Jerel thought guiltily, and looked around for him. He was leaning at a dangerous angle over the side rail, staring down into the village, Jerel thought, though what there was to see there . . .

"Hey, K-Kain!" she called, remembering his pretend-name at the last second. He turned around, and she held up the tube.

"Oh, great!" he said, coming over and taking it from her. "Just what I need! There's the weirdest flock of birds down here—" He turned back to his portion of railing, the tube already at his eye.

"Lady?" Masy said. Jerel turned and blinked. The girl was unfolding a pair of shears. "Be best to cut the burnt parts off," she said seriously, "and t'even up the rest. If gate-walking is as dangerous as Mauder and yer fanter agree."

Rule Four, Jerel thought, and nodded gratefully. "I should've done it myself," she said, "but we haven't stopped long enough."

Masy squinched up her face. "Might be best if I don't know much about yer bidness," she said, patting the chest. "Fanter says knowing another one's bidness makes ye party to their troubles."

There was, Jerel thought, something to that. She sat on the wooden chest, closed her eyes, and listened to the ocean and the crisp snip of the shears.

"There!" Masy said eventually, brushing Jerel's shoulders vigorously. "Short, but hair will grow, and yer young man will be glad of having his cap back."

Cautiously, Jerel lifted her hands and felt her head. Short, it definitely was, she thought, but she figured a bad haircut would attract less attention than half-burned-off hair half-hidden under a grubby cap.

"Thank you," she said. "It feels better already."

The girl grinned. "Welcome. It's good ye finally came to women. Wast there no sister to travel wit ye?"

"No, just me and Un—my father."

"And yer Kain," Masy said, with a slight frown.

"Oh, sure," Jerel agreed hastily. "Kain, too." She stood and stretched, starting to feel seriously hungry now. How long, she wondered, would the adults be at their business?

Kay was sitting cross-legged on the floor, rummaging through his pack. Jerel drifted back toward the railing, and crossed her arms on the rail, looking out over the sparkly sea. Birds that might have been the same ones Kay had been looking at were up now, dancing and calling on the breeze. There were a couple more boats tied up at various posts now, she saw. Squinting, she thought she saw even more boats farther out, bobbing bits of brown among the glitter.

Maybe she dozed, soothed by the breeze and the scents and the sounds. Whatever, she was brought to sudden and complete wakefulness by Masy's outraged cry—

"That be meen fanter's blade!"

Dern's brown skin was pale, her lips pressed so tightly together they were just a thin white line; Venren's good-natured smile had vanished. She stood, arms crossed over her chest, against the room's closed door. The skin around Erazias's eyes was bright yellow, and his fingers, too. Uncle Orned was mad—Jerel could hear it in the way his voice was way too polite when he asked Kay questions.

It was Kay that they were focusing on, though Jerel had said right away that she knew he had the knife. Apparently, they'd all expected her to say something like that; Dern had given her one of those heavy tips of the head and said bleakly, "Ye comport wit honor, lady"— and then forgot about her.

Kay himself was red-faced and stuttering, his pale hair still wind-rumpled, but he was sticking to his story, which was, as far as Jerel knew for herself, the truth. With the exception of the bones. No amount of badgering from Erazias or terse questioning from Dern and Uncle Orned had been enough to force Kay to mention the bones.

Which, Jerel thought, sitting ignored next to Masy on the built-in wall bench, was probably not a bad thing. If the bones happened to be Darnay's, who knew how much more trouble they'd be in?

Who knew how much trouble they were in already?

"It is plain," Erazias said, breaking into the fifth repeat of Kay's version of where the knife had come from: ". . . just laying there in the rocks. There wasn't anything else but rocks there, sir—you know that!"

"It is plain," the lizard man repeated, as all eyes turned to him. "The Lady Dern has lost a valuable resource of her family; a loss that rightly deserves to be balanced. We therefore shall, with Lady Jena's agreement, relinquish this boy and see him no more."

"What!" Kay and Jerel yelled at the same time.

Erazias raised a bright yellow hand. "It is just and reasonable. The boy claims that he has not harmed Lady Dern's mate, yet neither he nor we can prove so, while the lady continues managing the business of her clan handicapped by a lack of personnel. We rectify the matter as best we can, to show good intent, and to repair any actual damage that may have been caused by the removal of the captain's knife from its resting place."

"Zendig—" Uncle Orned began, but Dern overrode him, fixing Erazias with a grim glare.

"It's nowt a boy that I require, sir scholar. Hoebout I hold yer debt cleared with the payment of this one, instead?" She pointed at Uncle Orned. Jerel gripped the edge of the bench so tightly her fingers cramped. Uncle Orned only lifted an eyebrow and sighed.

"On the face, it appears a reasonable solution," he said, "especially in the first heat of anger. However, I feel compelled to tell you that you would not be able to hold me."

Dern smiled grimly. "Fraderione would hold you, well enowt. Unless you have a *vildegatter* in your pocket."

"I don't," Uncle Orned said seriously. "I am, however, a licensed killer, such things being legal on some worlds. If I were a cruel man, I'd wager with you that Fraderione would *not* hold me. As it is, I give you the respect due the eldest daughter and the high captain's mate. Data coin, Eldest." He moved his hand, as if he tossed something lightly to her.

"Hah!" Dern lifted her hand, fingers closing swiftly, catching the thing he hadn't thrown.

She stood quietly, then, looking down at her closed fist. Then, as if she had made her decision all at once, she snatched the blue-handled knife out of her belt and with a practiced move set the point of the blade against Kay's throat. Jerel started to stand up; and forced herself to sit down. She couldn't take her eyes from the scene in front of her: Kay's face was even paler than normal, but he didn't try to dodge away, and he didn't cry. He lifted his chin and met Dern's eyes.

"Hah!" she said again. "It might be the blade understands best. Boy! Ye'll swear to me that ye brought no harm to Darnay Dernsmate, nor to Pulvar Conikmin."

"I swear," Kay said, and if his voice quavered a little, his gaze was steady.

"Ye hear this, sister-next?" Dern called to Venren, who inclined her head from her position against the door.

"Eldest, I do."

"Also ye will swear, boy, that should ye find what came of Darnay Dernsmate er Pulvar Conikmin, ye'll not rest in yer efforts to bring that data to me. And, should ye find they've been dealt a death, ye'll not rest, not ever, ontil ye've dealt their killer likewise."

Kay swallowed.

"I swear."

"Dern Vasdatter, Eldest, I hear and accept yer oath." The blade was reversed in a bright twirl, the handle now toward Kay. "Yer blade, until ye return it to Darnay or use it to avenge him."

Slowly, Kay raised his hand, wrapped his fingers around the knife's hilt, and drew it from Dern's grip. Then, he bowed, low and with one of the complicated hand gestures his mom was always drilling him on.

"Lady, you have my oaths," he said quietly. "Know that it will be as you have said."

"Ach," said Dern, and turned away from him to face Uncle Orned. "Ye'd best be callin' that transport the scholar thinks he has, and take yerselfs far away from here."

CHAPTER ELEVEN

I never want to walk again," Jerel said, flumping down beside Kay in the shade of a dilapidated tin shed. They'd left the sea behind them, trudging down a sandy trail through a landscape of sharp brown weeds. That they were sharp, Jerel knew from unfortunate personal experience. That they were weeds, she assumed, because surely nobody would deliberately *plant* such ugly, nasty things.

In the shade of the shed, she opened the first aid pocket of her backpack and pulled out an antiseptic quick-seal.

"Get hurt?" Kay asked, slipping his pack off with a sigh.

"One of the weeds cut me," she muttered, struggling with the easy-tear activation strip. "There!" She unfolded the seal and put it over the scratch, carefully pressing the edges down. For a moment, it just sat there, an inert orange strip; then she felt a cool sensation around the area, simultaneous with the seal going from orange to the exact shade of her skin.

"Dune grass can be pretty sharp," Kay said. "At least it's just dune grass and not something poisonous."

Jerel eyed him. "There's poisonous *grass*?"

"Well—plants. Sure. All kinds."

"How do you tell them from the plants that aren't poisonous?"

"Study, mostly," he said, like it didn't make much difference. He sighed, and squinted around. "Hot."

That was true. They'd left the ocean breeze along with the ocean, and without it, the bright day was uncomfortably warm.

"How about Erazias trying to get rid of me like that?" Kay said suddenly, keeping his voice low, as though the lizard man could hear him from the middle of the field where he and Uncle Orned were having another one of their "talks."

"Maybe we should've offered to leave him instead," she said, pulling a water bulb out of its pocket. She held it out. "Want one?"

"Thanks."

She nodded, got another bulb out, pulled up the straw and had a sip. The water was warm, but not as warm as she was.

"That was pretty brave," she said, "to just stand there while Dern pulled that knife on you. I almost fell over— how'd you know she wasn't going to, you know, cut your throat?"

"I didn't," he said, giving her a sheepish look. "I was too scared to move. And I guess I figured your uncle wouldn't have let her hurt me too much." He drew a big sip of water. "Talk about scared! I hope I never hear anything scarier than him telling Dern about how he's a *licensed killer*, in that calm voice of his." He did an exaggerated shiver completely at odds with the sticky heat. "Good thing Dern believed him."

"Why shouldn't she believe him?" Jerel asked. "He *is* a licensed killer—that's what insurance men do." She sipped. "Well. You don't always have to kill somebody, Uncle Orned says, but if the client wants a permanent solution, then it's usually the way to go."

Kay stared at her. "I didn't think of that," he said slowly. "I mean, I know what insurance is and how it's regulated and all from Civics. And I knew that your uncle was in insurance. I just didn't—" He paused, his gaze wandering over to where Erazias and Uncle Orned were still talking.

"Wow."

Jerel finished her water, flattened the empty bulb, and put it in her pack.

"Does he tell you about his jobs?" Kay asked, finishing his water and handing her the squashed bulb to stow.

"Not usually," she said. "He doesn't like to bring work home."

"Oh." Kay squinched up his eyes, thinking. "Didn't you—hey, hear that?"

Jerel stared at the ground, listening. The sound of a rotor came faintly out of the clear, bright sky.

"Think that's our ride?"

"It had better be." Jerel sighed. "I hope, once we get to this city Uncle Orned is pushing us to, we can get a hotel room or something. I want a shower. And a real meal. And a good night's sleep in a bed."

"The fish was good," Kay commented.

"You can get sick from eating unprepared food."

"Well, you can. But that wasn't unprepared. Venren had cooked it up good." He gave her a sideways look. "They live on fish and seaweed there, pretty much. Couldn't do that if it made people sick. Though it is," he hurried on, when Jerel glared at him, "kind of weird the first time. I remember when we had to catch and cook our own fish for the basic bio seminar. I wasn't real sure, but I'd followed the directions and, honest, by that time we'd hiked in and set up and fished—I was so hungry I could've eaten the rocks off the ground. Raw." He pointed up into the sky at a rapidly growing dot. "There!"

In the field, Uncle Orned and Erazias were looking up, too. Jerel pushed herself to her feet, slung her pack over one shoulder, and ran a hand over her shorn head. She didn't like to fly all that much, but—shower, she reminded herself. Dinner. Bed.

Right.

The copter settled with a roar, hatch rising. Kay started out to it at a trot a little less brisk than it was at home, and Jerel followed.

Jerel squirmed in her seat as the copter lifted, and tried to think about something other than the fact that they were flying—difficult, since the pilot and passenger sections were enclosed by nothing more than a transparent bubble. She tried closing her eyes, but that only made her more nervous.

She'd taken a seat in the rear of the passenger section mostly because Erazias had chosen to sit forward and she didn't want to talk to Erazias right now. After all, *he* was the reason they were dodging the police through his stupid wild gates, with their tendency to just drop people in places they hadn't asked for or expected. If his gate hadn't malfunctioned, they would never have been on the world of rocks and Kay wouldn't ever have *seen* the knife—or the bones. And then to be willing—eager!—to just leave Kay with Dern . . . Jerel took a breath. No question, she didn't want to talk to Erazias right now.

Kay was a different matter, but Kay was up in the pilot's compartment, perched on the jump seat, talking
eighteen to the dozen at their pilot. Their pilot, Jerel
noted sourly, happened to be yellow-haired, tall and
busty—and not much more than a year or two older than
Kay. Jerel sighed, sharply, trying not to let her irritation
at Erazias spill over to Kay. Likely, he was sitting up there
because he didn't want to talk to Erazias, either—and because he probably thought Uncle Orned was still mad at
him.

Which, she thought, rubbing her wrist, he might well
be. Uncle'd been pretty sharp in his comments during
their walk out of the village, and while Kay had borne
the lecture pretty well, he couldn't be wanting to hear
any more.

The copter tilted; Jerel's involuntary grab at the snatch
bar didn't go unnoticed.

"There should be gum in the side tray," Uncle Orned
said, quietly. He'd chosen to sit in the back, too, next to
her on the two-person bench. It looked like nobody
wanted to talk to Erazias right now. He touched the
molded armrest on his side and a small section popped
open. "Here you are—" He handed her a blister pack.

She bit her lip. What a whimbo, she thought. Your father was a pilot and *you* need airsick medicine! She was
about to refuse the gum when the copter tilted again.
Sighing, she snapped one of the two blisters and popped
the gum into her mouth, handing the pack back to Uncle
Orned.

"Thank you," he said, and took the second piece of
gum for himself.

Jerel blinked. Uncle Orned raised a eyebrow.

"Not all of us have our space legs," he said, "and even
those who do sometimes need a little help when it comes
to unexpected motion in the atmosphere." He bent to put

the empty blister pack carefully into the trash slot. "Learn to take advantage of convenience and comfort when they're to hand, Niece, because you never know when they won't be to hand."

Jerel looked at him. "Does that mean we can check into a hotel when we get to the city?" she asked. "A shower and a real meal would be . . . convenient."

Uncle Orned smiled. "In fact, I was considering something very like that myself."

The intercom crackled.

"To the west, gentles, look to your left!" The pilot was almost singing. Jerel carefully looked out of the transparent wall to her left. Slightly ahead of their craft was a dark, funnel-shaped column in the air. Without landmarks, she couldn't tell how far away it was—or, in fact, *what* it was. It *looked* like a wind twist, but wouldn't any sane and competent pilot try to avoid such a thing?

"What is it?" Kay's voice came over the intercom, asking Jerel's question for her.

"Gyre-falks," the pilot answered. "Thousands of them, rising to take advantage on the oncoming front. We will give them a wide margin—the largest have wingspans wider than our craft!"

The maneuvering that followed made Jerel glad she hadn't been too proud to take the gum, for the pilot flung the craft about with a will. Though she said she was going to give them a wide margin, in fact they came close enough that Jerel could see the massive barred wings and the hooked beaks as the creatures swooped, dived, and danced. Some, she thought, were even watching the copter, as if considering whether it might be good to eat.

Apparently deciding that was enough of a good thing, the copter pilot put them into a long swoop out and away. Jerel looked down-cabin, expecting to see Kay with his nose pressed to the window, staring after the column of birds, but his gaze seemed permanently attached to the pilot's long yellow hair and pretty white blouse.

Creep.

"Jerel?"

Uncle Orned touched her shoulder. She started, and looked over at him. His face was serious, and she thought he looked tired, which was . . . disturbing in its way. Uncle Orned never looked tired.

"Jerel, I need to ask you something," he said, and her stomach clenched. The bones, she thought; he'd figured out that Kay wasn't telling everything. Though that was disturbing, too. He should know that she wouldn't give away Kay's secrets.

He was waiting, as if he expected her to give permission to ask his question. She took a breath.

"Yes, Uncle?" she asked, trying to be as quiet and serious as he was.

"Twice in a very short while, I have seen you pull your weapon. I wonder—and I do *truly* wonder, Jerel—if you were prepared to follow through."

Not about the bones after all, she thought with relief. But—

"Follow through?" She frowned. "You mean, fire my gun?"

"I mean," Uncle Orned said, "*use* your gun. Were you prepared to shoot a police officer, or one of the men in the alley?"

Ouch. Maybe it would have been better if they were talking about Kay, after all, Jerel thought. At least then she'd know what the right answer was.

She rubbed her left wrist and looked out of the bubble—the column of gyre-falks was a small smear against the bright sky—and then back to her uncle's face.

"In the alley," she said slowly, "I was pretty scared. And they were pointing guns at us—at me. I did think, yeah, that I should shoot one of them."

Uncle Orned's face changed, slipping through several expressions until it settled on one she couldn't say she'd ever seen before. She was used to categorizing people's expressions, as a sort of shorthand for what they were thinking or demanding, but this look was entirely new to her.

"I was scared, too," he said, and she got the impression he was being very careful, and choosing his words with even more deliberation than usual. "Being scared isn't reason to shoot someone by itself, though."

"But—"

He held up a hand, and she subsided, not really sure what she'd been going to say, anyway.

"It was not and is not my intention to bring you into the insurance business," he said slowly. "Your father wouldn't have wanted it, though that wouldn't necessarily have stopped me if you'd shown an interest and an aptitude." He looked down at his hands, folded neatly on his knee.

"Your aptitude was elsewhere and your interest followed—which is as it should be, since you are neither your father, nor me—nor your mother. You are yourself, Jerel Telmon."

He paused and it seemed to Jerel that she should say something.

"Yes, Uncle," she said softly. "I did wonder if you would want me to go into insurance."

He moved his shoulders. "I wanted—want—for you to be the very best Jerel Telmon you can be, utilizing your skills, whatever they are found to be, to insure your future happiness." He smiled faintly. "Or, since happiness is so often in short supply, at least a contented and prosperous life. However. You must know that there is a difference between what I do and taking responsibility for your own defense."

Jerel frowned. "So, I was right? I should have shot—"

He held up his hand again. "Should you have shot? That's a difficult determination to make, and often people err, because they must decide quickly and with too little data. Shooting someone should be, as nearly as it is possible for it to be, *a decision*. Fear"—he shook his head—"is not a good basis for a decision."

She thought about that, rubbing her wrist absently.

"That's why you didn't shoot *at* the police," she said slowly. "Because there wasn't any need to. You knew they could be—could be shouted down."

Uncle Orned smiled crookedly. "Let's say that I *hoped* they could be shouted down. It happened that I was right. But, had I been wrong and they advanced on us, I would certainly have shot one of them, though not fatally. Do you know why?"

"To scare *them*?" she asked. "To show you were serious and to—to up the odds? So maybe they'd pull out, because they were scared?"

"Exactly. Very good."

"What you have to remember," he said after a moment had passed and Jerel hadn't thought of anything else to say, "is that I am a professional. These decisions are not new to me, or strange. I have learned to recognize my fear, and how to use fear to gain advantage. For you—" He paused.

"For a person just beginning to take responsibility for her own life, who is traveling in the company of several people who have more experience in making decisions under difficult circumstances, perhaps the best first step is to promise yourself that you won't draw your gun unless you intend to use it. Does that seem reasonable to you?"

135

Uncle Orned didn't ask questions like this because he wanted her to agree; he asked because he wanted her to think about what he'd just told her. Jerel thought about it, taking her time.

"It seems reasonable," she said at last. "But—we got away, didn't we? The police won't come where they don't have jurisdiction, and the others—they can't follow us through the wild gates, can they? Isn't that why Erazias wanted to travel that way?"

"One reason, yes," said Uncle Orned. "But there's another thing you need to know, in order to aid your decision making, should it happen that you do pull your gun."

She frowned at him. "What's that?"

"The people who kidnapped you, and who followed us to the first gate—they aren't going to give up. They will try to follow us. I hope that we've given them the slip for the time being, by trying my contact here rather than going with the choice Erazias preferred. We shouldn't, though, assume that we've lost them forever."

"But why *me*?" she wailed suddenly. "I'm not anybody!"

"That's hardly true," he reproved her quietly. "You are the daughter of Parvair Telmon and Banin Vayle. In the eyes of some, that makes you very important, indeed, and for reasons that have nothing to do with who you are yourself. Those three facts I've just given you mean that you may find it necessary at some point not only to shoot someone, but to kill them. You may be required to do so in order to insure your own survival. If it happens that you are confronted with this choice, you must have no hesitation. You must act coolly and decisively, on the best data available at the time. Do you understand me?"

Jerel took a hard breath, surprised to find that her eyes were filled with tears. What did she have to cry about?

Uncle Orned was only trying to make sure she understood, just like he always had.

"Jerel?"

"Yes," she said and looked up at him. "I do understand, Uncle. Rule Six: *Shoot to kill.*"

His lips compressed and he closed his eyes tightly for a moment. Then he opened his eyes and smiled grimly.

"That's the right of it." He put his hand over hers and squeezed her fingers gently. "And don't fail for fear."

CHAPTER TWELVE

It is too public," Erazias argued. "We do not dare assume that we are not stalked, Hunter. They will be watching the datanets. As soon as they see you have rented a room, they will close."

"Which is why they won't see that I've rented a room," Uncle Orned answered calmly. "Really, Erazias, do you think I'm an amateur?"

"Surely not! It were only, brought away as quickly as was needful, with no time to prepare . . ."

"Erazias." Uncle Orned stopped right there in the center of the walkway, and turned to face the lizard man. "I am going to rent us a room. We are going to get cleaned up, rest, have a meal, *and talk*. This is not optional. Do I make myself clear?"

Jerel looked at Kay, who shrugged. Rule Four, thought Jerel. If they stood around on the sidewalk much longer while Erazias and Uncle Orned argued, they were absolutely going to attract attention. A couple of passersby had already sent them curious looks.

Maybe Uncle Orned had been betting that Erazias wanted to attract attention on the street even less than he wanted them to rent a room—like firing into the ground ahead of the police. If he was betting that way, he won, for Erazias fingered his staff nervously, and inclined his head.

"Lead on, Hunter. Our lives and the success of our entire enterprise are in your hands."

Jerel touched the panel in the shower room, and warm water gently sprayed out of the walls, soaking her, and making her face sting where she'd scraped it—how long ago?

Another touch and the spray was mixed with citrus-scented soap. She sneezed—soap up the nose—then lathered her hair, and used the brush provided to scrub the rest of her. Doing so, she discovered more scrapes, along with an amazing number of bruises. She sighed. Considering everything that had happened, it was no wonder that she was bruised, but, still, it offended her. She might not be tall and blond and busty, she thought, rinsing her hair in a spray of clear water, but she wasn't *clumsy*, either.

She touched the panel once more and the walls began to glow, drying the area, and Jerel too. When she was dry enough, she stepped into the dressing room, where her backpack waited. The door sealed behind her and would stay sealed until she left. Meanwhile, the occupancy indicator over the door to the shower room would have gone from blue to yellow, meaning that Kay, who had lost the toss for first shower, could use the facilities.

They'd been moving so much, this was the first chance she'd actually had to go through the main compartment of the bag. In the clean-clothes department, she found two pair of tough black pants, four long-sleeved shirts, and a hooded sweater that she had never seen before, as well as socks, and underwear. She chose a yellow shirt and snaked into a pair of pants. Uncle Orned hadn't done too badly in getting the size right. The pants felt a little loose, but she was used to wearing slideboarding togs, which were tight and stretchy, to cut down on resistance and to reduce the risk of a fluttering sleeve getting caught in something and making a problem.

Turning, she found a mirror—and almost burst into tears. Her hair! Masy had cut it short, all right. Gasping, she dove back into the depths of her pack, and in a moment turned back to confront the mirror again, brush in hand.

Brushing didn't do much good; what was left of her hair still wanted to stick out every which way. A more thorough search of her backpack failed to turn up any glittergel, which she could have used to hold it down—though she did find a lectriclibrary with about a million books listed in its index; a watch; a wallet containing cards and papers identifying her as Anatasha Morin, and a jaw-dropping amount of money, as cash and on debit cards.

Also, at the very bottom—a toolkit. Jerel opened it, blinking to clear her eyes, which had gone all teary. A number-three basic small units kit. With a gentle fingertip, she touched the tools tucked neatly into their loops and pockets. A toolkit. Uncle Orned was—

There was a thump on the door that led into the shower room.

"Hey, Jerel!" Kay yelled. "C'mon, I want to get dressed!"

"Hang on a second!" she yelled back, cramming everything haphazardly back into the pack. She'd have to unpack and repack it again, she thought, but she could do that in the common room while Kay got dressed.

"Okay," she called, triggering the door that led to the hallway. "I'm gone!"

Uncle Orned had rented a double suite, which was two sleepers-with-shower connected by a common room/kitchenette. The rental office had been automated, and the rooms were had simply by choosing a configuration and either depositing the appropriate number of coins, or running a debit card through the reader. Uncle Orned had paid cash. Jerel hadn't been quite able to see what name he had tapped into the guest register, but she doubted that it was "Orned Vayle," "Ondrew," or even "Chaklit Seven Chaklit."

She was in the common room, sitting cross-legged on the parlor's plushy rug, the contents of her backpack spread around her, when Erazias entered from the opposite side. He'd changed his blue robes for a sleeveless white shirt and blue pants that were full at the thigh, then buttoned tightly at the knee. His scales shone in the room's light, and his crest was high. He was carrying the gate finder and a datapad.

"*Terama*," he murmured, and Jerel blushed, realizing that she'd been staring.

"Hi," she said, and went back to ordering her pack while Erazias curled bonelessly into one of the room's several cup-shaped chairs.

For a while they worked in silence, Jerel rolling and packing her clothes, the Turlon writing notes onto the datapad's screen with a stylus.

The sweater, Jerel thought, should stay on top, in case she needed to get it in a hurry; the wallet and papers that belonged to Anatasha Morin she kept aside until she could talk to Uncle Orned about them. The toolkit she slipped into an outside pocket, noting as she did so that there were only two cereal bars and four water bulbs left. Now that they were in a real place—a city—she wasn't going to have to depend on what was in her pack, but, still, she liked to have some food on hand, in case she got hungry.

That left the watch.

She sealed the various pockets of her pack, set it aside, and picked up the timepiece. It was a standard multiuse with a slap-bracelet and an iridescent green face. At the moment, the screen was blank, waiting for her to code in the local time.

"Erazias?"

"Yes, *terama*; how may I serve you?"

She bit her lip, staring at the watch's waiting face.

"What time is it?"

He glanced up from his pad. "Did I not see a clock elucidating the local time in the sleep room? Indeed, I believe I did."

"No, wait." Jerel bit her lip. "What I'd really like to know is—how long have we been traveling, exactly? It seems like days, but I'm guessing that it hasn't been more than—twelve hours?"

"Ah, now *that* is a penetrating and interesting question, *terama*; I commend you." Erazias slipped the stylus into its slot in the frame of the pad and closed the cover. "You make inquiry into the very nature of the gates." He leaned forward slightly, his hands and the area around his eyes a dark and satisfied blue.

"To answer the base query—I would estimate that we have ourselves been traveling between two and one-half and three Galactic Standard Days."

Jerel blinked. "That long?"

"Indeed. Wherefore the nature of the gates comes into the equation. You must understand that when you enter a gate you do not, as your mind and senses report, instantaneously transition from one world to another. Though you are not traveling anywhere near so slowly as lightspeed, yet the transition requires time. Here the large, commercial gates, which are stabilized, buffered, and constant, hold a small advantage over our wild gates. For it is sometimes true that one may traverse more quickly, using a commercial gate. The advantage of the wild gate being, besides the transitory nature of its existence, that one may travel freely without yielding one's name, image, or retinal pattern to the authorities."

"Which is why smugglers—like Dern's husband—like them so much," Jerel said.

Erazias moved his shoulders in a sinuous shrug. "Indeed. Though it would appear in that case there is another who controls access to the gate and imposes a toll for its use, thereby creating a situation far inferior to that offered by the commercial gates. It is never wise, *terama*, to negotiate with persons of dishonor."

There was a click behind her, which was the door to the dressing room coming open. Kay came into the room, lugging his pack and his boots, sock-footed, his shirt comfortably untucked. He sat down on the rug, keeping Jerel between him and Erazias.

"Young Kay, greetings," the lizard man said.

"Hi," Kay said shortly, and was saved having to say anything else by the appearance of Uncle Orned, looking much the same as he always did.

"Well," he said, surveying them with one of his blandest looks. "We clean up nicely, don't we? I suggest we all have something to eat. Then, I believe it will be time for a chat."

The meal was done, the dishes recycled, the stools hung away, the table refolded into the wall.

Back in the common area, Erazias curled again into the cup-shaped chair. Uncle Orned took the chair that faced the door to the outer hallway. Kay dropped to the rug and stretched out on his side, head propped on one hand.

"Please, Jerel," Uncle Orned said. "Take a chair, and ask Erazias your question."

Her question? What did *she* have to ask Erazias?

The Turlon inclined his head. *"Terama?* Please, ask. I find your questions most worthwhile."

She sat, one leg tucked beneath her, and shot Uncle Orned a look. He raised an eyebrow, politely waiting. Touching her tongue to her lips, she transferred her glance to Erazias, still wondering—

"Why," she heard herself say, "are the police after me so hard? What did I really do? I adjusted my slideboard! I didn't kill Mileeda, and—and we could've proved that, I bet!"

Orned fixed Erazias with a stare.

"I believe that to be an excellent and worthy question. Let me put the weight of my curiosity behind it, as well. Erazias, please explain why Jerel is being sought by the police and by leftovers from the old order."

Jerel's stomach went weightless on her. Not because of the "old order"—that was just a bunch of crazies who wanted to bring the Oligarchy back—but because the Turlon's entire face bleached from dark blue to near green, almost instantly.

Erazias looked to his greening fingers, then to Orned and finally to Jerel.

"Terama, as your uncle declares, you ask a most worthy question. Pray do not feel that I have taken you or your curiosity in despite when I say that it may not be safe—for any of us—to share the fullness—"

"Erazias," Uncle Orned interrupted, his voice hard and cold. "You have put our lives in danger. Worse, you've been playing second-rate games with the life of your teacher's daughter and heir. I don't ask for your secret passwords. But I do ask that Jerel and I—and Kay, since he's chosen to accompany us—be told precisely what is at stake. Why is Jerel so sought?"

Erazias was suddenly and extremely still, unnaturally so, his face almost entirely yellow. Jerel was afraid they'd pushed him past some limit for his kind; that he'd shed his skin or molt, or have a heart attack.

He did none of those things. The moment passed. He resettled in his chair, his color gradually darkening, to gold, to green, to darker green . . .

"I will speak what I know of it," he said slowly; "as much as I can of what I know of it. Even more than joining us, young Kay, knowing these things may place you in danger. Do you wish to hear what I will say?"

Kay craned his head back, looking at Jerel mostly upside-down, then swiveled right-side-up to look at Uncle Orned, and, last, at Erazias. "Yes," he said earnestly. "Yes, I do."

Erazias twitched, then inclined his head.

"Very well. The part-story which you know is that Jerel's mother was a great mathematician and a great scientist. You know also of her mate, how he came to dissuade the scientist from her art, and remained to aid her in the war, as so many of us did, and for such good cause."

"The details of her science, I cannot tell you. And it is not simply that you should not hear them, but that you would not understand them. I was at her side for many parts of the work, and have passed the time since the last battle in scholarship—and I cannot duplicate what she wrought." He paused, looking toward a corner of the ceiling, though what he saw there, Jerel didn't know.

145

"But then," he said softly, "it comes that as the war progressed it seemed that, from time to time, there might be a . . . a spread of information. An infection. A leak. So, as we approached that battle which became the last, we came more and more to fear that the enemy might duplicate the work, else steal it. It was nevertheless necessary to test the device—a small test, to insure that all would operate as it should."

Erazias paused again, moving his gaze from the ceiling and fixing Jerel with a long look before continuing.

"At that time, you, *terama*, were as familiar a presence in the lab as your father or myself, and perhaps more than either of us, for as much as they feared losing the war, your parents feared losing you."

"So, for the small test, with the very tiniest of voltages and amps and watts and ohms and units of energy involved, your mother needed a security device that would not be easily duplicable, nor even discernible.

"Such a device was found."

"There were, at that test, seven of us, beside yourself. One was slain doing warrior's duty before the hour of the final confrontation; five of us were on *Valero* as the two sides massed to attack. The other of those seven witnesses was a Turlon of great reputation; in fact so great a reputation that he was needed on a world to bring them to the side of the revolution, and so he went."

"The enemy closed sooner than we expected after that test—that highly successful test. And the upgraded, the full-strength equipment was needed far sooner than we had supposed. It was built, rapidly, and enlisting all of the safeguards of the original. All of them."

"For all their love for you, *terama*, and their fear that you would be lost to them, yet you were required to be present on bold *Valero* at the start of the confrontation, for you were in fact part of the circuits. Both your DNA and your unique neural pathways . . ."

"Wait." Jerel held up a hand. Her stomach was tight and her head felt funny. "I'm part of some kind of super-weapon—a bomb? Is that what you're saying?"

"No, *terama*, you are not a bomb, and never were. You are Jerel Telmon, a wonder like no other in history. Please, if I may continue, I believe you will understand."

She took a breath, pulled her other leg up onto the chair, and waved at him, speechless.

"Yes." Erazias inclined his head. "I continue. The battle was joined, and your father having decided the moment, the process was begun. When your part was done, you were given into my keeping and with mere moments to spare we departed, leaving behind my comrades, your parents, and the fleets of the revolution and of the Oligarchy."

"The triumph is that the device worked as it was intended—and today we are free. The marks on your arms, *terama*, are the price that you paid for winning the war. That, and the loss of your parents." He paused, maybe waiting for another question. Jerel shook her head.

"So. The story is done, we would think. I would think so—and did. I have striven, in these years between, to be the proper student, and thus have gained some insights into the work we did. At my current rate of progress I may by the time your great-grandchildren's grandchildren are grown approach your mother's success . . ."

"And now we find that all is not done, for amidst the war, and in the aftermath, strange things happened. Explosions, bombs, assassinations and betrayals happened."

"Chuton, of the great reputation, who had been so staunch for the revolution—Chuton now lends the weight of his consequence to those who wish to return the Oligarchy. He, you will recall, was present at the testing of the prototype. And it has been told to me by those others who remain staunch for the revolution, that Chuton has found the means to duplicate the master's work, to the tiniest detail. In order to perform this work, he must have all of the components of the original device to hand." Erazias looked to Jerel and bowed his head, deeply, his scales a deep blue untouched by green or yellow.

"All of them."

CHAPTER THIRTEEN

Jerel woke up all at once with the conviction that she'd overslept and was going to be late for school. She flung the light blanket off, sat up, and swung her legs over the side of the bed. Maybe she wasn't so late as all that; if she used her board and took the shortcut through Inkale's Market, assuming she could dodge Inkale, who didn't like the kids using his open-air for a shortcut, then she'd be—

She blinked at the dim, bland room, with its pale gray walls and pale gray floor and pale gray blanket on a thin pale gray bed. Her bedroom walls were yellow, what could be seen of them between posters of ships, engine breakouts, tool sets, the Alley Rats—Simka's own home band—and shelves untidily stacked with music slims, infosource, and a couple of old plushies. This—

Memory struck, and she closed her eyes, suddenly tired all over again. She was late for school, all right. She didn't even want to think about what Tech Doyan was going to have to say to her about missing the series drills for the laser-micrometer calibration test.

Worse, she'd worked so hard to make lead tech on the Rebuild Squad for the annual Central Regional Engineering Competitions—if she didn't get home soon, the squad was going to be stuck with Firky Ives on lead. They'd never make it past the prelims with him in the headset!

She looked over at the next bed, but Uncle Orned was gone. It might even have been him leaving that had woken her up. Whatever. She *was* awake, and she knew from experience that she wouldn't fall back to sleep even if she did lie down again. Sighing, she stood up, and did her morning stretches.

Then, stomach grumbling, she went in search of breakfast.

Uncle Orned was standing in the common room, watching the newsfeed, green plastic mug in hand. He looked up as Jerel entered and raised the mug.

"There's chokaffe in the pot," he murmured.

Jerel nodded and padded in sock-feet to the kitchenette. She pulled a yellow mug from the rack and put it on the counter. An inspection of the condiment shelf yielded a flat-pack of dry soy milk; she sprinkled some into the mug, then filled it with chokaffe, letting the swirling liquid mix in the milk.

She tried a cautious sip, decided the beverage was still too hot, and carried the mug with her out into the larger area.

Her uncle still had most of his attention on the feed, now and then sipping absently from his mug. Jerel waited until she was sure she'd seen a line repeat twice and then said, "Uncle Orned?"

He glanced down at her. "Yes?"

She pulled Anatasha Morin's wallet out of her back pocket and held it up. "I meant to ask you about this last night, but we never got a chance to talk by ourselves."

"Ah. And your question is?"

She sighed. "Am I now supposed to be—whoever. Anatasha Morin. Am I supposed to be her?"

Uncle Orned tipped his head, giving the question serious consideration. "I don't believe that it would be particularly advantageous at the moment," he said finally. "In fact, you may never need to become Anatasha Morin, but—if you do—you should know that the identification and papers in that wallet, while good, are not proof against a thorough check. For the moment, I would suggest placing the wallet at the bottom of your backpack, or better yet, inside the lining."

"Inside the lining?" Jerel repeated and Uncle Orned sighed.

"I see that I've been remiss in certain aspects of your education." He glanced at the newsfeed, shrugged, and turned back to Jerel. "If you're not immediately hungry, we can take care of that detail now."

Jerel sipped her chokaffe. "Actually, I am pretty hungry," she said apologetically.

"Then you should eat. In fact, I should eat. Put the wallet away and we'll eat together, if you'd like that."

She smiled. "I would like that, thanks."

"We must," Uncle Orned was saying some little while later, as they ate companionably side by side at the fold-down table. "We must very soon, I think, press Erazias for the details of his plan. If my contact here will see us—and I think she will, for your mother's sake if not for mine—then it may become less important that we have those details. I'm not comfortable at all with the level of

. . . sharing . . . Erazias has indulged in thus far. He's right to be careful, but I think he doesn't want us to know what he intends."

Jerel frowned. "Why do you think that, Uncle? Last night—"

"Last night, Erazias related some history and warned us that Chuton believes you are necessary for something *he* is planning. Specifically what he is planning, and what Erazias is intending to do about it, we do not know. And we should. Most definitely, we should. Also . . ."

He paused to have a sip of his chokaffe.

"Also, *you* need to be aware that, when Erazias arrived at our apartment, inquiring after you, it was at that time his intention that *only* you should accompany him. Kay and I are with you on sufferance, and it may be that Erazias will yet attempt to separate us."

"But—" Jerel began, and cut off as the door to the second apartment, where Erazias and Kay were sleeping, came open.

"A most excellent dayspring to you, *terama*—and also to you, Hunter." The Turlon was dressed once more in his voluminous blue robes, and appeared quite cheerful.

"Good morning, Erazias," Uncle Orned answered calmly. Jerel waved.

Erazias started toward the kitchenette; paused and turned his head to consider the silently scrolling news-feed.

"I trust we are as yet unnewsworthy?" he asked.

"It would seem so," Uncle Orned answered. "We ought to be able to make contact with Sumelion this morning."

"As to that," Erazias said slowly, pausing at the side of the table and looking down at Uncle Orned seriously, "I would ask you, Hunter, to do me the courtesy of reconsidering the cojoining of logic and need which has produced this particular solution. It may be you will find, now that you have rested and fed, more merit in my suggestion that we proceed on to Nozarek." He inclined his head. "Please, consider, while I arrange a meal to break my fast."

Uncle Orned didn't say anything, just continued to eat his cereal while Erazias rustled around in the kitchenette.

"Is Kay still asleep?" she asked over her shoulder.

"Indeed, young Kay slumbers on," Erazias answered, most of his attention on the selection board. He touched a button, opened a hatch and extracted his choice. Another button, another hatch and he was back with them, carrying a warmer bowl and a bottle of water.

They ate in silence for a few moments. Jerel finished her cereal and her second mug of chokaffe and sighed, feeling—almost all right.

Uncle Orned finished his cereal, pushed the bowl back, and picked up his mug as he leaned back in his chair.

"I believe," he said to Erazias, "that it would be most advantageous and informative to pursue my contact in this place, if she can be located. Traveling on to Nozarek will take time, and increase risk. Perhaps, if Sumelion cannot be found, we should discuss Nozarek again."

The Turlon continued eating, the area around his eyes showing the faintest tinge of yellow.

"If I may," he said after a few minutes. "The being you wish to contact has expressed a promise to shoot me on sight, nor is she one to forget such promises, or fail to act upon them, given opportunity."

"That's easily dealt with," Uncle Orned said. "Since Sumelion has made no such promise concerning me that I'm aware of, Jerel, Kay, and I will make contact while you wait for us here."

Erazias sat quietly for a moment, head bent. Maybe, Jerel thought, he was watching his fingers turn green.

"Perhaps better for you to go yourself, and all of us await you here. The novices would, I think, be grateful for a longer period of rest."

Jerel felt her chest tighten. "No way!" she said to Uncle Orned. "We came all this way, and I want to see the city!"

He raised an eyebrow. "I think you have your answer," he said.

Erazias moved his shoulders inside his robes. Maybe it was a shrug. "Perhaps, then, we should all go. I will merely keep myself out of range until you are able to inform her that we are allied in this endeavor."

"All right," said Uncle Orned. He put his mug on the table and rose. "I'll go wake Kay." He patted Jerel lightly on the shoulder as he passed behind her chair, and strolled across the common room, hardly even looking at the newsfeed.

"Why," Jerel asked, "does—Sumelion?—want to shoot you?"

Erazias's gaze blinked from the newsfeed to her face.

"She misunderstands my role in bringing you to your uncle, *terama*. She and some others, in fact. They believe I ran from the battle, and thus was saved while my betters were not."

"Oh." She considered that. "So, she was a rebel . . . soldier?"

"She was—and as I suppose, still is—very much of the revolutionary mind-set; she knew many of the leaders and thus many of the plans. Oh, and she is remarkable for being a designer of low-cost weapons, and of multi-use items that were needed very much by our groups, for we hadn't the funding required to wage a full war at first."

Jerel leaned forward, her interest caught. "She sounds amazing! Is she still working?"

"So I would imagine," Erazias said, with a shrug. "At the time of the great battle, she was young for her species—quite young, in fact, yet entirely accomplished. An adroit and gifted engineer, but sadly given to flights of temperament."

A noise came from the common room. Jerel turned her head as Kay entered, yawning, hair rumpled and staticky.

"Hi, Jerel. Good morning, Erazias."

"Good dayspring to you, young Kay. I trust your sleep was sound?"

"It was okay," he said, moving past the table.

"There's chokaffe," Jerel told him.

"Hope there's lots." He pulled down a mug and filled it from the pot, then walked over to the selection board and punched a button. "Want anything?"

"I already ate."

He sat down, took a swallow of his drink, and fell to his sandwich as if he hadn't eaten in a month.

"Your uncle says we're going downtown pretty soon."

"In fact, as soon as everyone has eaten and made themselves presentable," Uncle Orned said, stepping into the common room. He paused. His attention, like Erazias's, was on the newsfeed; Kay's was on his breakfast. Jerel sighed and stood up.

"I'll go get my pack," she said to nobody in particular, which was good, because nobody answered.

CHAPTER FOURTEEN

They strolled around the concourse three times, each time with different companions side by side. The first time, Erazias walked side by side with Jerel, Uncle Orned close on her heels and Kay behind the Turlon.

The concourse enclosed all of the city's business district, creating something like a habitat, because it was climate-controlled and stable, and something not at all like a habitat, because the enclosing material was clear so it was possible to see out. There were even viewing stands set up at special recommended locations, complete with binocs rentable by the minute. From one vantage, the view was of the sweep of unprotected city, down to the glow of the commercial gate. From another, the airport could be seen; while yet another overlooked the long hillside on which the city was built, down to the glitter of water at the base.

No vehicles were allowed inside the concourse; signs posted at intervals listed precisely what sorts of things were considered to be vehicles, including "monowheels"—whatever they were—and "gyrostilts." Slideboards did not make the list, despite which there were none in evidence, which in Jerel's opinion was just dumb. A big protected place like this, enclosing all those offices and apartments—it was a natural for slideboarded couriers.

On the second go-round Jerel was paired with Uncle Orned, with him very much in lecture mode, whether he was discussing one of the trees in the park they strolled past, or the weapons on the belts of the rather obvious and ubiquitous security crews.

Their stroll took them past a series of open booths. At one—the banner over the booth read DIGITS—three people sat with their hands in the maw of an autosurgeon.

As they passed, the surgeon finished with one customer, who raised his hands, smiling as he admired elongated fingers, each with two extra joints. Jerel shivered and looked away.

Uncle Orned smiled faintly. "This place is tame, Jerel. I have been places where . . . well, no, maybe later."

They passed another booth, this one selling tiny, brightly colored capsules. Signs in three languages advised them to FORGET NOW, TEMPORARY OR PERMANENT!

Uncle Orned sighed this time, murmuring, "Some lives are more difficult than others, I must assume. My advice is not to use Forget-it. But, if you do, *never* as a lark in a public place."

Back through the park they went, and one of Kay's questions to Erazias reached them as they passed a bubbly pseudo-brook. "Are they natural fish in there? Or are they custom-grown . . ."

Uncle Orned's lecture moved from the general to the specific; he showed her the marked exits, the workers' exits, the emergency exits, and the places that could be used for short-term concealment. He also pointed out the entrances to the office complexes, explaining that they'd all have good ways out of the concourse—but only if you had the proper ID. . . .

"Did you get the triple or the quad?"

The third round, and she and Kay led the walk. It had been his idea, certainly seconded by her growling stomach, that they visit a food stop and try something good. He'd pointed out the multicream place, loudly, to Erazias the round before, so she wasn't surprised when that became their destination.

She wrinkled her nose at him.

"Triples are for whimbos. I got myself a quint. All natural flavors, too."

He laughed. "I guess, if you say so, but I got me an extra-size, and it's a quad."

The walked, Kay thinking his thoughts and munching his cream, while Jerel looked around, trying to keep Rules One, Three, and Four simultaneously in mind while she particularly noticed the exits, which she couldn't *not* notice, now that Uncle Orned had pointed them out, and thought about how the crew halls would be darker and have less obvious routes to safety while the public exit halls would have extra monitoring and built-in crowd control points. . . .

"Hiff!" Kay was staring at his cream, face screwed up in distaste.

"What's wrong, is it bad?"

"I dunno, not bad, really, but I think they gave me a triple with a couple extra blobs of C-fruit and called it a quad. Taste's all right, just not much of it!"

"Mine," she said seriously, "is perfect. But I watched them make mine. You were watching those girls go by. You're lucky he didn't just give you a double!"

Uncle Orned chuckled lightly behind them.

CHAPTER FIFTEEN

Excuse me, please," Jerel said politely. "Are you Engineer Sumelion Pel?"

She knew very well that the person she addressed was Sumelion Pel, since both Uncle Orned and Erazias had told her so. The part she didn't quite understand was how *she* got to be the one to initiate contact. She thought it had been all set that Uncle Orned would clear the way, while Kay and she waited with—

Right, waited with Erazias. Uncle Orned was *really* worried that the Turlon might try to sneak off with her. Jerel thought she ought to be offended, since it seemed like Uncle didn't think she had enough sense not to let herself get sneaked off with, but right now there was Engineer Pel.

She was tall—very, *very* tall. And very slender. She was wearing a scarf around her throat, and she had been gazing up into the trees as Jerel approached, standing by a park table bearing a tote bag, a furry-looking ball, and a lapcomp.

There was no reaction to her question. Jerel was afraid that perhaps she hadn't spoken loudly enough, for the Yliger was easily half again as tall as she was, and who knew where her ears might be?

She was just about to try again when the head bobbed in her direction, distractingly from atop a long, slim neck; and the eyes were not at all like the eyes of a human, but solid-colored—even beady. The eyes blinked several times at her, first the right, then the left, then both together, and the head twisted from side to side, as if each eye needed to perform its own independent inspection.

"I am who you name." The voice was something between a trill and a whistle. "Who might you be?"

"My name is Jerel," she said slowly. "I am to say that I have come with Orned Vayle and also Erazias, both seeking assistance for our party, numbering four."

The right eye blinked. The left eye did not.

"Erazias brings you here?"

"Yes," Jerel answered cautiously.

The Yliger's stance was impossible to read, for her head bobbed and weaved as she spoke, and she moved almost continuously. Her skin was—well, no, it wasn't skin and it wasn't fur, but might be, Jerel thought, feathers. Her face and hands were covered with them, and they held an iridescence that made it difficult to say what color her face was.

"I am amazed he arrives at all. That he does not arrive alone and carrying a story of great hardship is marvelous indeed! Have we proof that you are who you say you are, and that Erazias awaits?"

At this the Yliger turned entirely about, eyes scanning walls and halls hastily before she returned her attention to Jerel.

"His manners improve; he does not tempt me by being in my sight immediately." The left eye blinked thoughtfully. "Though how just any human child would know Erazias had threatened me with his presence, I am beyond knowing, so I will suppose a thread of reality runs through your feathers."

Jerel frowned—she'd been expecting a welcome, or at least careful neutrality, not an interrogation.

"My uncle Orned will vouch for me," she said, her voice sounding irritated in her own ears.

"Ah. The most excellent Orned Vayle is known to me. However, human kin groups seem remarkably unable to consider each other rationally, so this 'vouch' may not suffice. Yet, wait! Perhaps it is possible to attain independent corroboration. May I see your forelimbs?"

"My *what*?"

"Your arms above the hands. You have passed in front of me once before, if you are who you claim, and I would see . . ."

Jerel sighed, and looked around carefully. No one was taking undue notice of their discussion, at least not now. She had no idea what surveillance devices might be about, and if there were any paying attention to them, they'd have recorded everything they'd talked about anyway.

Annoyed, she pulled back her sleeves, exposing the marks on her wrists.

The answering twitter and flutter of limbs was bad enough, but then the bird woman laughed, which was truly unnerving.

"It is a good accident for us all that your mother branded you, is it not, and that you have not yet mated with any male demanding perfection in his pleasures! And yet it is just like Erazias to leave little things undone—those marks should have been cleaned from your skin before you ever came to space!"

Jerel had been trying to follow the rather flighty pattern of the Yliger's thought, but—the rudeness of this person, claiming she'd been "branded" by her mother, and then blaming Erazias for not removing the scars! What did Erazias have to do with it? The scars had always been there; if she wanted them gone, then she'd take care of it.

"I'm not sure I'm speaking to the right person," she heard herself say coolly. "I apologize and beg forgiveness for having misused your time."

The bird creature twittered; one eye, then the other, studied Jerel's face.

"Yes, yes, yes. Please be calm. I see you for who you are. The temperament is there, and the voice is close enough. Will you be an amazing scientist like your mother, or a revolutionary like your father?"

"I'm going to be a spaceship mechanic like my grandfather," she answered, shortly. "If you believe I am who I say I am, what about—"

"Erazias deserves the tortures of life," Sumelion declared airily, "since he clung to it so hard after those he was sworn to were gone. But he must be within easy reach, else he would not have sent the fledgling to face me first." She raised a thin, long-fingered hand and smoothed the air, as if it were alive.

"Calmly, please. We will discuss in this our first meeting small things, as if we have been properly introduced, as if there is no concern anywhere, nor need to watch behind us. So—I honor your goal in life, to be a mechanic and technician for spaceships. It is a fine occupation, though I wonder if you will find it challenging enough, in the long run."

Jerel sighed, not as soothed as the Yliger apparently wanted her to be.

"If it lacks challenge, then it does. But I want to learn, and to work in the field. Maybe later I could specialize in older ships, antiques, ships of historic interest . . ."

"Ah, yes, there is that sense again, like your mother. Learn the basics well, she would have it, and then move beyond and do more than anyone expects from those basics. Such a loss was your mother, to the movement, and to the galaxy!"

"Did you know her—my mother?"

"Indeed, indeed. She is kept among the most precious of my memories, and examined often."

Jerel sighed.

"I was too young to really remember her. Sometimes I think I remember leaving the ship . . ."

"*Ssss.* What useful memories humans have. Until they are filled up and sorted and truly conscious they can remember nothing of note. And I, tortured still by my sibling's pecks and scratches! I could count them. Were there cause."

The face glanced away. Now that she was used to it, Jerel didn't think it an unhandsome face, but it was neither human nor Turlon.

"Hold a moment if you would," Sumelion said. "I must refresh myself."

She stepped over to a tall gray tube planted upright in the ground some small distance beyond the table, and swiped a card through the reader at its side.

A whoosh of air shot out, quite forcefully.

Sumelion stared into the whoosh, turned her back to it—and Jerel had to work hard to keep from laughing. She was watching someone take a shower in the park, or at least an airbath.

Then Jerel did laugh, struck by a sudden idea.

"Are you doing this to annoy Erazias?"

There was a twitter. Sumelion reached to her neck and loosened the scarf, which was not a scarf at all but a long, black-feathered cape. There was a bright red patch on each shoulder, and the whole billowed and snapped in the whooshing air.

"Surely, surely," she sang, "you are your mother's daughter. The Turlon has earned his torture, and I will not be the one to withhold it. You and I, we will talk more fully in a moment. After, perhaps we will allow the males to join us!

"But please, permit me to use my hard-earned rest period and this expensive air. Air should not cost so much, even in the capital city!"

Sumelion Pel had questions. Lots of questions. Jerel tried to move the conversation around to Uncle Orned and Erazias again, but Sumelion deflected that easily. Jerel hadn't found it quite so easy to ignore the questions about where she'd worked, and how long she'd known Kay, and how much real experience she had with tools . . . and the next thing she knew they were talking about the intricacies of reprogramming slideboards and the joys of good tools.

Of course, Jerel had to admit that she'd needed to leave all her tools when they fled, though she did have a good number-three small in her pack; a confession that was met with a war story from Sumelion and . . .

An odd chirping whistle sounded from close by, but Jerel was in the middle of explaining the intricacies of the engineering competitions to Sumelion, and didn't think much more of it than there was a bird in one of the nearby trees.

The chirping came again; Sumelion twittered, and put one soft hand on Jerel's arm.

"I think perhaps we have baked Erazias enough for the moment," she said. "I am informed that he is making a sight of himself. . . ."

Jerel blinked at her, and suddenly remembered Kay and Uncle Orned and Erazias, stuck in a not-exactly-comfortable service bay while she chattered on for—how long? She glanced at her watch. Winced. Turned her head slowly.

Erazias was walking in tight circles near the niche they'd selected as a hide spot. When he saw she was looking, he stepped back into the niche and Kay came forward, looking worried. The whereabouts and probable state of mind of Uncle Orned, Jerel decided, didn't bear thinking about.

Once again, the chirping noise came—and this time Jerel located its source: the ball sitting on the lapcomp! Not only was it chirping and whistling, it was moving—stretching, really, and showing four small hairless feet. Jerel blinked.

"Ah!" the engineer exclaimed. "Please forgive. You should be aware, Jerel, that no longer does Sumelion Pel labor alone—but there, you have heard how my desire to work independently cost me several very fine sets of tools! I now have the felicity of a partner of great talent and insight. We did not properly make introductions because Vreet was working, and also because I felt it best for you to become used to me before meeting such a one. Now that work is for the moment put aside and you have accustomed yourself to the flighty Yliger we may observe the niceties." She moved her long hand in a complicated gesture.

"Jerel Telmon, I make you known to Vreet. Vreet, here is Jerel Telmon, the"—high-twisty-whistle—"of my so-passionate friend Parvair."

Vreet turned . . . itself slightly, rocking on its tiny feet. The fur covering the portion of its round body nearest

Jerel quivered, and two large blue eyes emerged, moving on short, flexible extenders. Simultaneously, a pillar—no, a hand and an arm as hairless as its feet emerged from its underside, elongating until Vreet had risen several inches above the lapcomp. The arm bent, Vreet bobbed and whistled while the big blue eyes looked at her seriously from two slightly different angles.

"Vreet expresses pleasure at making the acquaintance of one who proceeds thus gracefully from events of random beauty."

What? Jerel wondered; then forgot it as she bowed in turn. "I'm pleased to meet Vreet," she said politely.

"It is well done," said Sumelion. Vreet sank down on its arm until it was once again supported only by its feet; the blue eyes closed and withdrew into—wherever they had come from. It chirped, though Jerel could see no mouth, and Sumelion chirped in answer, before looking aside and twittering slightly to herself.

"Vreet suggests you acknowledge your friends before frustration incites randomization."

Jerel felt herself flush.

Once again, she glanced over toward the hide spot— and there was Uncle Orned, looking far more composed than either Kay or Erazias had, barely looking in her direction, as if the trio in the park was in no way odd, nor held any interest beyond something moving within his line of sight. . . .

Jerel nodded at him, very slightly. His left hand moved, very slightly. She sighed.

"Should they join us?" she relayed Uncle Orned's question to Sumelion.

There was a twitter, as Sumelion fussed with her cape, rolling it until it once again appeared to be a mere scarf about her skinny neck.

"So clever," she said, adding a nuanced whistle—maybe translating for Vreet.

"Allow them to know that they should follow us," she said then. "I suggest that it is not wise for all of us to be seen in the same frame, and while the cameras are not plentiful here, yet they sometimes do come among the trees.

"We shall proceed to a place less public. When we meet, it would be good if your kin were the one to speak with me, for my fingers flex when I consider the joy of having the Turlon's neck in my claws."

Jerel shuddered, and motioned vaguely with her right hand, trying to make the signal seem like part of the conversation she was having with the engineer. She also looked closely at the Yliger's soft, slender, taloned hands. . . .

Sumelion twirled and plucked the tote up. Vreet rocked itself off of the lapcomp, standing patiently on the table while the engineer powered the machine down. The comp went into the bag, and then Vreet did, a light whistle and chirp being answered by something similar from the tall one.

Suddenly, Sumelion turned, her face looming large in Jerel's vision.

"Words for you, not to be repeated," she said, both of her shiny eyes fixed on Jerel.

"I have no love yet for Erazias. Your mother, I hold in esteem and affection; I respect your father, whose understanding was quite nuanced, for a male. For you, who must carry on such important work with proper direction—you, I also respect. And so, for your mother, and your father, and for you yourself, I will do what I may to be sure that you have tools appropriate to the task when there is need of them. I am unsure if you hold those tools now." She made an adjustment to her scarf and settled the bag over one skinny shoulder.

"Come," she said. "Let us remove to the sunset side of the concourse, where the bribes of others will permit us to meet with fewer cameras upon us. From there, we will decide our next course of action."

CHAPTER SIXTEEN

Sumelion's "less public place" was a restaurant called Inaprio's, which was tucked into a cul-de-sac off a side hall in what looked to Jerel to be the Oldside of the concourse.

Slypo poured in jagged twists of sound out into the hallway, where several tech-heads sat at a table, a ganji board between them and drinks to hand all around.

Inside, a gaudy, flashing screen displayed the names of a hundred alcohols and other inebriants, while a smaller screen, beneath, showed the news.

Sumelion nodded at the Turlon behind the bar and kept moving, to the very backest, dimmest corner. She slid into a U-shaped booth, tote bag held high, Jerel after her, Kay and Erazias after *her*.

Uncle Orned remained standing while Sumelion fussed with the tote, removing Vreet and placing it on the table before her. When at last she looked up, he bowed.

"Sumelion Pel, I greet you, and express thanks for the kindness you have shown to a member of my nest."

"Hah." The engineer settled back in the booth, her head moving while she gave Uncle Orned her one-eye-after-the-other inspection. "Orned Vayle, it pleasures me to greet you. It has been too long since we have spoken. Please, sit here by my hand and let us renew our fellowship."

He bowed again and slipped into the booth from the other side, and moved round until he was sitting at Sumelion's left hand. Vreet expressed a quick series of chirps, and Uncle Orned tipped his head, one eyebrow raised.

"One's partner, Vreet," Sumelion said. "An emanation of honor is expressed."

"I am pleased to meet Vreet," Uncle Orned said solemnly.

"It is well," Sumelion said, and put one eye on Kay. "Fledgling, may I know your name?"

Wedged between Jerel and Erazias, Kay tipped forward in kind of a seated bow. "Engineer, my name is Kaydar Vanion; small-name, Kay."

"Hah. A fledgling most mannerly. It pleasures me to welcome you, Kaydar Vanion." The beady eyes moved, their gaze passing over Erazias as if he didn't exist. Sumelion turned back to Uncle Orned.

"I regret that there is little time for the observation of proprieties. As you yourself taught me, no place is safe for long. I therefore urge you to speak closely to the point. You sent to me your fledgling, begging assistance. In what way may I assist?"

"We find ourselves pursued by those who desire to reverse the effects of the revolution. In particular is the fledgling to whom you have shown so much kindness of interest. The person who produces this disruption is, I think, known to you as one who worked tirelessly for the cause, now reportedly holding an opinion much changed from the old days." Uncle Orned inclined his head. "I speak in generalities out of respect for our location."

"Understood." Sumelion sat quietly, her hands resting on the table close to Vreet. Finally, her head moved, almost a shake, and her glance once again slid over Erazias, who sat stiffly at the very end of the curved bench.

"*Ssss.* I have heard something of this in the wind— faintly, you understand, and without direction. If it is as you say, and they come now . . ." Her left hand fluttered to her scarf. "If they come *now* . . ." she repeated.

Vreet whistled high and sharp.

"Indeed." Her long neck twisted so that she could look down into Uncle Orned's face with both eyes at once.

"Friend, I will assist you and your fledglings. Another—"

"Is necessary," Uncle Orned said softly. "I regret, but our surest means of travel, should it come to travel, is at his hand."

Silence.

"So be it, then," Sumelion sighed; "though I like it not."

"I appreciate your forbearance," Uncle Orned replied, bowing his head.

"Hah. Too long, indeed. I believe it is time for us to depart this place. My nest is yours."

"We are," Uncle Orned assured her, "honored."

They followed Sumelion out into the larger room and past the counter, the flickering colors of the newsfeed inevitably drawing the eye. Knowing the distraction of the video, Jerel tried to ignore it. Kay, however, did not. He stopped and stood like he'd been turned to ice, staring at the screen.

"Jerel, look—" he whispered.

Frowning, she looked, saw a distant smoky plume displayed, followed by a quick zoom to a smoking pile of machinery—possibly a former high-speed transport—crumpled against a highway abutment.

A box bloomed in a lower corner of the screen, displaying a pretty face, with long yellow hair, as the background filled with the details of another twisted pile of metal—

"That's her," Kay's whisper cracked with horror. "That's our pilot!"

"Are you sure?" Jerel asked, but her heart wasn't in it. She'd recognized the face, too.

The news moved on to some other tragedy. Sumelion looked back, saw them staring at the screen and tossed a metal disk onto the counter. The Turlon barkeeper looked up at the sound of cash.

"Please rerun news," Sumelion said, "the last two items."

The bartender signaled *yes* without a word, and in a moment the news repeated itself.

The first story involved some incomprehensible local scandal. Jerel reached out and took Kay's hand; his fingers were cold.

The scandal story ended, and the picture cut to the twisted metal, while the off-screen commentator chattered on, bright and happy, as if she were reporting a birthday party:

" . . . several deadly accidents caused by the low-flying craft before it crashed and burned. The pilot is missing and presumed dead in the crash, which some witnesses said was preceded by an explosion. . . ."

Kay's cold hand tightened around hers so hard it hurt. "She's dead? How can she be dead? We just saw her. . . ."

There was a burst of whistles then from the bag, and Sumelion's beady eyes glared down at all of them.

"Vreet suggests we remove ourselves from public view as quickly as possible. Let us be quick!"

CHAPTER SEVENTEEN

Kay was avoiding everyone, Jerel thought as they quick-walked, perforce following Sumelion down the strange streets. It felt like he'd built a wall around himself with signs saying "I'm really not here" posted on all sides. He was walking all stiff, his pack hardly jostling, and if he kept that up, she knew, he'd have a backache, big time.

She shrugged her own pack into a more comfortable position, and walked a little faster to come up beside him.

"You okay?" she asked.

He didn't look at her. "Sure. Why shouldn't I be okay?" he said, his voice the politely patient one he used when his mom got to talking really crazy. Jerel frowned.

"Look, seeing that was pretty bad, but—"

"I'm fine," Kay said, still in that maddeningly polite voice. "I just don't want to talk right now, okay?" Stiff-backed, he marched quicker, almost walking on Sume-lion's feathered heels.

Jerel deliberately walked slower, worriedly watching the back of Kay's head. He *wasn't* fine. After all, he'd talked to the pilot, liked her, maybe even knew her name. To Jerel, she'd just been "the pilot" and an excuse to have a bad mood. . . .

Their path away from the transport station was meandering, but they were quickly away from a major thoroughfare and had very little vehicular traffic to contend with when they crossed roads.

Sumelion had promised "a walk of short duration," but with Kay being incommunicado, Erazias too nervous to say anything, and Uncle Orned too far behind to talk to easily she felt like she was in parade. All they lacked was a marching band. . . .

Having no one to talk to made it easier to practice Rule One and observe the area they were passing through. The streets were residential, and felt alien to her, not only because so many of the buildings appeared to be built out of wood, but because there was no uniformity to it. One house might be three stories tall and the next only one; one house might be as bright a blue as Erazias in a good mood, while the next was off-pink, and the next built out of stones.

The weirdness extended to the roofs. Some glistened like metal, some appeared to have a soft patchwork covering, and some you couldn't see the roof because the sides of the buildings overreached the top.

They walked on neat sidewalks, with a bright yellow curb on the access roadside and a white line leading to a neat white fence keeping them off the individual property they walked past.

She wondered what it must be to grow up actually *owning* land. Back home, the urb was the property of the urb, and maintained by the administration, the parks were central, so everybody could have access. Here, each house had a little park around it, and the plants were just as diverse as the houses themselves.

She realized that she was slowly closing in on Kay, not so much because she wanted to try to talk to him again—what else could she say?—but because she was wishing they'd get to where they were going. Grumpily, she wondered how much further they had to walk. The heaviness hadn't been as noticeable earlier in the day, but now she was tired, and her legs were starting to hurt. Worse, she was going to need bathroom facilities pretty soon.

They followed Sumelion across yet another street and left, the walk suddenly thinner.

Jerel stretched her legs. Kay didn't look at her when she passed, and she bit her lip, but kept going until she gained Sumelion's side, and explained the circumstances.

"This is not a difficulty," the Yliger told her from on high. "Indeed, we can now see the spot upon which we roost; it is the pretty building four walkways ahead upon your left."

From within the tote, Vreet added a long, eerie whistle. Jerel felt her face relax into a smile without quite knowing why.

"Very wise, is Vreet," Sumelion said, loudly enough to be heard behind. "Vreet observes that sometimes silence is best, but that after one has been silent, it is important to recall one's voice—and one's friends. We turn here."

The building they were approaching was very strange and not at all what Jerel would have called "pretty." The outside walls were dull brown wood, worn and rough; the roof was the same color, made of a material she couldn't guess at. It seemed at first glance much taller than the houses around it, as Sumelion was much taller than humans. On second glance, though, Jerel thought it might have been that the windows were taller; the proportions not exactly what she was accustomed to.

The house sat in a small, extremely parklike enclave of trees and bushes, and the walkway leading to the front door was a series of flat stones, arranged in order from small to large.

"When we arrive," Sumelion said to Jerel, "I shall open the door. There will be need for a slight delay as I disarm a device, and then you may go to the left, where you will find the bathroom as the first on your right."

Sumelion touched a keypad set on the door frame, then placed some object in her hand against a flat plate. There was a mechanical sigh; she pressed the object against the plate once more and the door opened.

Jerel felt immersed in flowerbeds as soon as the door was fully open. Beyond Sumelian's tall form lights glowed to life, and Jerel could see greenery growing up the wall, threaded with a silvery waterfall. A wide stone cup at the base of the wall collected the tumbling water into a pool around which flowers grew. The scent of the flowers reached out to her and Jerel stepped inside—but was blocked by the thin engineer, who reached out to touch something on the wall within.

Sumelion moved further into her house. Jerel, her way clear, went as instructed to the left, moving down a hall floored in wood that felt springy under her feet, breathing in the flower scents, and shrugging her pack off as she went. The hall ahead was dim, the lights coming up only as she passed them, but she thought she saw the doorway she sought, just a few steps ahead and to the right.

"Jerel!" Uncle Orned shouted from behind her, but he was too late.

A shadow rushed out of the shadow, the newly wakened light glinting off the knife in his hand. He lunged, knife flashing. Jerel swung her pack around by the strap, let go and dove toward the floor, arms over her head, and there was the sound of a shot, shockingly loud in the contained space—and another. Huddled against the wall, Jerel saw the knife fall, its point buried in the springy wood.

Then something heavy and wet fell on her, and she yelled.

There was blood everywhere, and Jerel felt sick to her stomach. The knife man was against the opposite wall now, dragged off by a white-faced Uncle Orned.

"Did he hurt you?" he demanded.

"I'm fine," she gasped, dragging a sleeve across her face to clean off the wetness, only to find that her sleeve was soaked with red. Gagging, she jumped to her feet—and promptly fell down.

"Jerel!"

He picked her up, as if she weren't any older than seven, and carried her into the bathroom. The lights came up as they entered. He sat her on the bench by the shower, and snatched up the towel draped over the end. Carefully, he used it to clean her face.

"Did he hurt you?" he asked again, and Uncle Orned *never* asked the same question twice, unless he thought you were fibbing—and why would she fib about—

She looked down at herself, realized that her shirt and pants were wet clear through, looked out into the hallway, where she could see the dead man—and her stomach rebelled.

Uncle Orned held her head while she threw up, and she was too miserable to be embarrassed about it. When she was done, he left her sitting, drained and shivering, while he went back to the dead man and methodically went through his pockets, recovering several packets of pills, a drug injector, a phone, another knife, and a thin wallet.

Sumelion's voice reached them from elsewhere in the house.

"They have destroyed my desk attempting to open it; my research media is strewn and trodden; my accounts computer missing! They have shredded flowers and cut vines without cause. And of course we cannot call for the security forces, for they would ask questions I very much do not wish to answer!"

From another part of the house, voice echoing hollowly, Erazias called out, "The identification forms . . . they are cheap. They might have been purchased anywhere. I did better work when I was an apprentice! Two knives. A stunner. Blast grenade. A forcing tool . . . operating-system rescrambler . . ."

Uncle Orned came back into the bathroom, carrying the dead man's things and her backpack. He set the pack by her knee and stepped back, not saying anything. Jerel looked up and saw that his face was still pale. She took a deep breath, but her stomach only felt hollow.

"Can I get up now?" she asked him.

"Certainly. Stand there a moment and we'll get you another towel."

Sumelion's voice came closer.

"Hah! The blood of brigands stains the wood of the roost." Her head on its long neck snaked around the doorway, one eye on each of them, though she spoke to Uncle Orned. "It is well done, my friend. Your fledgling—she is unharmed?"

"She needs to clean up," he said, sounding mild and matter-of-fact, despite his pale face.

"I shall attend to it," Sumelion said. "If you will please assist in the inspection of the outrages that have been performed upon my nest?"

"Of course." He glanced at Jerel, looking so worried that she tried to smile so he'd know she was okay—mostly okay.

"I need to get out of these clothes," she said, and he nodded.

"Child," Sumelion said gently, "press on the small wood panel behind you."

Jerel did, not sure what to expect. Not much happened; there was slight mechanical click and the door—which was what the panel proved to be—opened enough for her to see a stack of beautiful woven towels, intricately decorated.

"Orned," Sumelion said, "please watch for Vreet, who also investigates—"

But at that, Vreet appeared low in the door, two blue eyes in the front, and two green eyes in the back fully extended and looking in all directions at once. It rocked over on two feet, and its hand snaked out, fingers gripping the dead man's shirt.

He whistled and chirped briefly, and Sumelion translated for Orned.

"Vreet believes this locally made. If it were our intention to track him back, such information might be useful. Vreet suggests, however, that we shall be leaving shortly."

"That's a very good suggestion," Uncle Orned said, as Vreet continued to examine the body.

"Jerel, attend," Sumelion said crisply. "Please randomly choose some towels, and walk with me; we shall clean you up elsewhere. Orned, the stairs at the end of the great room will lead you to the damaged office. Kay can put you on the path; he has seen that much."

The towels were much too fine, Jerel thought, but then she saw that everyone was waiting for her, so she grabbed a handful of soft and fluffy fabrics, seeing wonderful pale cloth woven of intricate patterns. . . .

The act of moving made her realize that she felt stiff, her muscles overtense. Right. She did need to move. Bending, she picked up her pack, slinging it over one shoulder before following Sumelion, stepping over the dead man, and continuing up the hall to the left.

The door slid open to admit them, powered only by Sumelion's hand; and so powered it slid shut behind them.

This room, Jerel thought, *is Sumelion's most private place.*

Several baths and pools were tucked in among yet more flowers and vines, and a wooden rack, perhaps strong enough to support Sumelion while she sat beneath what might be misting shower heads or air sprays or both.

The light was oddly tinted, the flowers bright and heavy with scent; the floors and what might have been elevated walkways were of wood. An expansive skylight gave directly into the branches of a large tree.

"Some lessons," said Sumelion as she helped Jerel out of her bloodstained clothes, "will stay with you all your life, no matter how you remember. Some events change you for all of your life. This event distresses me and is a lesson to me; for I learn I have not been as secure here as I felt, not able even to protect a guest inside my own space.

"I offer you the apologies of my nest. Please, let me help you."

Sumelion helped her wipe away as much blood as would come off easily with a beautiful lavender towel, then threw it carelessly into a corner.

"Stand here."

Jerel stood naked on a single round tile directly under the skylight, and a pleasant burbling noise ran through the room. She looked around, trying to understand where it came from—

The wooden rack! The wooden rack was itself a shower of sorts, and a musical instrument of sorts, too, for as the water ran and bubbled and began to spray it made soothing sounds. Spray rained on her, then mist, thickening to fog.

Loud, musical gurgles came from the wooden rack; several sprays combined to engulf her all at once, and it was a warm embrace. The sounds and the water worked together and she closed her eyes. . . .

"Good," Sumelion said; "that is good. Let me hand you another of these, for I fear my favorite cleaning abrasives would not be as kind to you as they are to me!"

Jerel took another of the towels; it didn't do quite as well wet as dry, though the weave was luxurious. She closed her eyes again, listened to the music of the room, and wished she never had to leave—

Her eyes flew open and she looked to Sumelion, sitting content amid the pipes themselves, her feathers shining in the odd light, her gaze on the tree overhead.

"Vreet said—are *you* leaving? All of this?"

After a moment, Sumelion answered. It was at first a whistle or trill, then in words Jerel could understand.

"That is what the wind has blown me, it would seem. A chance to travel with one I despise and one I admire, a chance to find new heights. One moment, please . . ."

She reached among the pipes, making some adjustment, and the sound of the water through the wood changed pitch. A breeze gentled down from overhead, the music slowed, burbling gently into silence.

"There, my mechanic of spaceships. Just as well you leave those things which have been damaged here. Dry and dress yourself. Then we will find your uncle and your crew and discuss how best to go elsewhere."

CHAPTER EIGHTEEN

We have not the time for more than Quick Council," Sumelion announced, "and so I begin. We must leave here rapidly; it would be good if we moved with a plan. So far, as I determine, the planning of this venture has been . . . not so much." She glared at them one at a time, with both eyes. Jerel, sitting between Uncle Orned and Erazias at the low round table in Sumelion's so-called visiting room, frowned.

"There wasn't time to plan," she objected.

"Hah! And what does chaos beget but more chaos, in ever-widening circles? Flight without thought engenders accident." Another glare. This time, nobody said anything.

"Errors. Do I see disguises, subterfuge?" Her hands moved, fingers fluttering consideringly. "A little, a little. Some cleverness. Some care, yes. But to allow Jerel to remain marked thus—when all those who seek her must have been told the prize is a human female, of an age no older than the years since the Oligarchy fell, brown and slight, and with two unique and distinct identifiers, one upon each wrist! A lack of attention to detail is noted.

"More—Orned, you are a clever and resourceful individual. Do I see you in disguise? Have you sought to alter the appearance of the fledglings in your charge? Did you not think of cameras? Here, Planet Security takes images constantly; there are flocks of computers, which endlessly shuffle, match and rematch each. Have there been robberies in three places and one individual's image recorded nearby? A triangulation initiates. Look! Here is one buying a knife with a three-inch blade. Here—many seasons later—is another who has died by a three-inch blade. . . . Knock comes on the door. Planet Security watches the official gates. Further, Planet Security disapproves of smuggling, and so watches the areas of greater energy spill, as well. Modest disguise is sufficient to fool the match programs, for also Planet Security is lazy and does not wish to put itself to the effort of pursuing where the returned probability is less than 80 percent. And yet more! Do you say to your fledglings, be careful what you touch? It seems not!

"And Erazias! What do you think, to lead on through this gate and that gate and never conceal the use of power? Of course! There was a reason you were not placed in charge of projects—always you had your master to tell you what to do, or a manual to consult. It is amazing to me that you have managed as well as you have, with no master and no manual to guide you! Ah, yes, but you are a scientist, always experimenting this way and that way until, suddenly, something works. *Pawoo!* This way lies danger in what we do."

She paused for breath, then went on before anyone else could speak—not, Jerel thought, that anyone else looked like they wanted to. Uncle Orned sat with his hands

folded on the table before him, his mild gaze on Sumelion, a slight smile on his lips. Erazias had tucked his
hands into the sleeves of his robe and was glaring at the
table. Kay sat dejectedly, shoulders hunched, head bent.
Maybe he was looking at the table, too. Or maybe not.

"True," Sumelion scolded on, "you have also brought
the young male, and this will perhaps confuse the trail,
as legitimate lawgivers may consider that the whole matter might be only hormonal rampage at work! Yes, this is
good! You brought the child of your master out of an im-
mediate danger, and this is also good. But, I must ask—
where did you think to go?"

Erazias didn't answer immediately, which Jerel
couldn't blame him for. At last, though, he rallied,
slipped his hands out of his sleeves and placed them flat
on the table. They were, Jerel noted, blue, and, when he
raised his head, the area around his eyes was also blue.

"From here," he said quietly, "we are to go on to
Rifthalten. I believe that the gate balance will operate
usefully. However, I will require a few days to reconnoi-
ter and track power usage. . . ."

"There! You continue yet upon this flawed trajectory!
The gate this—the gate that! The gates are useful and
necessary, but sometimes they are not the best option!
And—Rifthalten? I would expect that one would wish
to discover the whereabouts of the laboratory where
the . . ."

"Yes," Erazias interrupted forcefully, "I would expect
so, too. That is why we travel to Rifthalten. For there . . ."

"For there is *not* where your master's laboratory was!
Has your memory departed you? Surely, the place to find
that which was lost is Damaka. You recall it, I am certain—it was there that you were apprenticed, and there
where I first met your master when she was brought to
the university as a bright wonder."

Erazias drew himself up straighter inside his robes.

"Engineer," he said frostily, "you think well. Alas, you lack key pieces of information, and thus propose a flawed course of action."

"Hah," said Sumelion. "Speak on."

Erazias inclined his head. "Damaka, I thought initially, as well. How could I not? Indeed," he said, with a bit of heat rising in his voice, "it was at Damaka that I stopped on my way to Arantha to retrieve *terama* Jerel—and thus allowed Chuton to come to her ahead of me, and very nearly succeed in bringing her away."

"This story I will have in fullness at some later time," Sumelion promised. "Recall that we are at Quick Council, and keep the facts for now pertinent to producing a plan of rational action from the hour and circumstances in which we find ourselves."

"Yes," Erazias murmured, no hint of green at fingers or eye, though Jerel thought he might have a right to be irritated.

"Damaka is hardly key at this point," he said, "even if the material is there. The key appears to be Vony, the master's most junior apprentice, who had been left to care for her interests at university while the rest of us went to war.

"When war came to the university, it was Vony who would have insured that the master's notes were safe— and it was Vony who apparently did just this. However, Vony is not on Damaka as far as one finds. Not at any of the colleges, nor at the university, nor at the business research campuses, nor is there news to be had, saving this: Some few-to-many seasons ago, Vony expressed an intention to return to his kin group to undertake a necessary growth ritual."

Here Erazias paused, savoring a fact for some moments before presenting it like a gift to the entire group, with nodded head.

"Vony's kin group is installed upon Rifthalten."

There was a small silence, then a barrage of questions from Sumelion, regarding search methodologies and other matters that Jerel didn't quite follow in the increasing flow of wordage between the bird woman and Erazias. It seemed to her that Uncle Orned was trying to offer information pertinent to the discussion, but was ignored by the primary combatants.

It was, Jerel thought, glancing at her watch, taking some time to get this Quick Council done.

A whistle pierced the air. Jerel jumped at the unexpectedness of it, and was relieved to see that Kay had, too, and was looking around with wide eyes.

Sumelion stopped her rush of chatter and issued a quick series of soft chirps, which were answered by an emphatic and extremely complex whistle.

"Hah!" Sumelion looked around the table. "Vreet sums up: Rifthalten is the place we should go to, for if we repeat a search on Damaka we will likely stir unwanted and possibly dangerous interest. If we attempt to search from afar, it is likely that we will be unsuccessful. And if we attempt to prevail against each other's arguments instead of doing honest research, we shall go nowhere, no matter where we go."

"I accept that summation!" Uncle Orned said briskly.

"I, too," agreed the Turlon.

"There, then, it is simple!" declared Sumelion. "We shall go to Rifthalten, there to explore for one Vony, and to discover the location of the master's artifacts. A plan has been achieved. It is well. However, we shall not begin this journey with a gate. We shall go where I have contacts, I think. Yes, very much so." She stood, and looked down at them, first from the right eye, then from the left.

"Before we leave, we must supply ourselves with lunch money."

Lunch money was a joke.

A big joke.

Jerel felt rich. And she'd thought Anatasha Morin's wallet had held a lot of money! She was carrying more cash on her than she'd ever dreamed of, some of it in electronic plastichits, some in ceramalloy coins of incredible denominations, some in pads of ornate paper which could be used in a block or stripped off in portions or single notes.

She had cash of some kind in every pocket, she had it tucked inside her bra, and in a so-called money belt that Sumelion provided, and more tucked into the inside pockets of the floppy hat Sumelion insisted she wear. She even had cash in her socks.

Kay had blushed when she asked him where he had stored all of his, but he did admit that he'd decided not to put any inside his shoes because it might hurt if he had to run. He had also been given a money belt, and he, like she, was wearing a necklace of a dozen Peblar coins.

"These belong in a museum," Kay muttered, touching the necklace with a light fingertip. "She doesn't really expect us to *spend* them, does she?"

Jerel shrugged, not being sure what Sumelion intended, beyond what she'd said—that the money was the last of the rebels' "war chest," and that she, as treasurer, had determined that using those funds in the present instance fell within allowable parameters.

Uncle Orned and Erazias both carried awesome amounts of cash, and Uncle Orned at least was disguised, if you could call a big shirt printed with enormous red flowers, and a stripe of blue glittergel in his hair, a disguise. Erazias was not disguised, nor was Vreet, unless the identification belt around its—neck? waist?—was a disguise.

Jerel's disguise was the floppy feathered hat. Kay had pulled his hair back into a tail, and used some of the blue glittergel to paint a lightning bolt on his left cheek, which looked, Jerel had to admit, pretty naugy.

Going to the place where Sumelion had contacts meant another trip on public transport, this time with Jerel and Kay side by side on the bench and Sumelion sitting on the aisle, her bulk shielding them from prying eyes.

Uncle Orned sat near the front of the car, a beat-up rucksack on the bench next to him; and Erazias was situated in a single-seat approximately midway between, working with his stylus and pad.

There was, at the moment, no one else in the car.

"How," Kay whispered, leaning hard against Jerel's shoulder, "did Sumelion get so big?"

"Well, the work vest," she began—and stopped, as Sumelion's beady left eye took note of her.

There was, in fact, more to Sumelion's extra bulk than the work vest, though that accounted for much, its pockets crammed with tools and cash. She'd also somehow scrunched her neck down into her shoulders, which made her less tall and more broad. And she'd also inflated her chest feathers, declaring, "I doubt that we will find on our journey even one person who will wonder why I am wearing a work vest while so obviously in search of a nest-friend!"

Jerel thought that might have been intended to make her laugh—she could even see where it might've been funny. Trouble was, she didn't feel much like laughing. She was so tired her eyes ached, but at the same time she felt almost quiveringly alert. And she couldn't get rid of a depressing conviction that she had failed some important test by almost getting stabbed, and then by being such a *kid* about being saved. Throwing up! You didn't see Uncle Orned throwing up, and he'd done the hard part. All she'd done was sling her pack at the guy—what good had she thought *that* was going to do?—and fall down, arms over her head—and what good, she thought again, had she thought *that* was going to do?

True, Uncle Orned hadn't lectured her, or made her go through it all step-by-step so she could revisit everything she'd done wrong in excruciating detail. She figured he'd given up on her. *Hopeless, that's what you are,* she told herself. *You're supposed to be so smart—this whole mess is because you can't even remember five stupid Rules!*

"Jerel?" Kay sounded concerned—and like it wasn't the first time he'd said her name.

"Sorry," she muttered. "Thinking."

"Yeah, well. If you're thinking it's all your fault that zwinget almost killed you, I wish you'd stop."

She blinked at him. "Who else's fault?" she sputtered. "If I'd been paying attention to Rule One—"

"You'd've seen him, what, a second sooner?" Kay sighed. "Jerel, he was trying his best to hide in the dark. Why would you—"

"It is possible," Sumelion chirped crisply, "that this may not be the proper venue for such discussions." She rustled and reached into her vest, producing two pamphlets. "Here. Information regarding our destination. Please study it closely."

Jerel and Kay exchanged a baffled look. Sumelion thrust the pamphlets at them and each snatched one in self-defense. Satisfied, the engineer turned away.

Sighing, Jerel pressed the top right corner of the pamphlet with her thumb. Immediately the blank gray imaging area deepened, perspectives shifting and swirling until she was looking at a scene of frenetic activity.

People of all description danced, ate, spun, hung, twirled, jumped, vanished beneath torrents of water, jigged between walls of living flame, and slid across limitless fields of ice. Fireworks exploded colorfully; bright, happy music beckoned.

"We're going to a fun-park?" Kay asked, his astonishment plain.

Sumelion fixed him with a beady glare. "A fun-park? Never should we undertake so bland and uninteresting an expedition! No, our goal is loftier: *We* go to Tolchester!"

CHAPTER NINETEEN

In spite of herself, Jerel was excited. She'd never been in space, and they were about to take a space flight! True, they weren't going all that far, but considering that she'd only been on a couple of suborbital trips for school, well—this was a big deal.

Sumelion had told them to pay for their flight tokens in cash, which had concerned Jerel—Rule Four—until she saw that *everyone* was paying in cash, and more than one with large denominations, as if it was some kind of game. The ticket-sellers acted that way, too, laughing and exclaiming over especially clever, or rare, forms of payment.

"This is a holiday, a party place we go to, fledgling," Sumelion from behind her in line. "Tolchester is a place people go to—oh, perhaps five or six times in their lives. It is to celebrate, to be reborn, to be someone else, to do things only someone else would do. A place to be amused. You will wish, as always, to be careful of accepting food or drink from the hands of strangers, but please accept freely if the offer is to buy for you your choice! Should you have an opportunity to experience the joy of buying for someone else—spend a little money, for that is what money is for!"

This was slightly at odds with what Uncle Orned had told her as they had exited the monorail:

"Jerel, you'll need to pay very close attention; you've never been to an amusement center like Tolchester."

"I've been to Pandari's, Uncle," she protested, and felt a wave of homesickness for her urb's fun-park.

Uncle Orned snorted. "Pandari's is . . ." He paused. "Pandari's," he continued, "is meant to mildly titillate the staid and stable citizens of an inner administrative hub. Tolchester is . . . life-altering. People make pilgrimages to Tolchester, in order to undergo change.

"It will be crowded, and noisy, and . . . boisterous. People will be dressed—or not—as seems good to them. It may be difficult to spot anomaly, since the whole place is an anomaly. Track me—that I know you can do—and track Sumelion."

"Not Erazias, Uncle?"

"Erazias—yes." He sighed. "Should we become separated—I don't expect this, but on Tolchester anything can happen and often does—should you and I become separated, please take Sumelion's directions as you would mine. She may seem somewhat unusual, but her judgment and intuition are excellent."

The line snaked forward and Jerel looked around, trying to be alert—but there was so much to see!

As spaceports went, Tolchester Station, as the sign over the entrance declared it, was tiny, and displayed not much of the machinery, grit, and noise of a working port. But, then, Jerel thought, it wasn't a working port. It existed only to move people from the surface of the planet to the moon called Tolchester.

The name of the moon seemed oddly familiar to her, and she said it out loud a couple times, trying to bring the memory forward. The pamphlet really hadn't been much help there; it had focused on the fun and excitement, not background or history.

Still . . .

The line moved again. She looked around her, no longer feeling that her floppy feathered hat was slightly silly. If anything, it might, she thought, be a little too formal.

The line stopped, leaving Jerel standing briefly by a sign advertising Zingle's CareFree at "Speiders Wall on Glorious Tolchester!" and showing images of people walking straight up a glass wall.

On the other side, another sign was spraying out a dancing cloud of bubbles, while a man's voice urged her to ride the Float on Beautiful Tolchester.

The line moved again, and there was the counter. Jerel fingered a ceramalloy coin out of her pocket. When her turn came she dropped it negligently onto the counter, like she had a whole pocketful of the things. Which, in fact, she did.

"One to Tolchester, please," she said, and was irritated to hear her voice shake, just a little.

"Nice one!" the young man behind the counter said appreciatively. "First time to Tolchester, *femisi*?"

"Yes," Jerel admitted, and his smile got even wider.

"I envy you," he said, and handed her an ornate green ticket, with tiny green lights sparkling from the borders, like gemstones.

"Here is your pass to all the marvels of Tolchester. Please keep it with you at all times."

"Thank you," Jerel said.

"Thank *you*, *femisi*! Have a cup of courage for me! Next, please."

"Here's our seats," Kay said, holding up his ticket. The gem lights on the border now showed deep red.

Jerel glanced at her ticket, saw the same confirming red border, threw her pack next to his in the overhead locker, and slid into the chair beside him. "Oh, good, info seats," she said, tucking her ticket carefully into the pocket of her shirt.

Sumelion and Uncle Orned sat in their row, too, filling out the four, and Erazias stood for a moment before consulting his ticket and slipping into the aisle seat directly across, and next to another Turlon, who immediately began speaking to him excitedly in what Jerel had to believe was their native language. Erazias looked just a touch green around the eyes, but he seemed to be holding up his end of the conversation pretty well.

The info seat, now—that was pretty good: the screen began to shimmer as soon as she sat down, and she saw the status light glow red as the comp read the chip in her ticket through the pocket.

Words formed out of the screen's shimmer. "Traveler 7964A, welcome. Is this your first trip to Tolchester?"

Jerel touched the Yes key, glad of the distraction and hoping maybe the screen would tell her why Tolchester sounded so familiar to her. She wasn't used to forgetting things and she hated the feeling of the thought hovering just outside the reach of her brain.

The info screen offered three choices: History, Accommodations, Amusements. She chose History and was rewarded with an image of an old-style spaceship silhouetted against a verdant moon.

Yes! That was it! Jerel smiled. *Now* she remembered! They'd studied the *Tolchester* in Tech History, as an illustration of how a spaceship could be brought through hard times by its pilot and its master techs. Damaged during transit by a meteor, the *Tolchester*, an excursion liner meant for light duty, was brought safely down to the surface of a barely viable moon orbiting a previously uncharted planet. A planet that—

She was on right now!

The crew, proud and brave, had survived, and so had most of the passengers—disallowing those few killed during the attempted mutiny, of course—and the planet was wonderfully suited for colonization.

Now, the info screen went on to relate, the moon had been upgraded to a recreational haven and—

Jerel got bored then, and leaned back in her seat. Passengers were still filing into the ship, looking at their tickets, rather than where they were going, and talking loudly to themselves, each other, the air. Their progress was somewhat impeded by the number of other passengers who, having found their seats, weren't content to stay in them, but walked—or in some cases, danced—up and down the aisles, singing, whistling, chirping, and occasionally bumping into each other.

A blue-haired girl wearing a necklace of blue flowers, a drifty blue skirt, a pair of transparent blue ankle boots, and nothing else wafted down the aisle. Nobody much stared at her, except Kay, who almost fell into Jerel's lap, he leaned over so far to get a good look.

Well, thought Jerel, *at least he seems to have gotten over his upset about what happened to our pilot.*

And somehow, that thought triggered a memory of the hallway in Sumelion's house, the figure lunging out of the dark, light shining along the edge of a knife. Her fingers curled hard around the arms of her chair; she gritted her teeth and forced her suddenly tense body to relax, like she'd learned to do at CapCour's Techniques for Effective Slideboarding workshop. To take her mind off her queasy stomach, she fixed her attention again on the crowded aisle.

Now, this is more like it. . . .

A dark-haired guy in purple lace tights and a sleeveless silver tunic was going down the aisle in the wake of the blue-haired girl. He walked nice and—

Somebody cleared their throat, practically in her ear. She glanced up and saw Kay following her gaze. He looked at her with a weird little smile on his lips.

"You'd think somebody that skinny would put on some weight before trying an outfit like that," she said, sounding defensive in her own ears.

Kay snorted, but she wasn't sure if it was at her or because his attention had been caught by two girls wearing tops that shimmered from red to see-through . . .

She turned her head and saw that Uncle Orned was relaxed bonelessly in his seat, his head against the rest, his eyes half-closed, as if he was sleeping. Beyond him, Sumelion was having an animated whistling conversation with Vreet, who was for the moment occupying the beverage tray that pulled out from beneath the info screen.

The guy in the purple tights was coming back. His hair was red-gelled into spikes, and looked sort of like a crown of flames. In his left ear a red LED flashed; in his right swung a Peblar coin. He ducked past a man in a tight green jacket, and—looked right at her. His lips parted, like he was going to say something—yell at her for staring, probably, Jerel thought—and then swung on by.

Mortified, Jerel looked away and heard Kay snicker. "He didn't look skinny to me!"

"We ask all passengers to please return to their seats at this time," a man's warm voice said over the announcement grid. "Attendants will be moving through the compartment to assist everyone to strap in. Please, all passengers return to your seats and await the flight attendants. You will be asked to display your ticket, so be sure that it is easily accessible and live."

Jerel touched her pocket and felt the reassuring stiffness of her ticket, which was obviously live, or the info seat wouldn't have responded to it.

"Do you think people try to sneak on with fake tickets?" she asked Kay, but it was Sumelion who answered.

"Fledgling, the depth of deception and deceit which fills this poor galaxy is beyond belief! How much better for all, if honesty and straightforwardness were so plentiful!"

Uncle Orned sneezed.

CHAPTER TWENTY

Hey!" Kay stopped so suddenly, Jerel walked right into him, impelled by the people on the ramp behind her.

"What's the holdup?" "Hey, kid, get moving; it looks even better up close!" voices advised, loudly, from the rear.

"*Kay*," Jerel gritted, pushing at his shoulder. "You're gonna get us crushed!"

He shook himself, as if he'd just woken up, and started to move again, Jerel still mashed uncomfortably against his side. At the bottom of the ramp, she grabbed his sleeve and hauled him off the path, letting the eager passengers swirl past them, some running as soon as their feet touched the moon's surface.

"*What?*" Jerel yelled.

Kay shrugged and looked around, frowning. "I thought I saw my uncle Karta, is all."

"Who?"

"Ah, there you are, *children*!" Uncle Orned put a hand on their shoulders and forcefully steered them further off the walk and toward a line of low, thick trees.

"Now, what was that about, please?"

"I thought I saw my uncle Karta," Kay repeated, somewhat heatedly. He sighed. "There's so many people here, it could've been anyone, I guess. Anyhow, I thought he saw me, but then he just walked away, so it probably wasn't him." He shrugged apologetically. "Sorry."

Jerel braced herself for a lecture, but instead Uncle Orned looked at Kay thoughtfully.

"Is your uncle Karta on your mother's side of the family, Kay? Or your father's?"

Kay looked down, and scuffed at the pinkish grass with his boot. His delay and apparent embarrassment told Jerel that he couldn't remember. She was wrong, though.

"I think," Kay said carefully, looking up at last to meet Uncle Orned's eyes, "that he's a . . . distant . . . uncle, sir. He used to visit a lot, especially around the time my mother got her quarterly pension payment. Usually, she'd send me out on a long errand when he came by." His mouth tightened. "It probably wasn't him; I'm a norf, and I'm sorry for attracting attention."

"And so," came Sumelion's voice, as that lady arrived amid them. "Are we receiving instruction?"

"We are receiving clarification," Uncle Orned replied, frowning slightly, and glancing both at Sumelion and the surroundings. "Kay thought he saw someone he knew— someone who visited his mother from time to time. In case the fact is of interest to you, I offer that Kay's mother was of the ruling Family on Arantha."

"Hah. The fact interests, I thank you." She considered Kay out of her left eye; Jerel out of her right.

"So, fledgling, you travel in company with the House itself. Are you not flattered?"

Jerel frowned, not sure if this was a joke or not. Kay didn't say anything, his face studiously blank, lips pressed tight. Jerel knew the look: Kay was mad.

"I'm not traveling with anybody's House," she said to Sumelion. "Kay's my best friend, and he wanted to come. He didn't have to—Uncle Orned gave him a choice."

"Indeed; and just because a choice has been offered and taken does not mean that it was correct, or should not be rethought." She raised a hand and smoothed the air. "Enough," she said to Uncle Orned. "These things mean more to us than to those who were still wet from the shell at the time of our trial."

"True. But there are others, to whom these things mean quite as much and who may be obliged, as we were, to use the tools that come to their hands."

Jerel realized that both Sumelion and her uncle were talking both low and *down,* as if they were making it more difficult for cameras or listeners to home in on them. Too, they were both quietly scanning the area, it seemed, with Sumelion somewhat more obvious at it than Uncle Orned.

Jerel shivered momentarily when she realized that Uncle Orned was not only watching for things the way he'd told *her* to watch, but that he carried his bag in a way that kept his hands very near his weapons pocket. She took the wariness to heart—after all, if he hadn't been fast there was no telling what the man with the knife might have done to her at Sumelion's nest!

A rustle of robes came from the left, as a shadow glided toward them, highlighted by the glare of the landing-zone lights.

Kay glanced up. He'd been staring at the ground as if he was still embarrassed—or mad—about the big deal the engineer made of his parentage.

"Hah." Sumelion turned her head. "Here is Erazias, the mathematician, who has finally charted a course to our lonely outpost. I had begun to consider you lost to us!"

"The port guardians spoke with me briefly about my travels, but we parted amicably, despite that my companions went on regardless of my fate."

Jerel had been around Erazias long enough to hear the complaint, and she could see the green tinges which showed something about the level of his concern.

"Yes, of course," said Sumelion, who Jerel saw had not lost the unhappy habit of baiting the mathematician, "we were busy scurrying away that you might be lost without us!"

Erazias *twitched*. That was the only word Jerel could think of to describe it. Not strong enough to be a shudder, but clearly visible, as if he'd help himself back from something. His eyes were getting a slight ring of gold.

Uh-oh. Jerel wondered what was bringing *that* up.

"Sumelion Pel." The Turlon said her name as if he were invoking some curse. "Understand me as I understand you. I was not fond of finding you involved so closely in this, but clearly, you have some uses, and I bow to Orned Vayle for seeing this."

He did exactly that, a bow of intense exactness.

"However, yes, I see a pattern I believe unwise, and that is a pattern in which I have less rather than more to say about arrangements, and a pattern in which your own words fill the ears of Jerel and Orned far more often than mine own. Should you go off on your own course you hardly know what needs done."

"This isn't a good place," Orned started to say, but Sumelion's rebuttal cut him off ruthlessly.

"The universe does not revolve around you, Erazias, as well you know. The accident of your being a student at the right moment gives you no right . . ."

Erazias raised both hands at once, gently. Jerel realized he wasn't carrying his staff, but saw his hands were turning green. She turned to Kay, who was doing his best to look somewhere else. Jerel followed his gaze; no girls there, so Kay must be feeling as awkward about the argument as she was.

"Sumelion, I will not argue that the universe revolves around *me*. It does, very nearly, for us and the movement, revolve around Jerel. *Terama* must be delivered to safekeeping, and she must be able to assist if the models prove true and the master herself may be recovered from the battle. Eventually, mine is the path that must be trod."

Jerel was still watching Kay when Erazias spoke; it took a moment for the words to penetrate. Kay's eyes got wide and he slowly looked at Jerel, and then turned toward the Turlon.

Jerel ran the sentence past her inner ears again, slowly.

What did he mean, *the master herself may be recovered?*

Sumelion's demeanor changed abruptly. She stood straighter, then looked directly at Erazias, and leaning toward him she spoke very quietly.

"You are sure enough to even suggest this?" The words were filled more with hope than challenge, in Jerel's estimation, and were received by the mathematician in the same way.

"Others are so sure, engineer, and others have begun the quest. My goal, as always, must be to hold to hope and do what needs done."

Sumelion startled Jerel—and perhaps all of them—by doing a little dance and twittering something. That twitter was answered by Vreet in his bag, not with a single syllable or two but with a veritable deluge of quiet trills, clicks, and whistles.

Looking about at all of them, she pointed across the grounds boldly. Jerel couldn't tell what she pointed out, but whatever it was was clearly in the distance.

"As we are now complete, and informed, I suggest that the pleasures offered beyond the western gate may suit us well. Understand that amusement is the duty of all who visit Tolchester. Should we stand too long, discussing seriously, we will draw the helpful attention of an Amusement Aide. This, we do not desire, for we are well able, my friends, to amuse ourselves."

Uncle Orned, Jerel thought, had been right. There was way too much going on in Tolchester, and *none* of it was usual or normal. Hard to spot an anomaly with so much around. Hard to stay alert when there was so much to see, hear, touch, and smell that she had a hard time fighting the desire to just *sit down* with her back against something solid and close her eyes.

The adults were walking behind them, in deep discussion about the staff Erazias had been carrying. The spaceport hadn't let him bring it through, and he was much distressed. So was Uncle Orned, who was talking about "tracing to original owner" and such when he'd pointedly sent Jerel and Kay ahead, out of hearing range, with the admonition "go straight until we tell you to turn. We'll be right behind you!"

Jerel had tried to follow all of Uncle Orned's necessities of being alert, but even the smells and the signs were distracting, not to mention the people with their clothes or lack of them.

Finally, she settled on watching where she was walking, which was harder than it should've been, what with people running, skipping, chasing each other. A human wearing body paint that mimed Sumelion's feathers darted past her, laughing breathlessly; a second human, this one wearing a skirt so short Jerel wondered why he'd bothered, cut right in front of her, almost knocking her over as he caught the feathered one around the waist, boosted him effortlessly over one shoulder, and bore him off into a cluster of the low, thick-leafed trees.

"One good thing," she said to Kay, who was walking beside her, his head swiveling from side to side so fast Jerel felt her shoulders cramp up in sympathy. "At least it's *lighter* here."

Kay skipped, bouncing higher than Jerel's head. "A lot lighter even than home," he said. "My pack hardly weighs a thing." He grinned at her. "This, I could get used to."

"Especially if they shipped out about 90 percent of the people," Jerel agreed grumpily. "There's too much going on!"

The crowd ahead swirled momentarily around a road-block of someone who'd dropped a drink, and then it spit out a really large person who abruptly changed the course in their direction.

"Excuse, *femisi? Masata?*" The person who approached them was wearing one of those supershort skirts, and sandals laced up to his knees. On his head was a red silk skullcap, the tiny propeller at its summit spinning lazily in the breeze.

Jerel tried to step around him, but he put out a hand to block her. She sidestepped a bit, and so did Kay, and now the crowd swirled around them as a roadblock.

"Please, *femisi*, a moment only. You need have no concern," he said, his voice soft, the irises of his eyes so dilated that only a thin ring of gray showed. "I see that you and your companion in pleasure are young, and surmise that this is your first pilgrimage to the Holy City, am I correct?"

Holy City? Jerel blinked at him.

"That's right," Kay said, in the so-patient voice he used when his mom got to talking really crazy.

"That is most excellent, *masata*; I thank you for the courtesy of your reply. I wonder therefore if you have considered dedicating yourselves to the Church."

"We hadn't thought of it, no," Kay said, "and I thank you for bringing the possibility to our attention. Certainly, we will seek the advice of our elder companions on the matter."

"Elder companions?" the man repeated, looking over his shoulder just in time to see Sumelion arrive at some speed."Ah, I see that you are well companied, indeed!" He bowed, which made the propeller in his skullcap spin faster, and moved aside, whistling a light melody.

Sumelion gave him the notice of her left eye, and a short, answering whistle.

"Come, tardy fledglings!" she trilled, catching their hands in slim, surprisingly strong fingers. "The wonders of the western fief await you!"

With a certain feeling of relief, they followed her. Jerel turned her head to look for the man with the propeller, but quickly he had disappeared into the crowd.

CHAPTER TWENTY-ONE

The Gravity Well was a tall transparent rectangle, surrounded by pleasure-seekers who were watching the dozen or more people suspended in midair. One or two were floating quietly, but most were bouncing off walls and each other. Among them was a woman wearing wings and a white iridescent unisuit, acting as a sort of combination traffic controller and zoo keeper.

"Step right up!" a voice called as they approached. "Always wanted to fly like a bird or float like a fish? Here's your chance. Step right up and we'll get you off the ground in no time. Think you're really made to fly? Try our Test o' Wings and win a trophy to take home with you. Step right up!"

Jerel was startled to see that a live human was sitting behind a desk at the entrance. He wore a cheek mike and watched the crowd closely, calling out challenges.

"Hey you, Skinny! You trying to make time with the pretty girl—no, not you, dummy, you there! Right. You can look, everybody knows what you're really here for."

The crowd laughed, including Jerel and Kay, and apparently Orned. Erazias stood to their left, unnaturally still in his blue robes, his crest seeming . . . a little wilted.

The man behind the desk pointed to a middle-aged man with his arm protectively around a younger woman. Sumelion seemed unmoved by the production, the rude comments, or the crowd reaction; she stood to Jerel's right, slightly behind Kay.

"But hey, you look kind of like an airhead. This'll be a natural for you! Give it a try! Bet you can't win the Test o' Wings. Go ahead, give up your chance for immmmorrtalitee on our Wing Winners list. Walk on, Skinny."

The crowd laughed, half at the caller, half at a poor man inside the cube who was gesturing for help as he floated head-down and struggling very near the center of the cube.

"How about you, *femisi*? You right there, wearing that silly hat!"

Jerel swallowed the laugh because the finger was pointing at her this time.

"Come on in, the air's fine—and bring your boyfriend!"

Jerel began to shake her head, only to hear Sumelion twitter, "Yes, exactly. This is what we will do. Please, fledglings, step up, and I will follow."

Jerel looked at Kay. He shrugged and they both walked forward, to various whistles and comments from the crowd. Jerel hoped that some of those shouted comments were for other people. She didn't think they were possible—or advisable—to perform while floating in view of hundreds of people.

Sumelion offered a pad of currency to the attendant, gesturing to include all of them—and finding one missing.

"There!" Jerel said under her breath. "Erazias is standing over there!"

Sumelion inclined her head to the attendant. "Our friend, there, will also join us," she said, then handed the rucksack to Uncle Orned and stalked off purposefully toward Erazias.

Jerel and Kay, with Uncle Orned behind, walked up the ramp. At the top, they followed a flight of holographic birds to a room where an attendant wearing pink glittery wings and pink glittery tights pointed them to a scale.

Kay was first; the scale not only weighed him but spun slowly as a light came on overhead.

The light faded. The attendant pulled a tray from the rack beside him and in a moment had expertly fit Kay with flexible waist belt, wristlets, and anklets, as well as a lightweight helmet.

"There you are, *masata*, we've got you weighed and analyzed, so we know where your center of gravity is. These devices are all carefully calibrated to help you attain the most pleasure possible from the Gravity Well. Move forward and we'll get your friends outfitted. . . ."

Jerel was next, then Uncle Orned, and by the time he was rigged out, Sumelion had arrived, a yellow-fingered Turlon in tow.

Jerel and Kay followed the flight of birds out of the fitting room to a hall lined with lockers. They opted to take a big one, and opened it and stowed their bags, waiting for Uncle Orned, who arrived very quickly. He put his bag and Vreet's rucksack into the locker.

"We're locking Vreet in?" Kay asked.

"Vreet will be fine," Uncle Orned answered, "trust me." He smiled slightly. "Why don't the two of you get started? I'll wait in case Sumelion needs any help with Erazias."

"Together?" asked a young woman wearing a pair of feathered wings. She rushed on without waiting for an answer.

"We suggest that you not try the wings first time—do either of you have experience with moving in zero gravity?"

Both Jerel and Kay admitted that they did not.

"The best thing, then," the attendant said, "is to simply let the gravity go away. You're not going to experience actual zero gravity; instead you'll be able to move around in a repulsor field that mimics zero g. You are absolutely safe; even in the event of a power failure—which is very rare!—not only do your personal repulsors have a latent charge, but there's a very good net and a compressed-air field to catch and hold you until safety personnel arrive. When you walk into the Well, you'll be launched by the compressed air. It's very gentle, but a little startling, if you're not expecting it.

"Your time and power is preset—when you reach 5 percent, your wrist cuffs will vibrate in warning. If you do not return to the floor under your own direction, the power will fade and you will slowly sink. It is easier on all of us if you return under power, for the floor becomes sticky over time.

"One more thing. Please do not transfer, throw, or otherwise remove the repulsors, nor should you throw things currently on your person about the Well. If you do, you may end up like the person being rescued right now by Serena—he kicked his shoes off attempting a flip!"

Serena was the winged woman inside the Well. Her wings, Jerel saw now, weren't feathered. They looked to be made out of leather, and had extra support ribs in them. Working wings, Jerel thought, and smiled.

"Why do you think . . ." Kay murmured as they moved toward the access port. "Why do you think we're *here*?"

Jerel glanced behind, relieved to find Uncle Orned following at a little distance, behind him the unlikely couple of Sumelion and Erazias.

"I don't know," Jerel began—and stopped talking as the floor left them.

"*Hey . . .*" she said softly.

"*Ahhh . . .*" whispered Kay.

The sounds within the Well were muted, but the shill's voice could be heard as if at a great distance urging more customers to come in, challenging them to fly.

They drifted upward slowly, and then Jerel twisted her head, looking for Uncle Orned—and started a slow spin, which was . . . surprising.

What was even more surprising was that she found Uncle Orned, not below them, where she'd expected him, but slightly above and at the opposite end of the rectangle. As she watched, he elegantly bounced off the wall with a simple push of his finger.

The repulsors weren't uncomfortable to wear, but they did feel funny, as if someone was gently holding her wrists and ankles—not to mention her waist—and tugging her a bit this way and a bit that way.

Somehow this kind of flying was a lot more comfortable to Jerel than being in the copter. Maybe it was because the air currents weren't so bumpy. Or maybe it was because no one else was in charge. Jerel considered this, feeling better about moving about with no visible means of support. Heck, this was even neater than using elevators!

About then Serena flew by, actually using her wings to propel herself, and one hand in a swimming motion, which apparently helped keep her on course. The other hand was holding on to the unfortunate shoeless man, pulling him along behind.

"I'm glad that's not me!" Kay said, and Jerel agreed. He was testing his ability to spin in place by moving his arms and hands. It seemed to Jerel that he was actually working out some kind of useful system, though she couldn't exactly—

"But, really," he went on, taking up their interrupted conversation. "You don't think we came here for fun, do you?"

"Nobody told me any more than they told you. It'd be nice if Rule Five went both—"

"Hey, look!" Kay interrupted. Jerel frowned, irritated, her eyes drawn against her will along the line of his pointing finger.

It was, she thought, a sight worth seeing.

Sumelion flew like she'd been born to it, wearing a pair of leather wings the twin of Serena's. She swooped and glided, dipped and turned, slowly, on the very tip of one leather wing.

Jerel turned her head to follow—and started to spin slowly again.

"Try twisting your right hand *this way* to slow down or stop," Kay advised.

She had to twist her neck to see what he was doing, which made her spin faster—and then slower as she copied his move. In a moment, with the help of a small additional adjustment, she was floating serenely in one place, just as Uncle Orned came by, face down, very slowly.

"Not quite zero g," he said quietly, "because you don't lose your sense of up-and-down entirely. Not quite frictionless. But interesting. . . ."

His voice trailed away and Jerel giggled, imagining him talking to himself the whole way down. About then Sumelion flashed past, did a loop, and sat cross-legged in the air next to Uncle Orned, who had effortlessly altered his downward drift and was rotating slowly in place.

"Guess it might be this is a good place to talk, and that's why we're here," Kay opined, drawing Jerel's glance. He was beside her, face down, emulating Uncle Orned's former drifting stance.

"Hey, look!"

"Will you stop that?" she said irritably. "Can't you at least say 'Look over there,' or maybe 'Have you seen this' or something?"

"Huh," he said, and flipped his hand, starting a spin.

"In that case, Telmon, have you noticed that the man I think is my uncle is staring at us, and maybe getting a video of me-or-us?"

"*What?*"

Jerel moved so suddenly that she began spinning in earnest. She was much closer to the transparent wall than she had realized, so her attempt to stop the spin bounced her out into the middle of the Well, where she almost ran into a couple who were busily staring into each other's eyes as they drifted up to the ceiling.

"You okay?" Kay was next to her; he was, Jerel thought, really good at this.

"What about your uncle?" she asked. "Is he still watching?"

"Look over in front of the restaurant with the big icicles hanging from the roof. There's a man wearing a bright green vest and silver shorts. He's off and on looking in this direction. Twice I thought I saw him . . ."

"Yes," Jerel said, twirling about slowly, this time on purpose. "I see him and he's definitely watching this way. Uncle Orned seemed pretty concerned about him. . . ."

"What's he think, Uncle Karta's a spy?"

As soon as he said that Kay's hand went to his mouth, eyes widening. He tumbled slightly as a result, and Jerel followed him, lazily turning with a flicker of her fingers.

"Let's look the other way," Kay said. "Point at some-body. Hey—look at that cute guy down there who's showing off his buns."

Jerel saw the guy he was pointing at.

"You've got a good eye. Maybe we should go lower and see if your uncle is still watching."

"You want to see if you can get close to the guy!"

"Don't," said Jerel, grinning. "But you'll have to get a better look at that uncle fellow before you can be sure it's him."

They drifted slowly downward in companionable si-lence until Kay rubbed his ear a second and glanced over at her.

"He *could* be a spy," Kay muttered. "He could. My mother's always talking about all the important people she knew in the old days, and about how she'd fix every-thing if she could . . . and I think the first time I remem-ber him visiting us was after we moved into the apart-ment we have now."

They continued downward, vaguely in the direction of the boy Kay had pointed out, who was just enjoying the sights.

"Now are you *sure* the guy out there is your uncle?" Jerel asked.

"As sure as I can be without going up and talking to him. Which I think maybe *your* uncle wouldn't like too much."

Jerel had to agree that he was probably right. Still, Kay had a good memory for faces—he hardly ever forgot one. She was willing to believe that the man in the green vest was his uncle. But—

"Even if he is a spy—what's that got to do with us?"

Kay gave her a wide-eyed look. "Didn't Erazias tell us that there's a—a movement to bring the Oligarchy back? I don't think my mom's part of it, but I'm sure she agrees with it. If Uncle Karta *is* part of that movement . . ."

"I get it." Jerel thought. "It would," she said, reluctantly, "be a pretty big coincidence for him to be right here, right now, where we are, wouldn't it?"

"Unless he was looking for us, and then it wouldn't be a coincidence at all, eh?" Kay finished.

Now they were leaning against the transparent side of the Well, using the resistance of their hands against the surface to slow them.

Jerel sighed. "Do you see Uncle Orned? We'd better—"

"I'm right behind you."

She twisted, immediately controlling the spin with a flick of her hand. Uncle Orned and Sumelion were directly behind them, and about a body's length higher in the air.

"What," her uncle asked lazily, "should you better do?"

"Tell you about the anomaly—Rule Three and Rule Five."

"Which anomaly," asked Sumelion, "out of so many?"

"The guy who looks like my uncle is over there at the Ice House restaurant," Kay said. "He's wearing a green vest and silver shorts and he's been watching this way. I think he was taking a video of me."

"Or of me," Jerel added.

"So . . . Yes, he does watch this way, does he not? But what of it," Sumelion continued. "Surely each of you is worthy of admiration as you move about so gracefully."

Kay snorted.

"The thing is, he still looks like my uncle to me."

"Ah. Well then, perhaps it is best we move on. My contacts will have been notified that we arrive."

Jerel and Kay exchanged glances.

"My wrist thing is vibrating!" Jerel said, surprised.

"Good. Then it won't appear that we're leaving the fun ahead of schedule," Uncle Orned said. He rolled slowly in the air, seeming to search. "Oh, no. Sumelion, can you retrieve Erazias? He's clinging to the top of the far wall."

"Alas, my friend, this must be your retrieval. I will be needed at the exit." She flexed her wings. "Come, fledglings, fly behind me!"

Jerel only wished she could fly like Sumelion, who was absolute grace. Clearly this was a place she'd visited many times in the past. She and Kay swam vaguely behind, and landed softly on the cushioned floor where she stood, eyes up, as if sorry to be leaving.

Following her glance, Jerel saw Uncle Orned patiently leading Erazias down the wall. She could see the yellow around his eyes clearly, despite the distance.

They followed the bird woman down a different ramp than the one preferred by the holographic birds. Two people waited for them at the bottom—one a shorter, plumper version of Sumelion. The new Yliger trilled out a song, which was echoed, briefly, by Sumelion. They appeared to bow or dance to each other, and then their attention was for the ramp, where Uncle Orned and a complaining Erazias appeared.

" . . . I do not understand why it was necessary that I be tortured—"

The human attendant wordlessly helped Jerel and Kay out of their repulsors.

"You do know, and that you do not agree is unbecoming!" Sumelion's voice was sharp. "This is a minor discomfort you have experienced, Erazias. But think how it would look should you go into the Gravity Well, and not take part? No one leaves here without flying!"

"Be that as it may," Uncle Orned interrupted. "I believe it would be best if we had this family discussion in a more private area."

CHAPTER TWENTY-TWO

The reception area for the business office of the Gravity Well *was* a more private area. Sumelion's twitter welcomed them, introducing them to Losteny, whom she described as "a fine friend of the revolution."

"Now it is come time, fledglings—and also my good friend Orned—to relieve yourselves of a portion of the burden you bore on behalf of the revolution! Please place half the funds you carry upon this worktable." She put her fingers lightly against the surface.

"You have done well," she continued, "helping to carry what was left of my small treasury for the revolution. Even 10 percent of what you held would be sufficient for many years' travel in the utmost of luxury. But now, the goal is seen to be both distant and costly. We have no mere 'Take Jerel here' and be done, but must needs fund the remaining math work, as well as accepting the possibility of funding major enterprises and even the raising of local forces. Hah! It is well, is it not, that the treasury was to hand?

"Here, now, local forces already stand guard, as they have for more years than you, my fledglings, have been alive. It is fitting that some of the treasury stay here."

Uncle Orned finished emptying his pockets and waved his hand, claiming Sumelion's attention.

"I've been considering the problem of Kay's uncle," he said; "and it's my opinion that the situation needs to be investigated more thoroughly and perhaps . . . corrected. If you or your assistant here can direct us to a sentinel viewscreen . . . ?"

"Please, such cameras are in the back office. Losteny will show you. The mathematician and I shall discuss a point of precedence in another office, where Vreet awaits us."

The back office was a forest of screens, with each of the half-dozen observers covering several banks. Some views were of the Gravity Well itself, while others displayed the surrounding walkways. Most, however, showed places that Jerel couldn't identify.

"Is it wise that we see this, I wonder?" Orned waved at the room. "It appears that we might risk the entire operation if we're caught. . . ."

The assistant trilled a moment, almost sadly it seemed, before lapsing into the common tongue.

"With the funds you have brought we shall soon be dispersing this operation. We cannot be sure that Sumelion's own computers and comm codes gave no clues about our nature. Tolchester would not concede the necessity for an active revolutionary council so long after the battle . . . and we cannot afford to concede that we are not needed.

"Thus, soon, very soon, what you say about this place will be of no consequence!"

Losteny claimed a single-screen and sat down, manipulating the controls with quick efficiency. The screen flashed blue—there was an image of Kay's putative uncle. The image periodically zoomed in, perhaps sensitive to degrees of motion—first his face, then the whole person, then his feet . . .

"Is this the person in question?"

"Yes," said Kay seriously. "That's him. You can even see the scar on his jaw!"

Losteny worked another few minutes with the machine, then sat back and made a satisfied clucking sound.

"The programs have already identified this person as questionable; look, here is the path he has walked since your arrival early in the day. . . ."

She touched a stud on the control panel and a ghostly image retraced its steps, rapidly.

"See, his first appearance brought no special alert, for tourists frequently stop and stare. It takes many of them a long time to attempt the Gravity Well!" She touched another button.

"Yes. Here is the start of the alert phase. The subject has moved back and forth, exhibiting signs of attempting not to be visible, while his face is 82 percent of the time watching." She spun the chair until she faced Kay and Jerel.

"Do you, as patrons, report that you feel you were being singled out for observation by this individual?"

Jerel nodded along with Kay.

"I did," she said. "He was staring at us when we got off the ship, and then he showed up here."

"And he was taking videos of us while we were in the Gravity Well," Kay added.

"I must ask: This is not someone to whom you owe a debt, or who you serve under a legal contract, or to whom you owe explanations for your movements in any legal sense?"

Uncle Orned leaned in.

"I am in fact acting in loco parentis for the pair of them; that's home-planet legal talk for 'I am responsible for decisions they cannot make themselves.' In this case, I certify that the person in question has neither permission nor concern that I'm aware of; I find his actions suspect at best and alarming at worst."

Losteny's head bobbed up and down, and she pressed several more studs on the panel, humming, or perhaps trilling low in her throat, as she worked.

"There. Excellent, even. We thus have concerned patrons, and it is not good to concern patrons on Tolchester. Let us see what happens . . ."

A box opened in the bottom of the screen. Another image of Uncle Karta appeared within it, and then a list—seven different names, three different homeworlds, three different ages, and a notation:

Known to be employed by successors to the Twenty Families.

Losteny whistled. Uncle Orned frowned and touched Kay lightly on the shoulder.

"It looks like your uncle may not *be* your uncle, Kay," he said slowly. "Have you been close?"

Kay snarfed a half-laugh.

"Close? Not so. Whenever he came to visit my mother would tell me to take a walk, go visit Jerel, go get some milk, go to the zoo. And I haven't seen him at all for a couple years until just now." He frowned. "Though I guess he could just be coming by while I'm at school or working."

"In that case," Uncle Orned said seriously, "I'm inclined to assume his attentions are not in the best interest of our party, and I will—unless you object—act to neutralize him."

Kay shrugged. "I don't object *at all*."

Uncle Orned smiled, then leaned over and tapped the screen.

"What can be done?" he asked Losteny.

"While we are in good standing, we continue to act as ever. Tolchester very much likes things to be regular, so that the tourists are happy and able to pay."

The Yliger pointed to a monitor across the room.

"My query has already resulted in a RFD—Request For Drive-by. A security officer will drive by to locate the individual, and if he is still in place, will drive by again in some time determined by the officer. If the individual is still in place at that point, a summons for questioning can be issued, or a summons for loitering, or even an arrest for misuse of public property."

Uncle Orned frowned slightly, his eyes on the screen . . .

"It's a shame we can't be more active about this," he murmured.

Jerel glanced at Kay, eyes wide. He looked back, grimly nodding in acknowledgment. What he was imagining she couldn't know, but she'd already seen what happened when Uncle Orned *wanted* to shoot to kill.

"The man is an easy . . . and yes, he is a very easy mark, isn't he? That's . . . disturbing. A man with so many names, and so many contacts . . . I wonder if you can tell me if any of your other cameras have spotted anything odd? Even borderline odd? Can you compare his walkabout to others?"

Losteny considered him out of her left eye, and then her right.

"Have you much security experience, may I inquire?"

He said nothing, merely fished a small badge out of his pocket, displayed it quickly, and returned it to his pocket.

The Yliger let out a series of cheeps, and bounced, just a little.

"I see, sir. I see. Your question is a good one; let me take a few moments to do the compare."

"Oh, priceless!" Kay burst out laughing. Jerel jumped, then looked at the screen he was pointing to. It was an image of the Gravity Well's interior, looking up from floor level, and there was the guy in the purple tights and flame-gelled hair, giving himself a pretty bad time. He was spinning, fast and faster, his overshirt billowing away from his body. He was spinning, but it was clear that he wanted forward motion.

"It looks like he needs to pay better attention," Kay said. "People all around him have it figured out. . . ."

Jerel nodded, watching the screen, something tickling at the edge of her—

"I think he's faking it!"

"I think so, too," said Losteny, from behind them. "It is rare that one can achieve such complete disaster through mere ignorance. Let us look at this backview. . . ."

She touched a button and the image ran backward until Purple Tights entered the Well, then reversed itself.

From his first step onto the floor until he rose to midlevel he'd appeared to be entirely under control. It was only after he'd gotten height—and looked in the direction of the winged attendant—that he began to act oddly.

"Put that image on hold, please," Orned requested.

Purple Tights hung still in the air.

"Thank you," Orned said politely. "Now, if I may, let him spin, very slowly, just once. And can you zoom in a little tighter?"

The image shifted, his legs and shoes gaining prominence. Soon he filled the screen.

"Boy, they are tights, aren't they!" Kay muttered.

"Well yes," Orned agreed, "and they are inappropriate to security work. After all, let's look for bulges." Orned paused, and Jerel felt his gaze sweep her and Kay.

"Actually, we're looking for bulges of a less obvious nature, Jerel."

She glared at him as Kay tittered, but the image on the screen helpfully expanded once more.

"See that, Kay? Not only is the gentleman a little paunchy in the stomach . . . he's got a strange bulge on his left hip."

The image expanded once more, and the purple hip filled the screen.

"Yes. There. That's a fair-size energy gun, I'd expect. Note the barrel. That's not really required for most energy guns—except it's an excellent aid in quick-sighting and long-range work. Not a toy, nor a tool for a novice."

"Good, can we let him spin? Ummm, fine, I'm sure that's a nice view, but how about stopping at the other hip?"

The spin stopped.

"Odd, isn't it? What do you suppose?"

"It doesn't look much like a gun, or even a knife," Kay ventured.

"No, very good. That's not what you see. And Jerel?"

Jerel shook her head. The hip definitely bulged, with several crescent-shaped items pressed close together under the garment.

"Not surprised you don't know it. It looks to me like a mechanical wrist-restraint system. Might have a stun element built in—those are illegal in some spots. But legal or not, what we see is someone prepared to take a prisoner."

"Ah!" said their assistant. "Look at the pattern!"

The other screen was now showing two images. The first, labeled Subject One—Kay's uncle-or-not—

coincided nicely with the debarking of the guy in tights, now labeled Subject Two. While One loitered near the restaurant, where he'd have a good view of the Gravity Well, Two walked entirely around the facility before stopping and passing a brief word with One, going from there directly to admissions.

"Instruct the attendant not to notice this one for some moments, or until his time runs out," the Yliger said into the speaker by the screen. She touched the off button and turned to Jerel's company.

"I must make arrangements," she said starkly. "Please come with me! Quickly, before the change of fliers."

"*What?*"

"It looks likely that we've got a tail on us, at least," Uncle Orned said. "We'll wish to hurry. I think it time we reacquaint ourselves with friends Vreet and Sumelion."

Vreet was in fact waiting for them in a hidden room behind the shelving of a hallway. Or maybe not waiting for them, exactly, since it was sprawled out across the screen of a lapcomp, making small burbling noises, entirely different from the whistles and chirps it exchanged with Sumelion.

"I didn't know Vreet snores!" Jerel said, laughing.

"And he does not," Sumelion replied. "That is the sound Vreet makes while interpreting the mathematical data necessary to a current project. As I understand the process, it is a form of checksum."

Kay rolled his eyes, and Jerel had to bite her lip so she didn't laugh again.

"I see," he said, exaggeratedly serious. "Vreet's checking the computer's figures."

"Indeed, young Kay. Exactly so. Vreet does very fine work, and I'd have it no other way!"

Losteny interrupted, chirping a few quick notes at the engineer. She replied in kind, glancing around the room as if counting them—or checking something they couldn't see.

"Now," she continued, her voice taking on a businesslike tone. "We arrive here as a working party. To begin, we must calibrate the *awfengat*. The description I have of its recent awkward operation concerns me greatly. Here, we have the necessary equipment."

"If Erazias will produce the device, we may—"

But Erazias, Jerel saw, was fading to green, his hands withdrawn entirely, his robes rustling and rippling as if he were making sure that certain items were sealed in hidden pockets.

"Erazias," Uncle Orned said softly from his lean near the secret door. "We've taken on some risk to arrive here. Do we now find that you mistrust our fellow revolutionaries?"

The rustling and rippling halted abruptly. Erazias pulled himself stiffly upright. His bright green hands emerged each from its wide sleeve, smoothed the front of the robe once and folded themselves primly.

"You mistake me, Hunter," he said with dignity. "This is a matter not so much of trust as of practicality. The device I carry is one of the originals which the master ordered modified. It is irreplaceable. I cannot allow it to be abused, and perhaps damaged, by jerry-rigged calibration equipment. . . ."

There was a short, sharp laugh—Sumelion's.

"Thus speaks a scholar bound by university! Hear me, Erazias: This is the field, where accidents are not theoretical, but produce real injury. We have no time to engage in petty debates of property." She fluttered a hand.

"Ah, but here—allow me to reassure you!" She bowed in his direction, quite formally. "I promise I will take proper care of that device, and treat it with the respect it is due, for I was of the working group that modified it, and have touched it with my own hands. Additionally, Vreet and I have both studied the schematics of this and follow-on models—"

The robe rustled as Erazias shrugged. "How can I know this?"

Apparently, Jerel thought, exchanging a glance with Kay, trust *was* an issue.

"Pah!" Sumelion twisted her head, inspecting him with one eye, then the other, slowly, perhaps intending insult.

"You doubt my word. I will recall. For the moment, however, I say only if you are so concerned of my clumsiness, open it yourself."

Despite the disparity in accents and vocal equipment, Sumelion's disdain was obvious. "You are technician enough to do what is needful, if you will take direction, though we would all be better served if Vreet did the work. If you will not do what is necessary or consent to have Vreet do it, then perhaps you will allow your master's heir to do the work. I believe her hands equal to the task."

Jerel glanced down at her hands involuntarily, wondering what special, undiscovered, powers they might hold. If they just needed somebody to use the tools and follow Sumelion's instructions, well, yes, she could do that. She wasn't afraid of tools.

"Here," Sumelion continued, "view this!" She reached to the lapcomp Vreet lounged on, snoring—calculating—undisturbed, and emphatically tapped the top edge, simultaneously chirping a few notes.

Nothing happened for a moment; then Vreet grumbled more deeply, and shifted, half-rolling, half-falling off the screen. From the edge of the table, Vreet leapt to the floor, landing quite softly, and strode with firm tiny steps to the hem of the rustling blue robe. Vreet's hand appeared, holding high, and with an air of challenge, a small neo-magnetic rotator. A pair of eyes on stalk scanned the Turlon up and down all the while.

"When you open the case," Sumelion said to Erazias, "you will find that the design on the tech screen will match that on the back plate, excepting the number also inscribed upon the plate. If you do in fact carry one of the devices modified for Parvair, and not, as I begin to suspect, some clumsy counterfeit of your own devising, it will be one of two that were with her at the moment of the event. Thus, the number of your device will either be five or three.

"Number Two was tested to destruction at my hands; it no longer exists. Number One remained at the laboratory; we do not know its current location. At last report, Number Four was with Chuton."

She considered Erazias from both eyes at once.

"Will you continue or will you require Jerel to do the work?"

Jerel had counted to twelve before Erazias sighed, bent, and accepted the proffered rotator. The eyes watched the process, then retracted as Vreet moved discreetly toward Sumelion.

"If it must be done, then I will do it. I point out that my questions are unanswered. How do I know the equipment here is properly calibrated? How do we . . ."

"I vouch," Sumelion interrupted. "The equipment here is of the finest; I myself have used it on more than one occasion. More, Vreet has assisted in the writing of the manuals for the entire suite."

She whistled. Vreet pivoted on its hand and waddled to a conspicuously convenient accumulation of boxes and packages, then climbed to another workbench.

"Vreet will be your second," Sumelion declared. "Then all parties will be certain that you have a proper *awfengat* in your keeping."

"Can someone please explain what's going on?" Kay's plaint was loud in the room as Erazias silently followed Vreet to the bench and began work.

Sumelion whirled, and bent her face toward his. The iridescence of her facial feathers made an interesting contrast to his hair, which was at once brighter and blander.

"A challenge!" she trilled. "A challenge from young Kay!"

She flipped her left hand extravagantly, and a small crest rose on top of her head.

Jerel was impressed. What a way to get someone's attention!

"In fact," Sumelion continued, "as this may well be the only occasion we have for some time to speak of such things, let us do so! Young Kay—enlighten me! What is it that *you* think is 'going on'? When you have told me, I will correct or amplify what I may, and Erazias—who I am certain is able to listen while he works—will be available to verify or correct our joint understandings."

Kay reddened, probably thinking that he was being made fun of, Jerel thought—and for all she could tell, he was right. Sumelion bent her head closer, and looked at him first from the left eye and then from the right.

"Please," she said, softer, "all of us here are embarked upon the same mission, and if our reasons are not the same, yet the mission itself should bind us. So begin, and we shall be enlightened."

Kay glanced at Jerel. She smiled at him and nodded, hoping she was right and Sumelion really was serious.

"Right." He took a deep breath, and saw he had the direct attention of everyone except Vreet and Erazias—and

it was hard to know about Vreet's attention, anyway—
then looked directly into Sumelion's face.

"What I *know* is that someone tried to kidnap Jerel, and
they probably killed Mileeda because they kidnapped
her first and she *wasn't* Jerel. Jerel got away."

He paused, maybe hoping that stating the obvious was
enough, but Sumelion showed signs of having been a
teacher. She moved her hand in a circle, asking for more.

Kay went on, slowly at first, but picking up speed as he
went on.

"That was the start I knew about. Jerel was already in
trouble because of the slideboard, but I don't think that
was part of the problem, and besides, I'd warned her not
to do that. Anyhow. After Jerel got away from the people
who had killed Mileeda, she went home, and Erazias had
come to rescue her because he'd heard that people were
out to get her because she's Parvair Telmon's daughter."

Sumelion inclined her head solemnly, but said nothing. Kay took another breath.

"The people who are mad at Jerel for being Parvair's
daughter are leftovers from the Oligarchy. They blame
her—well, her mother—because the Oligarchy lost the
war. When my mother told me the police were looking
for Jerel, I thought it was because of the slideboard, at
first, and went to her apartment to warn her, because
she's my best friend ever." He paused and frowned at the
floor before continuing, slower again—

"After that, things got rushed together. My mother explained that it was my duty to help Jerel—my father
would have wanted me to. She . . . she was really sure
that Jerel would have to go someplace else to be safe, so
she had me pack my backpack, and she gave me some
money and stuff, and told me that she was proud of me."

Kay stopped, looked at Erazias, who had his back to
the room.

"And besides that, Erazias says that we need to keep his *terama* healthy so that his master can be retrieved and Jerel can meet her mother."

He cleared his throat and looked back to Sumelion.

"So, that's what's going on—we're helping Jerel get to someplace safe."

Jerel blushed, wondering if she deserved to be anyone's "best friend ever," especially Kay's. If he'd stayed at home, he wouldn't have had to give an oath on his honor; he wouldn't almost have been left with fisherfolk; he wouldn't have met the pilot and then had to be sad. . . .

Uncle Orned was still leaning against the wall, his arms crossed over his chest, his head tilted at the angle that meant he was, on the surface, listening to what you were saying, but underneath was doubtful. Erazias stood tall and motionless at the worktable, eliciting a noise that Jerel took to be a complaint from Vreet—and was staring at Kay without comment.

"It is the nature of reality," Sumelion said suddenly, peering at Jerel and Kay out of her right eye, then canting her head to peer at Uncle Orned from her left, "to attach itself to each mind differently. I suspect that we might each give our interpretation and have it slightly different, but on the whole, I think that perhaps some things need to be made extremely clear, so that we share at least some of the same realities as each day strikes us in order." She looked only at Kay, now, with both eyes.

"Surely, we all wish to keep Jerel safe. Indeed, it is a task to which we shall bend our most ardent efforts. However, effort is expended in service of a plan. What we plan for in keeping Jerel safe is far more than merely prolonging her life in a hostile universe, though failing to do so may ensure other failures, and thereby doom the plan."

Kay frowned. "You're saying that there's something you want from Jerel, in—in *exchange* for keeping her safe."

"Never will it be said that the ruling House of Arantha failed for faulty genes!" Sumelion exclaimed. "Excellent, young Kay. We do indeed want something from Jerel—something which only Jerel can provide."

"I don't have anything," Jerel said, hotly, "except what's in my pack, and you can have that, if you want it!"

"*Ssss.*" Sumelion's right eye focused on her, while the left remained on Kay.

"In such transactions as these, it is most often immaterial things which are exchanged. Would you put a price, in gemstones or cash, upon your safety?"

Jerel frowned, and looked to Uncle Orned. He raised an eyebrow, politely waiting for her to answer.

"No," she said shortly to Sumelion. "I wouldn't know how—I don't think anyone does."

"Also excellent; you are mother's daughter. And, lest we forget, your father's. There was a man who understood the exchange of commodities with a nicety too seldom enjoyed! So, tell me, daughter of Banin Vayle—would you find it wrong to repay in like coin those who had preserved your safety?"

Jerel sighed. "No," she said again. "I don't want people to lose because they helped me, but—"

Sumelion raised a hand. "A moment. Weigh the price. For keeping you safe, we ask, so I believe, your assistance in determining whether or not we have won the war."

"But the war's over!" Kay protested. "The Oligarchy lost its fleet!"

"As did the revolution. Yes, for many years this seemed to be so. Now it appears that reality may be severely elsewhere."

"How," Jerel asked carefully, "could it appear to be otherwise? Has somebody found the ships? That would've made the news, and—"

"Indeed, indeed. The discovery of the fleets or any part would have overflowed newsfeeds and popular media for months! That we have not heard of such a discovery, nor even the rumor of possibility of such a discovery, is proof that it has not been made.

"However, another discovery *has* been made, or—more accurately, theory posited—and it is, oh, so small and dry and technical a thing that no one has bothered to examine it, saving a few mathematical scholars and an odd engineer or two."

Jerel looked at Erazias, standing motionless and entirely blue by the workbench.

"Yes," Sumelion said softly. "Very good. Erazias understands what this small, dry theory may mean. He is, in his own way, quite a good mumbler of mathematics, and his master labored perhaps not entirely in vain to awaken creativity within him."

Sumelion paused; standing with no apparent strain on one foot, she used the other to scratch the back of her leg, while she studied Jerel and Kay closely.

"As far as my understanding of these matters—what is 'going on'—I believe that there may be contained in this small, mostly ignored theory a way to remove the field invoked by Parvair and Banin, and which has for fifteen years held two great war fleets in stasis."

Jerel looked at Uncle Orned, but he was wearing his I'm-not-here face, and a glance at Kay showed that he was as baffled as she was.

It was Erazias who broke the silence, speaking more, it seemed to Jerel, to her and to Kay than to any of the others.

"Engineer Pel simplifies somewhat, though I believe her understanding both nuanced and complex. What you, *terama*—and also you, young Kay—must understand is that this *plan* is more of intent than design; it is more hope than certainty."

He bowed, very slightly, in Sumelion's direction.

"This mumbler has, in the study of some recently published material on the maths of gates, determined that when activated at the moment of decision, the device fabricated by the master effectively created a special-case gate. Let us, in the service of illustration, allow it to be a gate that is both steady-state and almost entirely self-contained. This is entirely within the bounds of the observed effects following the use of the device: that is, there were only minimal, almost vestigial signs of the battle fought by the fleets. All reasonable search patterns based on known trajectories, and on standard orbital mechanics, found nothing—no dead ships, no jettisoned safety pods, no wreckage, no messages.

"This leads us to acknowledge that both fleets were involved in the same event, an event which left only the tiniest of radio signatures for study. The event from which my master sent me forth, in order to preserve the life of her child."

"On the whole, this is nothing new," Uncle Orned objected. "It took some months to piece together, but it was clear that the Oligarchy was broken, and that . . ."

"No," Sumelion interrupted. "Forgive me, my friend, but it was clear that the bulk of the forces of both powers *were missing*. What was missing with the revolution was the ships of the fleet, the crew of the fleet, and some few leaders. What was missing of the Oligarchy—hah!

"Almost without fail the leaders of the Oligarchy wished to claim their own glory from a battle they knew they could not lose. So their leaders, all pecking at each other's strength, threw all of their ships and all of their reserves into the fight."

Now Sumelion startled Jerel—and apparently Uncle Orned too!—by performing a dazzling spin accompanied by a low whistle. The down of her face shimmered and seemed to fluff.

"Thus the preparations we had done for victory and peace were ready when the Oligarchs failed to return. . . .

"Yet, with all of the fanfare, there was no true answer, aside this one's assertions to we inside the revolution of how the Oligarchy was on the way to victory when the the master's work bore fruit. The assumption of a broken or desperately lost fleet ignored physics. Physics, however, has not ignored the assumption."

Erazias took over again.

"And the enemy has not ignored the journals or the information that such an anomalous state as a self-contained gate might possess interesting properties. One possible property, not yet determined experimentally, is that it might be bound by gravitation, and thus be in orbit around the system where the battle was being fought, at a point. A locatable point."

The Turlon paused, warming to the lecture mode, his face and hands a brilliant blue.

"Another possibility is that the whole of the battle scene was instantaneously relieved of the burden of the gravity field and is in motion, speed and direction unknown, mass unknown, in what we shall call a geometrically straight line, from the moment of inception. The volume of space to be inspected in order to prove that possibility is an expanding sphere—potentially as small as the solar system in question, potentially thirty light-years across. We are assuming, of course, the that fleets were in real space at the time, since I was able to leave, and that they were not accelerated by the process, but englobed."

Now Erazias scratched thoughtfully at some skin behind his left ear while formulating his next statement.

"I'm still confused," Jerel said, taking advantage of this small pause in Erazias's lecture. "What does a hypothetical sphere thirty lights across have to do with me?"

She looked between Sumelion and Erazias, and finally at Uncle Orned, who sighed and straightened out of his lean.

"I think what we're hearing is that both sides are trying to do the math and search the search and that when they find this anomalous bit of space they want you there," he told her seriously. "And when the point has been discovered and you and their devices have been assembled, they imagine that they'll be able to open the containment field and let whatever is in there . . . back out into the wide universe."

There was a silence punctuated with Vreet's thrumming. Erazias opened his mouth as if he might be going to speak, then closed it.

It was Kay who broke the silence this time.

"But there's two whole war fleets in there, right? I mean, are they still fighting after all this time?"

He'd directed his question to Sumelion; she looked to Erazias silently.

"The math . . . does not tell us that, not . . . precisely," said the Turlon, a slight ring of green growing around his eyes. "It . . . let us say that it hints . . . that the pocket of anomaly that was formed at the inception could be at exactly the state it was in when it dissolves. That is, for those within, if any are, it may well be that no time has passed at all."

Kay's face was suddenly alight with understanding. He turned to Jerel.

"Listen, your parents are in there, and so's my dad. Maybe we can get them out!"

Maybe they could, thought Jerel, but—wait.

"Kay, they might've already killed each other. And there's something Erazias isn't talking about." She looked at the Turlon. "What else does the math hint?"

Erazias looked at Orned, and then at Sumelion.

"*Fffttt. Terama*, this mathematical model, it is not quite complete. However, you ask a worthy question; it is only my answer which must be unworthy, for lack of complete proofs.

"So—another possible outcome is that the act of dissolving the anomaly will release the entire contents of the pocket in a single event of undifferentiated energetic particles."

Kay's face lost some of its glow.

"You mean that trying to get them out could make everything inside the—the pocket—explode?"

"You might describe it that way, yes, but the process is quite different."

There was a hard yellow line directly around Erazias's eyes.

"What else?" Jerel persisted. "Is there another possibility besides the explosion?" Erazias flinched.

"Yes, *terama*. Several possibilities. The best possibility is that the pocket will simply open. The chances favor that. The explosion is much less probable. Also related to that is the chance that the . . . pocket . . . leaks energy, the way a black hole does. If that is the case, eventually, over days or over aeons, the particles will come out individually and whatever is inside simply . . . dissolves."

He paused one more time, fingernails showing green and yellow.

"There is one other possibility that we must look toward, and this is the area I have not finished solving."

Jerel waited; Uncle Orned didn't.

"This other possibility you speak of, Erazias. Can you share that with us?"

"Merge."

The Turlon appeared extremely uncomfortable, and again Jerel waited for more, unsure if the sound had been a word or a verbal shrug. Finally her patience shattered.

"What in farkation is wrong with you? Answer the question!"

Jerel was probably as surprised as anyone else in the room at her outburst. She bit her lip and watched a kind of green-yellow wave move across Erazias's face.

"*Terama*, I have answered the question. I must model this carefully, and I hesitate to speak on such a weak theory. However, your will is clear, and so I will speak of it. If the fields are not precisely aligned and balanced when the attempt is made, we may not properly open the closed anomalous pocket."

He paused, but apparently realized by looking at their faces that he still hadn't said enough. He gestured, an expansive hand-waving motion, as if he was pointing to something they could actually see in front of, and all around, them.

"Instead of producing a counterfield, so to speak, it is possible that we will produce a second pocket, and that instead of dissolving each other, these pockets might merge and become one, larger, pocket."

"Ah," said Sumelion. "So there exists the danger that we might join those we are trying to pry out."

Erazias twitched again—or maybe he was just trying to nod an affirmative.

"That does appear as a possible outcome," he said softly. "Yes."

Uncle Orned spoke immediately, and in the tone of voice he took when he tried to take control of a conversation.

"But what you haven't said is that if this can be done you would materially affect everyday life as we live it today. After all, the Oligarchy is quiescent; we live free. There is no fleet of doom weapons hanging over our heads at the moment—it's been neutralized. There's very much benefit to letting things go on the way they are, Erazias. The things you speak of might be possible, but are they desirable? I suspect that reconstituting a pair of war fleets might have some unintended consequences!"

"But Hunter," the Turlon answered, "if this is what you want—if you wish to insure that for most people the universe goes on as it does—why should we take any chances at all? We have the means at hand to do this. Simply use your skills as a hunter on young Jerel and incinerate her remains. Poof—until such time as another genius comes along, no one will be able to attempt the opening."

Jerel was shocked at the suggestion, and found herself starting to boil inside.

"That's a bad idea"—Kay tried to butt into the conversation but Uncle Orned's voice was up to smoothly taking control.

"Erazias, what you offer us is theory with vague possibility. Jerel herself is not a threat to the universe, though it's apparent that she's threatened by those who think it may be possible to use her as a tool. I suggest that affirming the status quo is the most responsible thing we can do. Use your math skills to disprove the potential. Surely a mathematician such as yourself can convince . . ."

"Stop it!

Jerel's voice echoed, and enforced its own order. Only Vreet's slow burble could be heard for several heart-stopping moments.

She found herself standing apart, ignoring Kay, her glare switching between her uncle Orned and Erazias.

"I'm pretty tired of this, you know. None of this was my idea. I didn't ask to be swept away from home. I didn't ask to have some guy with a knife come after me. I didn't ask to come to Tolchester. "

She had their attention, and had it good.

"In fact, everything that's happened so far has happened because someone else made a decision. Erazias decided to *rescue* me. Kay decided that he should come with me. Uncle Orned decided to find Sumelion. Sumelion decided to come to Tolchester."

Jerel matched Erazias and Orned glance for glance.

"We've been running for days and about all that I've been allowed to decide is what I was going to eat. Now you're trying to decide where I'm going to be dragged off to, or if I am, and why, and you haven't asked a really important question."

She paused to catch her breath, and a cowed Erazias said, "*Terama*, which question is it that we have not asked?"

She lifted her hands to shoulder height and shook them, causing Kay to shrink away as she nearly growled the answer.

"You haven't asked, 'What does Jerel think we should do?' You haven't said, 'Your life's at risk, what chances do you want to take?' You haven't asked *me*!"

She paused so slightly that no one could break in, found some direction to the ideas she wanted to articulate.

"What I have to say is this. I think that if I'm at the center of this, I need to make some of the decisions. I think there's a Rule Seven no one's told me about but I'm making it up and I'm going to use it. Rule Seven is *choose your own path*."

She glared at them, found herself pacing as she thought rapidly.

"So, what I think, what I think is that if we can, we should see about getting to Kay's dad and my parents—and everyone else who might be in there. And if the Oligarchy was winning, then they might win, I guess—so what we need to do is make sure that when the pocket is opened there's a way to stop anyone from fighting. There must be a way. Do you hear me?"

"Jerel, we *do* hear you!" Uncle Orned stood straight and spoke without any of the syrupy soothing that he could do. "And you're right, I'm sure that Erazias agrees—we must be sure, that if the pocket is found—that releasing the ships doesn't restart the war. You're very much your father's daughter, and yes, we'll work with you!"

For his part, Erazias bowed.

"*Terama*, true *terama*! I hear. I shall make the best effort to follow your path, as I always made the best effort to follow your mother's path."

Sumelion twittered a moment, leaning first toward Jerel, and then perhaps toward Vreet.

"We have decision, and this is good. But see, time presses, and we must also decide to continue projects begun already."

Sumelion inclined her head once again toward Jerel.

"Lady, with your permission?"

Jerel smiled, feeling much lighter than she had been somehow.

"Of course. We need to continue."

CHAPTER TWENTY-THREE

Under the renewed threat of having Vreet do the job, Erazias was at the workbench. He'd popped the back off the *awfengat*—it actually sounded much like a wine bottle being opened.

"Five," he said, glancing over to Sumelion.

"That perhaps explains some of the difficulty," she answered. "It was the last that I sealed, under, as I recall, circumstances less than ideal. It is surely in need of calibration after these years, and the use it has recently borne."

Erazias nodded and went back to work, Vreet at his elbow. Sumelion turned to Jerel and Kay to say something but stopped when the door opened without warning.

Losteny reentered the secret workroom, taking in Sumelion, Erazias, and Vreet crowded around a monitor jacked into the *awfengat*, its insides visible on the tech screen and several leads running to it from devices on the worktable.

"Captain," Losteny began.

Sumelion held up a single finger, silently indicating *Wait!*

Losteny made an urgent motion with her hand; Sumelion repeated hers, and turned her back.

"Well," Jerel murmured, repeating one of Tech Doyan's remarks from class, "a lead tech always stays in charge once a project is started. That is, barring death or dismemberment, and dismemberment doesn't always qualify. . . ."

Of course, that was spaceship on-duty stuff Doyan had been talking about. On the other hand, maybe this was the equivalent of spaceship on-duty stuff happening right in front of her.

She leaned forward, trying to get a better view. Sumelion's left eye saw her, and the engineer turned slightly and gave her a peremptory sign to join them. Jerel eagerly went forward—and out of the corner of her eye she saw Uncle Orned put a hand on Kay's shoulder to stop him from crowding in as well.

Erazias was bent almost double, his hands encased in what looked like nanogloves, his eyes on the screen as he made tiny adjustments to the last two numbers on a grid of fifty. It seemed to take him a long, long time. Finally, he was done. He pulled his hands out of the gloves, stood up straight, and stepped back from the table. His face, Jerel saw, showed no hint of yellow or green, but there was the palest of blue, or moleskin gray, bordering his eyes.

"Engineer, check me, please."

"Hah." Sumelion stepped closer, scrutinizing the screen with both eyes. After several moments, she raised her head.

"Jerel, if you will be kind enough to observe columns four and five here, and speak to me of your findings."

She stepped closer, squinting at the series of six-digit numbers—matching, matching, matching . . . "Item five is not a match!"

"Indeed, it is not. Alas, this column is well into the decimal numbers—a difficult match. Even Vreet confesses uncertainty of success, should Vreet attempt the manipulation. I must ask if you will assist us. The tolerances, they worry me. . . ."

"Me?" Jerel blinked. "I have no idea . . ."

"Indeed you do have an idea," Sumelion said crisply. "And we have no time for games of shyness. Please use the glove set and I will explain what you must do."

The glove set was in fact nothing less than a Thuyle nanowaldo with logarithmic digital verniers. Jerel blinked again, hand hovering—

"Yes," Sumelion said, "it is a very nice tool, Jerel. Please, you are allowed to touch it, and I would urge you to do so. Quickly."

Blushing, she made sure of the connection between the set and the *awfengat*, then slid her hands into the gloves.

In front of her was another screen, displaying a series of colorful geometric objects, with something that looked like a large pipe next to one triangle-shaped thing that looked like it was supposed to fit even closer to a slip gear than it was.

"We have locked the nanomover," Sumelion said; "it cannot go out of true by more than two full units. That is easy enough to fix, if it comes to that, any of us may do it. What we do not prefer is to have anything less than nine-digit agreement. This unit has been hard used and most items were two or even three decimals off. No wonder you have left blazing records across gates! So, try the pull. Again, it is locked against a large disruption; we are attempting to put the alignment as exactly as we may utilizing so awkward a unit."

Awkward unit? Jerel was in awe. The nanotouch at school couldn't get reasonably closer than five units, and here she was being asked to budge . . .

"Tell me what the mover bar is?" she asked.

"Good! An excellent question! It is a microshaved cat whisker. It has some give, and will not cause whiplashed joints if stressed. You may continue."

Jerel took a breath, then another, calmed herself, concentrated . . .

Slowly, she closed her hands, feeling the pipe within the box, knowing that some of the finest electronics possible were reducing her motions, and feeding back to her hands, the impression that a sliver of a cat whisker was an object the size of a pry bar.

She pulled slowly and the pipe budged; she pulled some more and realized she needed to twist it a bit to try to get some torque on the edge of the triangular gear. She got the torque, saw the triangle jiggle and move. Almost too much.

She realized she was sweating.

Unexpectedly, Erazias spoke from behind, with encouragement.

"*Terama*, we all feel that the torque needs to be applied after the touch has begun. We have none of us quite managed; certainly the unit is usable as it is. Of course, the more accuracy the better."

Your nanotouch, now, came Tech Doyan's voice in her head, *your nanotouch can make or break a spaceship repair. When you get right down to it, almost touching is just as bad as touching too hard, because of the way those molecules start to jumble about and vibrate when you throw the power on. These tolerances are so close that we're using lithium ions for grease; too many of them and we're building a charge we don't need. If you have a knack for this kind of work, do it, if you don't, you better be ready to call in an expert if you want it right.*

Jerel remembered the lecture; she also remembered that was why she'd gotten headset in the rebuild squad she'd never get to compete with. In the regionals you competed against a clock. Time and accuracy together . . .

She paused, withdrew her hands, and looked up at Sumelion.

"Time pressure, tech," she said. "Your crew needs your attention real soon."

The engineer bobbed her head several times.

"I am informed. The portals are not yet breached; we have no alarms. Therefore, I request you to try again."

"No pressure," Jerel muttered. But hey, if she ever *did* get to see Doyan again, maybe she could get some extra-credit points. Nine-digit hands-on work with a Thuyle Model 93 SuperSci ought to help make up some of the grades she was missing—if she could do it.

"Goggles? Can I get this a little bluer? I've got some blur to compensate for."

Someone, she didn't see who, adjusted the target illumination, and Sumelion handed over a set of video goggles, which she put on immediately.

Now she felt better as she leaned into the gloves. At school the goggles helped keep all the distraction of the other students out of her eyes. Here, it was as if they made the device she was looking at the only thing in the world.

She pulled with the left glove, pushed just a bit with the right, and instantly saw the motion deep within the device through the goggles. She felt like she had better depth perception now, and through amplified feedback, the tiny touch of the cat whisker against the edge of the triangular gear was jarring. She kept the pressure on, though, and twisted, the left hand going forward, right hand backward, the wrists struggling to keep even pressure.

In the goggles a sudden motion! Jerel remembered to relax her hands slowly as she saw the plane of the gear was as flat as could be against the plane of the ratchet.

Around her came a sense of collective relaxation as success clicked in.

"Hey! Did you do it, Jerel?"

That was Kay, still trying to peer in over shoulders.

Jerel felt drained, as if she'd been doing real work, instead of moving something that weighed a little more than a few molecules of vanadium. She pulled the goggles off, nodding in his direction, and ran her fingers through her very short hair, wrinkling her nose to find it damp.

"It is done," Erazias said, "and well done, *terama*."

Sumelion twittered something in Yliger to her colleague and then chirped a couple of lines of something to Vreet, who mumbled back at her, then curled up as if to sleep where it was.

Sumelion looked at each of the crew around her then, head bobbing, as if counting them off.

"Now we close the case and get on with the important news from the outside world."

Kay started to say something, but the up-to-now patient Yliger burst into a torrent of sounds, so much so that Jerel turned away so they wouldn't see her laughing. Then Sumelion joined in and it seemed they were both talking at the same time.

Sumelion and Losteny continued, full speed, and Jerel wondered if they could process right ear/right eye information separately from left eye/left ear information. It certainly looked like they were holding two different conversations with each other at the same time.

Altogether the workroom sounded like a rookery at high speed, with clucks, cackles, and whistles. The whistles brought Vreet back to attention, and then to action, as it suddenly leapt to the floor, heading for the ruck-sack.

"Hah!" said Sumelion. "The portals are yet un-breached, I think, but as I understand it, the police are on their way and will wish to be interviewing staff. It would no doubt be better if we were not on the premises when they arrive. Collect yourselves, fledglings! The moment Erazias has sealed the case, we move!"

CHAPTER TWENTY-FOUR

Moving had sounded more interesting than it was; the service tunnels under Tolchester were as bland as the aboveground was exotic, right down to the hokey signs pasted on the beige cermacrete walls.

HAPPY TOURISTS SPEND MORE, one advised; and CLEAN IS GOOD, SPOTLESS IS BETTER, SMILES PAY YOUR TAXES, and BAD LANGUAGE SPOILS EVERYONE'S DAY! Jerel yawned, and looked around her for anything interesting.

The early part of the trip had been fraught with sudden noise and sudden haste—the sounds of emergency responders, heading toward the Gravity Well—and several quick detours when those responders had rushed by them, some on foot, some in electric carts, and most recently a few on the rails that paralleled their course.

"We'll not wish to be seen rushing," Orned pointed out when Sumelion hustled them into what turned out to be a dead-end power-gauge room while a dozen foot cops approached with cameras on their helmets.

"Ah, but now we are safe—and they are busy," the engineer replied. "They are not looking yet for our mixed group!"

Along the way Sumelion had provided them with badges, with TEMP WORKER printed on them in ugly block letters. No pretty gem-light borders on this ticket, Jerel thought, though the chip glowed an alert orange.

"Please make certain that your badge is secure," Sumelion trilled, and led them through doors with large yellow letters declaring, in a number of languages, "Authorized Personnel Only."

"Won't these badges interfere with our tickets?" Jerel asked.

"An excellent point. The passenger tickets will show up on security screens as moving in the wrong areas. This we wish, for we will hand them off shortly, and will then require quick alternate ID to hand."

"Hand them off?" Kay repeated peevishly. "Are we done?"

"Indeed, fledgling. We are done as tourists for this small season. Alas, we shall not have the rocket ride I was planning. It appears we must make use of other facilities. . . . Perhaps we will all happily return this way another time."

Sumelion then had pointed out a microphone and camera pod on the ceiling some distance down the hall. "Shhhh. No talking about important things!"

The occasional robot vehicle passed them on tracks set on the left and separated from the walkway by a low wall; about the only relief from tedium they provided was a change in the low hum that constantly infused the halls.

The other regular sound was the noise of their walking. Jerel really missed her slideboard; she could have been on the other side of the moon by now. All this plodding was getting boring.

The sound of their footsteps, though—that was inter-esting. Uncled Orned, well behind them, walked almost silently, and she wasn't all that noisy either—though not as quiet as he was.

She glanced back at him, saw that his hands were empty and his eyes busy. Then she saw he dared to wear his backup gun—it looked like a clunky old phone—on his belt. Her stomach began to feel the now-familiar weight of slow dread. She would be really glad when they got to someplace safe!

Sumelion's steps in the lead were fast and clicky and constantly changing speed—but she didn't really move in a straight line either, but sort of wandered from side to side as she walked. Jerel's first thought was that the en-gineer was being awfully clumsy, but a second look made her realize that the side-to-side walk let Sumelion watch, first from one eye and then from the other, with-out appearing overobvious, unlike Uncle Orned, who needed to sometimes turn to glance behind.

Kay's steps were extremely regular, nearly as tidily straight as the rails that ran past them. He seemed not to be doing much more than walking, and it struck her that she didn't know if he had a weapon besides Darnay's knife. For that matter, she didn't know where he might have the knife, or if he'd use it. Grimly, she realized that he was sworn to find out what had befallen the dead man, and the only way he could do that was by surviv-ing whatever they came upon himself.

Erazias, somewhat in front of them but not too close to Sumelion, was the one who really plodded; she hadn't noticed that before, and wondered if he was tired. He had weapons, she was sure, but it seemed like he missed the staff, and she felt sorry for him.

The interplay of the various walking styles and echoes was subtle—but it seemed they never marched to quite the same rhythm, so there was a changing background of sound.

The lighting changed subtly from time to time, too. As they walked, lights in the two rows on the ceiling ahead of them would come on and brighten while those behind would dim and go out. While they never faced an entirely dark hall, Jerel had the impression that they were walking in darkness.

Kay, walking beside her, was amused by something, the sound of his occasional soft giggling a counterpoint to both the sound and the necessity of their march. Jerel looked around, trying to spot what was so funny.

At first she thought it was the automatic trains, because some of them were festooned with tags, bar codes, and warning stickers. But he wasn't looking in that direction most of the time; he was looking at the other wall, or the ceiling.

Then she thought it might be their echoes. . . .

"What, are we funny?" she finally asked in a hushed voice, putting her hand in front of her mouth to soften the sound.

"No," he whispered, "we're not funny. But somebody's been leaving graffiti all over the place."

She blinked at him, at the blank beige wall, and back at him. "Where? I don't see any!"

"Haven't been paying enough attention, then, have you?"

She glared at him, suspecting a joke at her expense. "It looks like they clean this place four times a day. Besides, there's cameras, and—"

"There!"

Jerel didn't see anything. There were the lights overhead, a camera pod, an access gate for the robototes . . .

"Still don't see it."

"Wait, I'll show you in the next section."

She sighed. "What do you mean, section?"

"This place is marked—right now, we're in section DHT419. Have been for a while. There—see the tag in front of the light fixture there: DHT419 and a couple smaller letters? Here comes the next section."

Jerel looked where he pointed. In fact the new section was DHT418. Now that she was looking for it she found it inconspicuously but consistently displayed on the light fixtures as well as on the divider wall; there were even small tags beneath some of the posters. The posters themselves were free of extraneous writing.

"Still not seeing any graffiti," she muttered.

"Slow down. Look at the base of the wall. Watch what happens when we set off the lights ahead."

Jerel watched, and as the lights came on an ornately lettered series of words appeared in a beige barely distinguishable from the background color. When the next set of lights came on, the words disappeared.

"I saw it, but I couldn't read it," she said to Kay. "What did it say?"

"Well . . ."

She glanced at him. She was starting to be able to read his blushes as well as she could read Erazias's blue-to-green-to-yellow changes.

"Yes?" she coaxed.

He grinned weakly.

"That one was an invitation for . . . anyone wanting a particular kind of good time to be at a certain place. But it was for yesterday, so you're too late," he finished, his grin suddenly wider.

"*What?*" She glared at him, though she remembered to keep her voice low. "If you don't tell me I'll . . . I'll go back and look."

He reddened some more, but shook his head.

"Here, watch ahead," he invited, obviously trying to distract her.

This time as the light changed the message was clear: someone's ex-boyfriend was fond of doing something really disgusting. Thing was, Jerel didn't know which of several possibilities *phooter* covered, so she didn't know how mad they were at the ex, or how disgusting he really was.

The next couple of messages were boring, and the one after that—

Kay stopped in his tracks and Jerel almost ran into him.

"*Now* what?" she hissed.

"Look! Can you read that one?"

She squinted at the wall " . . . 'is returning'?"

"Look higher!"

"'Prepare yourself, '" Jerel read, "'the Oligarchy is re-turning'?"

"Let's keep up!" Uncle Orned's voice came briskly from behind them. "Pick it up!"

Jerel stayed stubbornly put, Kay beside her.

"Uncle, have you been seeing the graffiti?"

"I have. It's about as stupid here as anywhere."

"Then look at this one!" Kay's voice was strained.

Uncle Orned was beside them. He paused and considered the wall, lips pursed.

"Well," he said mildly. "You're right, Kay. That one's different." He moved his shoulders. "All right, then, you two, let's all of us walk together. It might be interesting to keep an eye out, in case there are any more of those, or anything with a timetable attached. In the early days of the collapse, it wasn't unusual to see messages like that, though I agree political statements seem a bit . . . out of place in Tolchester. Not that I've been studying the information here as hard as Kay has. I rather suspect he knows where to go and who to ask for. . . ."

Kay blushed fiercely and Uncle Orned laughed. "Sorry, but I could see you noticing. Have you figured out how it works?"

Kay admitted that he hadn't.

"Some of the lights have a higher UV ratio, and some have a higher infrared. The markers that were used to write the graffiti absorb the energy at different rates, and you can only see the words for so long before they disappear again. I suspect that during shift change the words are invisible except by accident—because the lights would be on all the time in heavier traffic."

"But how do they get there with all the monitors?"

"A good question. Perhaps they're written by someone moving very slowly, or perhaps the cameras aren't live— or are live on an easily obtainable schedule. I'm afraid we're not going to be here long enough to find out, though. We've probably come three-quarters of the way to our exit already."

"Where are we going?" Jerel asked. "Do you know?"

"Yes," he said. "But I don't know how good the microphones may be." He tapped them both gently on the back. "Now let's close it up with Erazias. We don't want him to think he's lost us all!"

Steps echoed ahead, and the lights were already bright. Not only bright, but wider, and Jerel soon saw what looked like a station for the robotrains, with more than a dozen tracks side by side and more feeding off to the right.

The hum of the trains was louder here, and there was actual clatter as some cars found each other and coupled into a longer train, while other trains decided to divest themselves of a car or two, which were shunted away onto the sidetracks. Jerel thought it must be some kind of distribution center, and it was much more interesting than the service tunnel.

There were other people there, too, all bent on their own business and taking little note of passersby. On the wall opposite the trains and tracks was a bank of elevators, and also a pair of escalators. This was a space through which a lot of people moved, then, Jerel thought, and felt oddly comforted.

Sumelion halted her small group by the tracks, and they leaned against the train wall as she spoke to them, her voice weaving through the ambient noise.

"Here is where we will need to have some luck. Will you"—this asked of Uncle Orned without mentioning his name—"collect these items and place them all in this envelope as we stand in a circle so the camera cannot quite see us?"

These items were their original Tolchester tickets, which Uncle Orned gathered without fuss while Sumelion looked over their heads. It was hard to tell what the engineer was looking at, Jerel realized, unless she was staring right at you, which she wasn't at the moment.

She surprised Jerel then, by leaning in close to Erazias. They spoke a few moments, possibly closer to each other than Jerel had ever seen them. The Turlon made an openhanded gesture with his right hand while his left remained within the folds of his robes.

The tickets were collected, the envelope sealed. Sumelion received it without acknowledgment, her attention ahead.

"Orned," she said, "another moment of your time. Erazias, you will do the honor of standing with your *terama*?"

"Of course," he said, bowing to Sumelion, and then saying "Hunter," and bowing Orned on by him.

Jerel watched her uncle and Sumelion converse in a low whisper, both alert, both deceivingly calm. Uncle Orned was *holding* the stealth gun.

"What do you think?" Kay asked Jerel, leaning close.

"I think I'm scared," she admitted. "You got Darnay's toy?"

"This one?" he asked, glancing down toward the front of his jacket.

The knife hilt was showing, tucked in a drawable position in the front of his pants.

"And you?"

"In my pocket."

"Wish I knew what or who."

"Me, too," Jerel agreed, wondering if Kay knew Rule Six. She looked beyond Kay and the dread in her stomach got heavier: Uncle Orned was strolling casually down the hall, away from them!

Erazias moved close then; Jerel could catch the scent of him, a scent reminding her somewhat of the fishing village. He spoke, keeping his face lowered and looking away from the more obvious of the monitoring cameras.

"*Terama*, your uncle the hunter goes to view the environs. It is, indeed, the kind of work in which he is expert. On my side, I wait and watch patiently, as should you."

Jerel nodded. Waiting seemed indicated, after all.

Kay leaned in and said, "We're all waiting, but I'm not sure about the patience part." Then after a moment's pause he blurted out, "Can you tell me what '*terama*' means?"

There was a small noise, and Jerel realized it was Erazias, emulating a chuckle.

"There is that proof the engineer would have that I am an academic! I have never thought that you didn't know. And you, Jerel, do you know the word?"

Jerel blushed. "I should have asked, but no, I don't."

Again the chuckle.

"Some concepts are very difficult to translate. Words are much harder than mathematics, you know!"

He paused, and in the distance Jerel could see Uncle Orned bend down as if adjusting his socks within his boots. Then he stood, turned, and started a leisurely stroll back.

"*Terama*," Erazias finally said, "is a word reserved. It is nearly a name in itself, but it is a description. Let us say it is translatable as 'child of highest promise' or perhaps as 'the one who will grow to fullest potential.'"

"Child?" Jerel asked gently, almost chidingly.

"Child, youth, one born of a house. You are born of the house of a master, therefore you are *terama*!"

Jerel felt the blush anyway. *Child of highest promise* was a bit of a load for anyone to carry!

Kay rescued her from reply.

"Do you know what we're waiting for? What's happening?"

"Not fully, young Kay. I can say that Sumelion has come to see that her original plan—which was to involve us in several days of travel aboard a small space freighter, and then a smuggler's path among several space stations—is perhaps too ambitious. So we use a backup plan. This plan has some small risk, but has the advantage of boldness. It also involves gates, of which Sumelion is less than fond. I honor her willingness to alter plans!

"And as to plans, I was not able, being at work, to finish my description as we spoke earlier. Do you see, not only do some of the enemy conspire to mold you to their necessity, as you might expect, but some within the movement are also not pleased with my plans."

"Which plans, Erazias?"

"*Terama*, it is my plan to arrange, when the bubble is clearly located, for the *Valero* and the other flagship to be isolated and removed first from the matrix of energy. I have readings made of the ships just before it transitioned; I have the closest records of location and power levels. But see, some of those within the movement would have us fall before we attempt so daring a plan."

"What? Why would they want to stop us?"

Erazias looked over his shoulder, saw that Orned was approaching rapidly. He spoke quickly.

"Consider, Jerel, what would happen to those who are comfortable with how things are, if your mother and father could be brought out? Imagine the changes? Imagine those who would be exposed as power-grabbers? And so I beg you to stick with my plan. We can save your mother!"

"My father, too!" Kay looked thrilled. "My father is on the flagship. If you can pull them out, we can make them talk with each other. We can stop the war."

"You must stick with me, *terama*," Erazias said, and then stretched to his full height just before Orned got back.

Sumelion came to them.

"Attend me now!" she said, suddenly speaking quite loudly, her voice easily discernible over the noise. "Your attentions, please, upon this train, which is almost stopped."

Startled, Jerel looked, and so did Erazias and Kay.

"You will note," Sumelion went on in lecture mode, "that these cars are crafted of spun fibers, so they are light and strong. You will also note that they become stained with use, and are subject from time to time to accident. Most are repaired and returned to service."

The train in front of them stopped momentarily; then two cars—under their own power—reversed themselves, heading for the siding. Another car joined them there, and the newly configured three-car train whisked importantly away, clattering through a set of switches until it joined an even larger set of cars.

"Yes," Sumelion said excitedly, leaning over the wall. "See, here before us is such a repair!" She touched the side of the train, running her fingers over a gnarly patch near one of the bar codes.

"Why, that feels quite solid!" she exclaimed. "They do good work here!"

The train began to move almost immediately, slowly accelerating down the hall they'd come up.

"Ah. It delights me that we were able to see the repair so nearly! Often the trains are not so accommodating as to stop when they are the topic of discussion!"

Kay snickered lightly, and it was then that Jerel realized their tickets were traveling away from them quite handily. She also noted that the engineer assumed the cameras and microphones *here* were entirely functional.

"Now, in order to learn the job properly, we will be visiting a cargo gate. It is important that all remain close to me. The area of the gate is very busy and one would not wish to be in the way of a shipment. More than one person has been inadvertently transported to some unsuspecting world, as I understand it, and—it is unfortunate, but true—others have been injured badly, and a few fatally. Alertness is imperative.

"Follow, now!"

Sumelion led them to a lift marked AUTHORIZED PERSONNEL ONLY. NOT A CARGO ENTRANCE. CARGO ADMINISTRATION ONLY, and pushed a card into the slot. The lift door opened obediently and they entered. Sumelion delicately placed a finger in front of her face as each of them went by her, apparently indicating silence. She reached into her cape and brought out bright yellow passes with the word "Visitor" on them in black and green and mimed putting the passes on, which they did quickly.

The lift accelerated impressively, and Jerel's feet almost left the floor when it started to slow. Talk about a high-speed elevator!

They exited into a brightly lit area nearly as large as the warehouse they'd jumped into at Fraderione. Unlike the warehouse at the fishing village, the door here looked to be gasketed and air-secure. They passed between two bored armed guards, one on each side of the lift banks. Jerel thought that if he hadn't been a guard the one on the left would have been cute.

Sumelion waited for them at the entrance to the hall. Remembering the instruction to stay close, Jerel hurried to her side, and looked out over the whole of the hall.

The area gave the impression of meticulously hygienic upkeep. The walls and floor were an even, brilliant white, unlike the halls below. Even the air smelled fresh; Jerel wondered if it was because the gate here was steady-state and leaked ozone, or simply because the place was so clean.

At the far end the clatter of automatic trains was punctuated by strange whines, whooshes, and whomps. The now-familiar robot carriers were moving through the gate in both directions, keeping to a strange digital rhythm that required each departing car to come to a definite halt before continuing into the gate. The entering trains came in one car at a time. Each car paused, then moved forward to lock on to the car ahead of it.

Sumelion walked toward the gate, and Jerel followed. There was something nearly hypnotic about the shimmer of energies that stretched soundlessly and without pyrotechnics from the floor to the ceiling.

Set into the floor around the gate was a confusing web of rails; it looked to Jerel as if there were a hundred different sets. Multiple tunnels led in and out of the hall, and though individually the transports made little noise when they were all running at once the noise was awesome.

Rather than the cermacrete half-wall that firmly protected pedestrians from the rails in the underhalls, here were bright red stanchions connected by wide yellow and white ribbons of mesh wire. Not only were working sections of rail set off from pedestrians by linked groups of stanchions, but there were also stanchions blocking the track nearer the gate, so that only the dozen or so active rails in each direction were unimpeded.

"You will see"—Sumelion was still in her role of instructor, lecturing—"there is no true 'nonstop cargo railroad to Risiglia,' despite the advertisements which overflow our in-boxes. In effect, each of these rail-mounted containers becomes, however briefly, an independent spacecraft in its passage through the gate, though its journey to our eyes is barely a few meters. When the carrier comes to a rest at its destination, it re-couples with the container in front of it. Besides that stop, there is one additional, where the train tunnels go through a pressure lock to reach this hall, so that in the event that the gate—either by accident or necessity—locks to a low-pressure or high-pressure world, damage will be contained."

On the far side of the gate was the control tower, its window reaching almost to the high ceiling, and it was in that direction they slowly moved, clustered about Sumelion, and obediently gawking at those features she pointed out here and there around the hall.

"Understand that it is not merely fancy that makes the cars into individual units for the passage," Sumelion lectured on, "but that one does not wish to attempt to run power cables between the stars, and conductive train rails would in fact be power cables, as would continuous trains themselves. It is far better that nothing directly connect power sources or permit a current across such distances, for the effects can be disastrous."

"What effects?" Kay was wide-eyed, like he was trying to take the whole room in at once.

"A prudent question. The effects are difficult to predict, for they tend to be high-frequency electrostatic in nature, as well as magnetic and gravitational. Energy, broadcast wildly by the spin of galaxies. These are called Tesla effects: you may look them up, and most earnestly hope that you never experience the like."

Sumelion looked down at Kay.

"There is a large field of study encompassing such things. But here, where we do not condone such dangerous events, all is calm, quiet, and ordered!

"On the tracks at the left side, you will notice incoming items. These will largely be fruits and vegetables and perhaps wines; we do not get our water from Risiglia, that comes through another channel. Also on the left side you will see the security officers and equipment prepared to intercept incoming items that are out of order. Generally this is not a problem, but occasionally one of the detainee fieldworkers will attempt an unauthorized visit. Of course, on the return side such are not required since returning cars are, for the most part, empty.

"There is, after all, not much here that would be worth sending to Risiglia. Tolchester exports very little, since we exist to provide luxury and amusement. Why one would wish to travel to a world largely populated by automatic growing equipment, farmers, deportees, and technicians I could only wonder!"

Sumelion sounded smug, and disdainful, but Jerel thought she could see where this was leading.

"So, now—observe the process. You can see across the interface. What looks to be a slightly smoky view into a mirror image of this room is in fact a view into a planetary structure some forty-four light-years from here.

"You will note that the rails stop before they reach the gates. So—the sounds you hear? The electric brakes on this side as the cars are received and slowed—that is the pitched noise. Then you have the sound of the compressed air as the cars are accelerated and launched across the divide—you cannot see the plunger from here but it physically pushes each car into the gate. It is fortunate that air pressure on the world at the other side of the matrix is quite close to ours." She turned, moving her hands as if shooing them along before her.

"In a few moments, our visitors' passes will be noted and we may expect to be invited into the control room, located above the ramps there."

She pointed ahead of them, toward an area rising out of the maze of tracks sunk into the floor. Actual railings—not stanchions—gaudily painted in yellow, black, and red warning stripes edged the ramps leading to a set of doors that Jerel thought looked like airlocks.

"Words and time are at premium in keeping commerce between the stars optimized, and thus I will answer any and all questions from the staff while we are in the control area. We should also expect to receive a tour of the interface itself; this has been arranged with Shift Leader VanGunten, who fully understands our program."

She'd emphasized *fully,* and now she paused, looking at each of them in turn before adding primly, "I am certain you will all follow my lead in the proper way to behave at the interface!"

Uncle Orned murmured, "To hear our leader is to obey. We are prepared to act as you indicate. You shall be our model."

Jerel dared to look at Kay; his half-exasperated return glance showed that he'd gotten the message. Erazias, trailing close behind, was showing just a bit of green around the eyes, which she took to be a good sign: apparently the prospect of running the gate with security in sight wasn't *too* scary for him.

Jerel sighed. She was hoping it wasn't going to be too scary for her. She'd never been afraid of police and security before, and thinking of them as being *on the other side* was hard. For that matter she wasn't really used to there being anyone to call *the other side*.

"Jerel? Jerel!"

Kay's whisper sounded desperate. She half-turned toward him and he grabbed her arm, leaning in to whisper directly into her ear.

"It's *him*, the guy from the Gravity Well!"

He used his head to indicate a direction. Behind them, she saw Uncle Orned catch the gesture and glance aside about the same time she did.

The guy in the purple tights was walking with someone who had an air of authority, both flanked by security personnel in full uniform, with firearms on their belts. The whole crowd of them was moving briskly toward the security station, on the wall opposite the control tower.

"Maybe they caught him?" Jerel ventured, which was stupid—she could see that he wasn't in restraints.

Uncle Orned whistled lightly, tunelessly. The lilting sound startled Jerel but was sufficient to attract Sumelion's attention. The engineer's head bobbed briefly, then she was looking ahead again, chirping a whistle and lengthening her stride.

She said, seemingly to the air, "I expect the shift leader will be able to explain security operations and options to us if necessary. . . ."

Jerel was trying not to be obvious, but she wanted to watch what was going on. Uncle Orned shifted and blocked her view. She frowned and he raised both his eyebrows, then slowly and deliberately shifted his gaze until he was staring beyond her and ahead.

Right. Fuming, Jerel looked at Sumelion.

"What are we *doing*?"

Kay stretched out the "doing" until it was almost a bell-like note. He, too, was trying to cast inconspicuous glances toward the security office, ignoring Uncle Orned's attempt to instruct him. On the other hand, Uncle Orned's location at the rear of their group made it hard for Kay to walk slowly and look back without getting his heels stepped on—hard.

"I guess we're going with the plan," Jerel murmured. "Just keep on walking. We're supposed to stay close to Sumelion, remember?"

Kay frowned, then nodded tightly and walked on, passing Jerel until he was next to Sumelion. His attempt to look nonchalant made Jerel nervous. She hoped she hadn't been so obvious!

Uncle Orned moved up, taking Kay's place at her side as they strode on at Sumelion's new, quicker pace.

"We have at least one anomaly," he said pleasantly, his voice so light Jerel had to strain to hear it. "I'm tempted to say, several anomalies, and we among them. You will want to follow Sumelion's lead, unless you have a plan of your own."

She stared at him, trying to figure out if he was joking. It seemed like the wrong time for a joke, though.

"That's what I told Kay," she answered, talking as softly as she could. "We're going with her plan."

"Good, this time. But you've already shown that you can make your own plans work when you put your mind to it. Don't forget that!"

Jerel frowned. "Is that going to be another rule? Plan ahead?"

He laughed, almost silent.

"That's your decision to make, Jerel. You're up to it."

First a joke and now a compliment? Jerel bit her lip, feeling like there was something she should say, or ask. Then her attention veered as Sumelion's pace abruptly slowed.

They were at the edge of the ramp. Sumelion cocked her head, and now Jerel heard it, too. One of the large air-lock-style doors was opening!

"Easy . . ." Uncle Orned murmured, so softly it might have been a memory.

The airlock hissed again and a mixed if well-dressed group of people exited, heading down the ramp without really looking where they were going, and talking loudly among themselves. A few words made it through the general racket, and Jerel realized they were arguing.

She looked beyond them, into the door, and saw that it really *was* an airlock, big enough to hold about six people, and that it was cycling through again.

" . . . I still say," the man with the Tolchester Corporation symbol on his jacket was insisting, loudly, "that this is a criminal waste of my time and the time of my crew chiefs! Unless someone's going to be promoted or demoted, this could all be done with a simple screen meeting. Just because the new security chief has a rich sense of his own importance doesn't mean the rest of us—" He looked up.

"Well hello, Sumelion!" He quickened his pace, speaking rapidly over his shoulder to the rest of the group. "Hold a moment, please—we'll want to wait for the rest of them anyway."

"Shift Leader VanGunten!" Sumelion trilled as he reached the base of the ramp. "We are on our way to see you, as agreed, and as I advised!"

The shift leader was tall for a human, but he still had to look up at the engineer, which he did after glancing incuriously at the rest of her group.

"Did you? When? The message never reached my desk."

He turned toward his companions, who were coming more slowly down the ramp, their argument put away for the moment, and nodded at a Turlon in plain yellow robes. "If your people are *helping* me again by only passing messages from names they recognize I do hope you'll encourage them to stop. It appears we'll have to put this so-important meeting off since I have previous arrangements . . ."

"That is not possible," the Turlon said. "The word has come from the Board itself: The issue of the stolen children is of the highest priority. Think of the damage, should it even be rumored that Tolchester is utilized by child stealers and slavers!"

The airlock cycled again and another group of people stepped onto the ramp.

"Anomaly!"

Jerel hadn't realized she'd whispered it out loud, but Uncle Orned's attention had been on the shift leader. His head jerked, and he went *quiet* the way he could.

Kay hissed under his breath and Erazias began to go green in the fingers.

Three people exited the dock: a Turlon in workeralls, a human woman wearing a tool belt—and the man sometimes known as Uncle Karta.

"Kay!" he yelled. "You're safe now, son!"

Kay gaped, cheeks flaming. Uncle Orned shifted ominously beside Jerel. Erazias also moved slightly, the rustle of his robes lost in the larger noises.

Shift Leader VanGunten looked down at Kay, a quizzical smile on his lips.

"He doesn't appear to be unsafe in any case, Inspector," he called up to the man at the top of the ramp. "Do you know these people?"

"Know them! These are the stolen children! I have met the boy on many occasions."

Incredibly, the shift leader burst out laughing and turned to Kay.

"And have you been *stolen, masata*?"

Kay's face was even redder now, but he managed to blurt out. "No, sir, I am *not* stolen!"

"He seems certain!" VanGunten called. "And I for one do not call him a *boy*." He glanced over his shoulder at the silent group of his companions.

"Return to your stations," he said quietly.

"You are out of order!" Karta yelled.

"No, sir, *you* are out of order!" the shift leader yelled back, and turned back to frown at their group.

"*Femisi*," he said to Jerel, "do you know this lad? Are you with him?"

Sumelion moved her hand. "This group is—"

"Let the *femisi* speak, please, Sumelion."

The Yliger folded her hands together.

Jerel felt the weight of more than a dozen eyes upon her. She swallowed and looked up into Shift Leader VanGunten's face.

"He's with us, sir," she said, pleased that her voice sounded even and calm. "We're all together."

"And are you stolen, *femisi*? Have you been brought here against your will, under the burden of threats or actual physical harm?"

"No!" Jerel said indignantly.

"I see. Thank you." He looked about him.

"There is no problem. They are together, and they are here. I don't care about what archaic age rules may be in place elsewhere. I mean, look at them! Both of these young people are obviously old enough—and interesting enough, for that matter—to give someone a good tumble if they wished to, and if they wish to do so on Tolchester, then they've come to the right place!"

Jerel felt *her* face heat, now, as several of the onlookers sent appraising glances her way.

"The boy is younger than he looks," Karta rapped out, "and he's been reported as kidnapped by his mother!"

Shift Leader VanGunten shrugged, to Jerel's eye, monumentally unconcerned.

"A mother's worry about a young man's experience is not my concern, is it? The *masata* tells us he is not kidnapped! And surely he is old enough to know his own mind, and to understand his own actions!" He looked to Kay. "Are you over thirteen regulation years old?"

Kay stared, and Jerel could see he was mad clear through.

"I'm fifteen-point-seven regulation years old," he said coldly. "And I have ID which proves it."

"Fifteen-point-seven. An excellent age, *masata*. I hope you'll be enjoying your stay on Tolchester." He paused, and gave Jerel serious consideration, a slow smile growing on his face. "I know I would!"

Jerel felt like sinking into the floor; then she caught Uncle Orned's grin from the side of her eye and got mad instead. She *really* didn't like being looked at as if she was everybody's favorite party!

VanGunten turned away, calling up the ramp to the one Kay knew as Karta.

"Inspector, this is a farce. I'm shift leader, and that means the gate dock is mine. On this dock, safety is my concern, and my say. If security wishes to talk to me, or to my *guests*, they can wait until we're off this dock."

He looked at the still-waiting group of people. "What are you doing here? You've been released to your stations! Don't make me do paperwork!"

At the top of the ramp, Karta pulled a gun. Erazias went green all over, while the Turlon on the ramp beside Karta went gray.

"The meeting is on," the man with the gun said sternly. "Those two children are being searched for across gate-span; there's a reward offered. Security will . . ."

The Turlon beside Karta moved, trying to knock the gun out of the man's hand; and suddenly there was hand-to-hand fighting going on among the group members.

"Heads up!" Uncle Orned's voice was in her ear. She looked at him and he jerked his head toward the gate.

The gate? Jerel thought, and looked to Sumelion, who was standing—

A shot rang out. Another. Jerel jumped, then grabbed Kay's sleeve to drag him behind the slim cover of a call pole. "Get *down!*" she hissed, as two more shots sounded. Someone screamed.

Jerel looked around the pole. Karta stood over the downed Turlon, his gun in hand. Shift Leader VanGunten lay at the bottom of the ramp, blood pooled around him. Sumelion was nowhere to be seen.

"This dock," Karta shouted, "is under police control. Bring the children to me!"

Everyone was quiet, shifting nervously in place. Up on the ramp, Karta's head moved, as if he were tracking something. . . .

Jerel realized suddenly that the presence that was Orned was gone. She spun—and saw him rushing across the dock toward the gate. He'd never stopped!

Guards came running from the security shed, some with guns in their hands; Purple Tights was among them, lugging a long-arm.

"Let him go," Karta yelled. "We've got what we need!" But the guards kept running.

"Let us help this one—he requires aid." That was Sumelion's voice. She whistled, and a sound that was Vreet answered. Jerel turned, and saw the bird woman bent over the fallen VanGunten, Vreet half out of the rucksack—but she had to see what was happening at the gate.

She came unconsciously to her feet, watching transfixed as Uncle Orned jumped a stanchion, ducked in front and then away from an incoming railcar.

"Aiding and abetting child slavery," Karta called down from the ramp. "All of you will be deported or put to death!"

Away among the muddle and confusion of track and train, Uncle Orned paused, turned—and dodged behind a car as two security guards raised their guns and fired.

He grabbed a stanchion, blocked an outgoing track with it, then blocked another, watching as the trains bore down on him, ignoring the shooting men . . .

Vreet screeched, high and terrible. The blue Ready light on the call pole exploded, raining bits of glass down on Jerel—and then they were down, Sumelion an unexpectedly heavyweight pinning them to the floor, chattering and whistling in languages Jerel didn't know.

She struggled to get her head up, to *see*—

Uncle Orned staggered. He wasn't running now, but he was grabbing yet another stanchion. . . .

A railcar hit the first blocked section, pushing the stanchion and its mates along. At the entry to the gate, it paused, as they all did, oblivious of the impediment; while on the second rail a car carried its blockage forward, the stanchion striking sparks from the floor. It too paused; then both cars shot across the gap in unison, carrying stanchions and webbed ropes with them.

For a heartbeat, nothing happened.

The floor—moved, sparks raining upward from the embedded tracks. One of the security guards was suddenly in the air, a railcar reversed its course, slammed into another—the alarms went off, and a railcar rose straight up into the air and blasted through the ceiling. Other objects were in motion, in the air and on the heaving floor. The lights flickered, and water sprayed from somewhere. . . .

Jerel saw Orned, crouched low amid the sparking rails, gun out, aiming at something. . . .

"Tesla effects!" Sumelion cried. "Wild charges! We must leave!" She was up, dragging Jerel with her, and shoved her toward Erazias as she pulled Kay to his feet.

"Stay low, fledglings! This is very bad!"

Karta was yelling, but the noise was fierce now, and electricity flowed in waves over all the free surfaces close to the gate, glowing and throbbing in blue streamers.

Uncle Orned. He was a target, as the security guards stalked him still through the pandemonium going on all around—but his real danger was flying things. An empty car shredded itself against the walls, shedding plastic shrapnel.

There was fighting on the ramps, and Jerel thought she saw the injured VanGunten pulling the Turlon into the airlock with him. Sumelion's voice carried above the noise as she herded Kay, Jerel, and Erazias toward the lifts.

"This way is blocked to us," she said, and Jerel saw uniforms among those trying to bar their way, and heard distant clanking noises she could only assume were more accidents caused by the interstellar overload.

"Gate!" yelled Sumelion, pushing her forward as the floor heaved again.

Erazias! He'd pulled his device and was trying to make it work in this maelstrom of power.

Sumelion pushed Jerel again, and perhaps there was shooting behind them, and Jerel felt something push her hard, fell to her knees. Sumelion pulled her up by one arm, pushing Kay, urging both forward, toward the scintillation of the gate's formation. Erazias stood as if a statue in the nave of a temple, in his hands the *awfengat*, blue lightnings dancing among the folds of his robe, grimly ignoring the hyperstatic discharges that now seemed to engulf most of the hall. Jerel could feel her hair on end and jolts of power rushing over her.

It was raining fruit one second, and pieces of metal the next.

Jerel rushed toward the wrinkled-looking space in front of Erazias, expecting at any second that it would expand, would brighten, would . . .

An explosion shook the hall, a dark cloud rushed up borne on insane breezes; she had no idea what had exploded, but the acrid odor and smoke swept past her.

Jerel saw Kay trip, stopped to help him up, saw that he had blood on him. They all had blood on them; she wasn't sure if he'd been shot in the leg or gashed himself as they'd tumbled over debris.

He looked at her wild-eyed—realized who it was, and actually grinned.

"Doesn't hurt yet," he said, calmly matter-of-fact as he, too, noticed the stain. "But we have to move!"

She pushed him, saw Sumelion waving, saw a properly flat-planed gate in front of them. But tiny, so tiny.

Jerel risked looking back. Uncle Orned was on one knee, looking in their direction. Then he fell, or ducked, as a railcar zoomed by low to the floor. In a moment he was up again, running in their direction!

"We mustn't tarry," Sumelion was saying, and Vreet's whistles and chirps were frantic from within the bag.

Behind them—Karta, gun out, racing toward them, and Jerel realized that Uncle Orned's angle would put him between the rushing gunman and Sumelion.

Jerel yelled a warning that echoed Vreet's.

Karta stopped, braced his legs against the rippling floor, raised his gun—and the gun's barrel was suddenly the focus of wispy blue lightnings. Screaming, he tried to let go—the gun exploded as he was launched toward the ceiling, his arms pinwheeling away from his body, by the wild charges.

"Now!" yelled Sumelion.

"Uncle Orned!" Jerel yelled back, but the engineer shoved her toward the tiny gate.

"Come!" Now Erazias, too, was waving at them urgently. Beyond him, the gate, as tiny as it had been, was shrinking. His face was nearly green, his eyes embedded in yellow. "*Terama!* Only seconds, *terama!*"

Kay tripped again, and Jerel grabbed his arm and pulled him on, the gate right in front of her.

"Rest," he panted, but Jerel wasn't having that. Ignoring the sound of another explosion and constant firing, ignoring the waves in the gate itself, she swept past Sumelion, pushing Kay in front of her relentlessly.

Through the gate they went, into sudden silence, the pair of them staggering as the gravity shifted.

Kay fell to his knees; Jerel tugged, sobbing, and got him out of the path just as Sumelion leapt through, carrying Vreet's bag, bloodied worse than Kay, and also stumbling, graceless and wild.

Erazias was next. He hit the ground and spun to face the gate's ghostly surface.

He stood to one side as if waiting for someone else, and the heartbeats went by, the gate still empty, peering at the action that could barely be discerned there. Jerel tried to see what was going on, tried to convince herself that the rumpled heap on the floor beside the crushed shell of a railcar was not Orned.

The lights began to go out, or the gate to fail. . . .

Hesitantly, Erazias looked directly at Jerel, and back at the faded view of the chaotic hall. Then he looked at Sumelion Pel.

"Engineer!" he cried. "Advise me!"

Vreet whistled and clicked from his bag, Sumelion stood uncharacteristically still, her feathers bloodstained, staring at him and the gate with one eye, and perhaps at Jerel with the other.

"Seal it, I advise," she said quietly.

Erazias raised the *awfengat*, touched a quick series, and the little gate faded to black.

ABOUT THE AUTHORS

Sharon Lee and Steve Miller are the authors of the award-winning Liaden Universe® novels. Their most recent novels are *Crystal Soldier* and the forthcoming *Crystal Dragon*. Steve was the founding curator of the University of Maryland's Kuhn Library Science Fiction Research Collection. For three years, Sharon served the Science Fiction and Fantasy Writers of America, Inc., as executive director, followed by successive year terms as vice president and president. Sharon and Steve live among the rolling hills of Central Maine with a large cast of characters and four muses in the form of cats. Both play on the Internet way too much, and they have a Web site at www.korval.com.